Kathryn Wallace is an experienced blogger, whose writing career pinnacle to date was when a little blog post she wrote about her front bottom's run-in with some mint and tea tree Original Source shower gel went viral and ended up being read by more than 30 million people globally. #lifegoals

A full time working parent, Kathryn somehow finds the time in between regularly losing her shit and screaming 'TEETH! HAIR! SHOES!' on repeat to update her blog, *I Know, I Need To Stop Talking*, which has around 140,000 followers on Facebook and is growing rapidly.

In her spare time, Kathryn likes to lie face down on the sofa screaming silently into a cushion or attempt to convince her children that urination really doesn't require an audience.

ABSOLUTELY SMASHING IT

Kathryn Wallace

sphere

SPHERE

First published in Great Britain in 2019 by Sphere
This paperback edition published by Sphere in 2020

1 3 5 7 9 10 8 6 4 2

Copyright © Kathryn Wallace 2019

The moral right of the author has been asserted.

A CIP catalogue record for this book
is available from the British Library.

ISBN 978-0-7515-7498-2

Typeset in Caslon by M Rules
Printed and bound in Great Britain by
Clays Ltd, Elcograf S.p.A.

Papers used by Sphere are from well-managed forests
and other responsible sources.

Sphere
An imprint of
Little, Brown Book Group
Carmelite House
50 Victoria Embankment
London EC4Y 0DZ

An Hachette UK Company
www.hachette.co.uk

www.littlebrown.co.uk

For Jamie and Beth,
and Wrenfoe,
because without you guys
none of this would ever have happened.

One

It was two o'clock in the afternoon on the day before the children were due to go back to school, and all hell had just broken loose.

Gemma covered her eyes with her hand and wrote FML on the roof of her mouth with her tongue while she counted backwards from twenty. The day counting backwards had ceased to work on her children as an effective parenting technique had been a dark day indeed. On the plus side, it was surprising how useful it had become as a mechanism for calming herself down whenever she found herself on the brink of losing her shit completely.

'What do you mean, you're not ready?' She looked at Sam and Ava in despair. 'I told you to get everything ready.'

The children responded as though she'd just announced she was going to be quitting her job to become a YouTube star: Sam appeared utterly baffled; Ava simply looked appalled.

'But we didn't know,' grumbled Sam. 'How were we supposed to know that we had to get stuff ready?'

Gemma looked at her son, standing there in his pyjama bottoms – actually getting dressed was apparently very overrated when you were nine years old – arms folded in front of him, and not for the first time wondered if she spent half her time speaking Klingon.

'You're right. I've only mentioned needing to get everything ready for the start of term – ooh, every thirty minutes for the ENTIRE CHRISTMAS HOLIDAYS. I can completely understand how the fact you would be required to have your school stuff ready for tomorrow would come as completely Brand New Information to you.' Sighing in exasperation, Gemma mentally counted down the hours until she could legitimately open a bottle of wine and wondered how yet again they'd managed to get themselves into this situation.

Slightly over two weeks ago, the children had broken up from school for Christmas. Two long, arduous, and mostly pissing-down-with-rain weeks of dealing with the fallout of a nine-year-old and a seven-year-old who were hyped to the point of hysteria by the thought of Father Christmas's arrival. Sam was torn between wanting to be grown up enough not to believe in Father Christmas any more, and hedging his bets just in case being a non-believer meant you didn't get any presents. Ava was mostly losing her shit over the thought of an old man with a beard turning up in her bedroom in the middle of the night.

Now though, at least, the last day of the holidays was here and the end was in sight. There had just been the small matter before the children went back to school of the traditional End of Holiday Rituals to overcome.

Earlier in the holidays, Gemma had made the fatal

mistake of smugly convincing herself that this time it would be different. Learning from previous end-of-term debacles, this time she had not trusted the children to empty out their book and PE bags on the last day of term, instead standing over them as they tipped their festering PE kits into the washing machine (boil wash with bleach for three hours, minimum) and dolefully emptied their book bags of unsigned permission slips and, in Sam's case, seven large rocks.

Quite why Sam felt the need to carry rocks to and from school each day Gemma had never entirely understood, but extensive questioning on the subject had merely resulted in him shrugging and clutching his rocks to his chest, so she'd accepted that this was just going to be one of the many parenting battles that would transpire to be more hassle than it was worth.

Even the holiday homework had been tackled early on. Ava had had to draw a picture of her family (Gemma particularly enjoyed her daughter's attention to detail, with the nipples she'd drawn on Gemma, which – cruelly yet accurately – hung at around knee height) and Sam had had a hideous-looking worksheet which required him to correctly identify a split digraph, a gerund and a fronted adverbial. Being someone who would struggle to identify a fronted adverbial if it had come up to him and punched him in the face, Sam had completely lost his shit, as had Gemma, and eventually they had compromised on under-lining random words in a wild guess before banishing the worksheet to the depths of Sam's book bag and vowing never to mention it again.

It turned out, though, that Gemma's idealistic hopes that

3

this time they might have collectively managed to get their shit together were just that.

'You haven't done my sponsorship form,' complained Sam, his hair – which regularly looked as though he'd been electrocuted – looking more madcap and out of control than ever. Shit, she should have got his hair cut. Were there any barbers open on Sundays?

'What sponsorship form?'

'My sponsorship form,' Sam continued belligerently. 'You have to fill it in. Ava's got one too.'

'Well, you haven't given it to me. How can I fill it in if you don't give it to me?'

'Here's the form, Mummy. This one is mine, and this one is Sam's. It's for reading. Will you sponsor me five million pounds?' Ava, blonde curls haloed around her head, and wearing nothing but a pair of Sam's boxers – she refused point blank to wear 'girly knickers' – stomped across the room and deposited two scrunched-up forms into Gemma's hand.

It turned out the sponsorship forms were for sponsored reading, for the reading that the children should have been doing *all holiday*! 'Daily reading will be an important way to maintain your child's literary skills over the Christmas break,' read the forms. 'We recommend a minimum of an hour's guided reading each day. Choose whether to sponsor your child by word, by sentence or by book. Make sure to set aside reading time each day and, above all, HAVE FUN!'

The words blurred before Gemma's eyes. An hour's guided reading per day? One hour? Per child? Which would mean *two* hours of guided reading per day, for two full weeks, a total of *twenty-eight hours of her life – ONE ENTIRE DAY* – that she would never get back, that she would have to spend remonstrating with Sam to please, please, read something – anything – other than Tom Fecking Gates, the collected series of which he could recite off by heart. Not to mention the slow, painful torture which was sitting next to Ava, encouraging her to sound out words and instead being faced with a series of 'D-O-G' – 'And what does that spell?' – 'Ummmmm ... ummmmm ... PINEAPPLE!'

Anyway, even if she had been willing to put herself through that particular hell, it was all null and void as there were now a mere nineteen hours until the new term started and the sponsorship forms would have to be handed in. Staring at them, baffled, Gemma wondered why this hadn't been raised on the class Facebook groups. Surely this would have been the perfect opportunity for some passive-aggressive Mummy-on-Mummy gloating?

Panicking, she texted one of the mums in Sam's year whom she knew reasonably well.

Hi Heidi, hope your Christmas was good. Sam has just handed me a sponsorship form. Something about a reading challenge? Is it compulsory, do you know? Love Gemma x

She followed it with a series of emojis, ambiguous enough to allow her to recover the situation if Heidi turned out to have a dark side and was appalled by her lack of organisation and inability to set aside an hour's (*an hour's*) guided reading time per day.

Heidi replied within seconds.

LOL. You've seen the Sponsored Reading Facebook page, right? Hang on, will add you. Hx

A Facebook notification popped up almost immediately, inviting Gemma to the Redcoats Primary Sponsored Reading Challenge page.

Her heart pounding, Gemma waited for the page to load. There were eighty-four members, most of whom she recognised as other parents at the school. Scrolling down, she saw to her horror a series of posts – an exhibition display of Mummy-on-Mummy gloating at its finest.

Is anyone else finding out that an hour simply isn't enough? Tartan and I are having such a *tremaze* time reading our way through *Great Expectations*. *A Suitable Boy* next!

Looks like our sponsorship total is going to hit the four-figure mark. If every parent managed similar, just *think* how many books we'd be able to buy for the new library!

Four figures? *Four figures?* That's what I should be getting paid for listening to this shite, thought Gemma, her eyes landing on Ava's latest *Biff and Chip* offering. A literary classic it was not.

In the office, Gemma was used to taking decisive action in the most challenging of circumstances. Not for the first time, the parallels between managing a large team of employees and parenting hit her as she pulled out her chequebook and started writing Guilt Cheques.

Guilt Cheques were a parenting tool which Gemma often thought she could patent. Too shit to remember your child is supposed to have made cupcakes for a cake sale for the homeless at school? Too unwilling to put yourself through the hell which is a Year 3 ukulele concert? No bother! Write the school a painfully large cheque instead and assuage yourself of any guilt! You might have to survive on Tesco Value baked beans until payday, but at least you won't get blacklisted by the PTA!

Gemma wrote a *lot* of Guilt Cheques.

Sponsored Reading crisis averted ('Just write down some books that you've read on the form.' 'But I haven't read any books.' 'Then just write down any books that you've read, ever.' 'But that's lying, Mummy.'), the next inkling Gemma had that the start of term might not go quite as she'd hoped came when Ava came downstairs clad in her school uniform. The winter uniform that she'd last put on a mere two weeks ago.

'Mummy, my uniform is a bit short.'

Understatement of the fucking year: her daughter looked like she was about to audition for Spearmint Rhino.

'Ava, you must have a bigger dress.'

'I don't.'

'And my shoes have holes in, Mum.'

'What do you mean, they have holes in?'

'Look.' Sam stuck his entire forearm clean through the sole of one of his school shoes, which, from memory, Gemma had bought no more than three and a half weeks before the autumn term had ended.

As a result, a frantic dash to the local Tesco before it closed at four p.m. was required. Gemma was an experienced enough parent by now to know that supermarket shopping with small children in tow was a bad idea at the best of times; these were certainly not the best of times.

'Come on, Mummy, this way!' An enthusiastic Ava – now wearing her Barcelona football kit underneath her bunny rabbit dressing gown, an outfit designed to maximise the mortification levels of the rest of her family – raced into the store as Gemma grabbed Sam by the scruff of his neck to prevent him from trying to go back down the 'up' travelator. 'LOOK AT THAT REALLY FAT MAN, MUMMY! WHY IS HE SO FAT? IS IT BECAUSE HE HAS BEEN EATING TOO MUCH CAKE?' A young couple sniggered as Gemma groaned in abject mortification and attempted to explain to her daughter, not for the first time, why we didn't always speak our inner monologues out loud. Just they wait. She'd be having the last laugh when they eventually decided it was time to breed and their toddler squatted down to take a dump in the Free From aisle.

Inching their way around the supermarket in an attempt to avoid the poor man Ava had just fat-shamed in public, Gemma divided her time between explaining to Sam the reasons why no, he couldn't put anything he fancied into the trolley, and bodily holding onto Ava to prevent her from marching up to people who weren't using reusable bags and informing them, 'You are killing the baby whales.'

Eventually, they made it to the checkout, where she paid for a brand new school uniform and a pair of school shoes while Ava solemnly informed the checkout lady that 'My mummy is also killing the baby whales, because she never brings a reusable bag with her. She is a murderer.' Ignoring the appalled look the checkout lady was giving her, Gemma took out her wallet to pay. The school uniform and shoes combined cost more than she'd spent on shoes and clothes for herself in the last five years; the total flashed up on the till and she had to fight back the urge to clutch at her chest and gasp. People often remarked jealously how lucky she must be having such a good job and having all of that disposable income to spend on herself. Gemma didn't like to point out that, as a one-income family, the only thing disposable about her income was how quickly the children managed to spend it.

Finally, by seven p.m., Gemma thought she had it nailed. The book bags, PE kits and water bottles were lined up in the hall. The children had eaten tea – a beige freezer food special – and she'd managed to get their hair washed, despite Ava's shrieks of 'YOU ARE TRYING TO KILL ME. WHY ARE YOU TRYING TO KILL ME?' as she did so, which left her devoutly grateful that the house next door was currently empty. In the absence of any barbers being willing to open on a Sunday in order to cut the hair of small boys whose parents had failed miserably to get their shit together, she'd given Sam's hair a cursory trim, remembering this time to wash the kitchen scissors before she used them so that he didn't smell like rancid bacon for the next week.

And then, just as she was about to tuck them into bed and say goodnight, her mobile phone pinged with a Facebook notification from – who else? – Vivienne.

When Sam had first started in Reception, Gemma was met at the school gates on his first day by an intimidating-looking woman with a strident voice, who was accosting all of the new Year R parents in order to get them to provide their personal details on a clipboard she was brandishing. Said woman turned out to be Vivienne, mother of Tartan (a choice of name which surely counted as child cruelty), also starting in Year R. Vivienne had two other children in the school, was chair of the PTA (naturally) and self-proclaimed queen bee of the playground.

If you believed everything you read on Mumsnet, the universal uniform of queen bees in playgrounds the world over was all patterned-lining raincoats and striped Bretons. Gemma's first thoughts on meeting Vivienne were that she'd taken school-run fashion to a whole new level. She was less Boden and more bondage, with her skin-tight Seven For All Mankind jeans accessorised with what appeared to be a rubber sweater, the latest Mulberry on her arm, and skin so perfectly porcelain and line-free that there was no way she wasn't a regular at some expensive Harley Street Botox clinic. Around her were a group of three or four similarly attired mothers, giving the impression that Gemma had walked onto the set of the remake of *Charlie's Angels* rather than the school playground.

Such was Vivienne's terrifyingly persuasive manner that Gemma was swiftly and effectively intimidated into handing over so much personal information that she thought there was a good chance Vivienne would be able to embezzle her way into both her bank account and her soon-to-be-ex husband's bed by the time the bell rang for first break.

It transpired that the primary reason Vivienne had wanted to collect everyone's personal details was in order to set up the Redcoats Primary Year R Mummies' Facebook page. When she first received her invite to join, Gemma couldn't decide what she was most appalled by – the horrendously twee use of the word 'Mummies', the fact Vivienne had chosen to use a photograph of her own (Botoxed to fuck) face as the group profile photo, or the already-thriving discussion about how much homework the children would be getting in Year R. Most of the 'mummies' appeared to believe that at least an hour a night would be necessary if their offspring hoped to make it to Oxbridge one day. Gemma, meanwhile, looked at Sam and thought it was probably more important that he focused on not leaving skid marks in his pants and actually learning how to flush the toilet rather than completing his first doctorate in Latin by the end of KS1.

Despite her initial horror, though, there was no denying that the Facebook pages – first for Sam's class, then, latterly, Ava's – had had their uses. Although she had had the very best of intentions to run a tight ship as a parent, Gemma frequently failed miserably. Channelling all her organisational efforts into her role as operations director for a once-small-but-now-growing-rapidly start-up, the chances of her remembering that tomorrow was Pirate Day, or that next week Sam would be required to take a colander to school (reasons unknown) were fairly non-existent, were it not for the passive-aggressive reminders on the class Facebook pages.

Now, though, Vivienne was in serious danger of crowning off a thoroughly shitty end to the holidays in style. Gemma scrolled down to her post.

> I just couldn't wait, I hope no one minds, I just wanted to share Tartan's model that he's made of the London Eye. It's been an absolute labour of love

and has taken the whole family the best part of a
week to assemble, but it's been worth it – see how
it rotates!

Below the text was a video of what was almost an exact
replica of the London Eye, made from discarded match-
sticks, which did indeed rotate.

Below Vivienne's post a flurry of comments was starting to form.

That's so amazing, I wish our Tower of London
looked that good.

We've got to work out a way to get the River
Thames into school tomorrow without it leaking
everywhere, wish us luck!

The blood in her veins turning cold, Gemma spoke in
what the children – and certain members of her team at
work – frequently referred to as her Scary Psycho Lady Voice.
It was calm, and controlled, and exceedingly threatening.

'Sam?'

'Yes, Mum?'

'Was there any other homework that you had to do?'

Sam thought for a moment. 'Ummmmm ... I don't
think so.'

'What do you mean, you don't think so?'

'Well, there might have been a little bit.'

'What do you mean, a little bit?'

'I think we might have had to make a model.' He glanced
nervously at his mother.

12

'What kind of a model is that?'

'Um . . . I think it was a London landmark.'

'You had to make a London landmark?'

'Um . . . yes. Out of recycled materials.'

'And you decided it would be a good idea to wait until now to mention this, because . . . ?'

'Um. Um. Um. I forgot?'

For a moment, there was silence, other than Ava in the background belting out the lyrics to 'Blurred Lines' to herself, and the rest of the street. Ava had a knack of ensuring a direct correlation between the volume she chose to sing at and the inappropriateness of the lyrics she was singing.

There were, Gemma considered, a number of options open to her. She could totally lose her shit, which, from the look on Sam's face, was exactly what he was expecting her to do. She could drag Sam back out of bed and force them both to sit downstairs, working through the contents of the recycling bin in order to find something which wasn't an empty wine bottle to create some kind of half-arsed attempt at a London landmark.

Or she could stick a metaphorical two fingers up to the whole thing, write a note to Sam's teacher to explain the situation, say goodnight to the children and drown her sorrows in the no doubt slightly vinegary and headache-inducing bottle of wine she'd picked up in Tesco earlier . . . Dry January already being but a distant memory.

She had fought enough battles for one day. Startling Sam into silence, she kissed him goodnight and told him not to worry about it. Leaving her son gripped by a gaming

13

magazine which had DanTDM's face blazoned across the front of it, and her daughter twerking in her bedroom, she went downstairs, poured out the largest glass of wine imaginable and collapsed onto the sofa.

Truly, it had been an absolute fucker of a day.

Two

Becky looked through the windscreen impatiently as the removal van pulled into the tree-lined street ahead of them. This entire situation was very much less than ideal. The plan had always been for them to move at the start of the previous summer holidays. Of course, the house-buying system in the UK being what it was, their chain had collapsed three times, and despite Becky's pleas – varying from flirtatious at the start of the process to downright aggressive by the end – to estate agents and solicitors on all sides, it seemed nothing could be done to move their completion date forward any earlier than the first day of the spring term.

Frankly, it was a wonder that they'd made it to completion at all. Becky and her husband – known universally to their friends and family as Lovely Jon, on the grounds that he was, really, just lovely – had moved house eight times since they'd married fifteen years ago, and had never known a chain like this. Their buyer's buyer had been struck down with typhoid and had been hospitalised for four weeks, meaning nothing could be signed or progressed during that time. Their buyer's buyer's buyer had suddenly decided to do away with all material possessions and join a cult in New Mexico, meaning a new buyer's buyer's buyer had to be found. Becky didn't so much want to consign the house-buying process to Room 101 as hurl it in there, kicking and screaming and throwing a stiff-bodied tantrum as she did so.

Somehow, though, the fates had finally aligned and now they were actually moving, moving into what Becky sincerely hoped would be a house she might actually be able to call home. Lovely Jon's job, whilst exceedingly lucrative, often required him to move across the country at a moment's notice, and therefore they had never really had the opportunity to put down roots. Outgoing and gregarious by nature, Becky had done a sterling job at building relationships in her local area, but had each time had these cut short as the next promotion or opportunity came calling for Jon and the familiar trawl of Rightmove started up again.

This time, though, he had promised it was going to be different. Having done his time in the regional offices of the large conglomerate he worked for, he had now been promoted into the London head office and given a small team to head up. The golden boy of the Sales division, his path to the top looked certain.

Provided he could continue to churn out those eighty-hour weeks, that was.

From the back of the car, Rosie started up another chorus of Are We Nearly There Yet? Rosie was seven, bright as a button, and had adapted surprisingly well to being continuously shuttled around the country. That didn't mean she hadn't had quite enough of being sat in the car for the time being, thank you very much.

Next to her, snuggled into her car seat, sucking her dummy furiously, was nine-month-old Ella, and in the boot, panting and slobbering for all he was worth, was Boris, their absolute fucking liability of a golden retriever. Boris was excitable, affectionate and a complete and utter moron. Which put him neatly into the same category as a surprising number of Becky's exes.

As the removal van pulled up outside the front gate of number 48 – their new home – and Becky parked their four by four neatly behind it, the door of number 46 swung open and a harassed-looking woman staggered out. Looking out of the window curiously, Becky could barely make out the features of the woman who was presumably her new neighbour, so adorned was she with book bags, PE kits, water bottles and what looked like enough empty wine bottles to start up her very own branch of AA. Springing out of the car to say hello, Becky raised one hand in greeting and was about to call over when she was drowned out by the woman's voice.

'SAM! AVA! Get downstairs, NOW. Have you done your TEETH? HAIR? SHOES? Come on, come on, come on, we're going to be bastard late again. No, I haven't seen Lego Optimus Prime, and nor do I give a shit about his whereabouts. Sam, will you stop winding your sister up and take this model of the Shard that I painstakingly sat up and created for you last night so that I wouldn't be in trouble with your teacher? I mean, so that you wouldn't be in trouble with your teacher. No, it doesn't smell of "dirty wine". Okay, maybe it does a little bit. Look, Sam, I haven't got time to argue. Just hold your nose and get in the car, please? AVA! TEETH! HAIR! SHOES!'

The woman unlocked the grubby white Fiat Punto parked just behind Becky and hurled book bags, PE kits and water bottles into the boot as a tall and skinny boy with the craziest-looking hair Becky had ever seen climbed into the front, clutching the empty wine bottles, and a beautiful blonde girl with a face like an angel, who must have been about the same age as Rosie, got into the back holding a slice of toast and jam, which she was eating messily. Becky gave the odds on her getting to school without wearing most of it as so low as to be non-existent.

Before Becky could try again to make acquaintances, the engine revved and the Fiat Punto sped off, chucking out large clouds of black smoke as it did so. Lovely Jon got out of the passenger side, holding the keys to their new abode.

'Looks like she's got a bit of engine trouble there. I'll have to take a look at that for her.'

Not for the first time, Becky found herself thinking just how lovely her husband really was.

And wondering when 'lovely' had started sounding quite so derogatory as a descriptor.

Rosie was tapping on the car window, impatient to be let out. Her dad opened the door and she bounced onto the pavement, as Becky unstrapped a sleepy Ella from her car seat and held her in her arms.

'Mummy, Mummy, they go to my new school! I saw the big tree on their book bags.'

With a flash of recognition, Becky realised that her daughter was right. The bright red book bags with their distinctive silhouette of an oak tree were indeed the ones she, Lovely Jon and Rosie had seen when they'd visited the local primary school in the process of securing a place for Rosie. They were, they were told, extremely fortunate to be able to obtain a place at such short notice. The school – Ofsted outstanding – was heavily oversubscribed, and indeed, the catchment area for new Year R students had reduced to just 400 metres. Becky shuddered at the thought of having to get Ella in in four years' time, given that she was just a tiny bit too young for a guaranteed sibling place. She would have to persuade Jon that making an obscenely large charitable donation to the PTA would be the right thing to do. Or get him to sleep with the headmistress. One or the other should do it.

Fortunately, Rosie's year had been a particularly low birth year, and with another Ofsted outstanding school at the end of the road opening a bulge class, Rosie had been offered a place to start in January. Becky and Jon had debated long and hard whether this was the right thing for their daughter. And by 'debated', what they really meant was 'totally lost their shit with each other and threatened divorce proceedings'.

Lovely Jon was absolutely convinced, bless him, that their children should be privately educated. After all, it had worked out pretty well for Becky and him. He himself came from a long line of English aristocracy; it had been taken as read that he would go to the local Eton-equivalent. Becky, meanwhile, was the overachieving product of her Filipino parents, who had come to live in the UK in their early twenties as a result of her dad's role with the bank he had worked for ever since. Nothing was too good for their little girl, and they would invest whatever resources were necessary for Becky to have the best education that money could buy.

Lovely Jon had excelled himself, proving himself fully worthy of his parents' faith in him. Meanwhile, Becky had gone totally off the rails, shagged her way around the neighbouring state comprehensive and had got hauled up in front of the headmistress for suspected possession of cocaine. (It was actually some Elizabeth Arden talcum powder that her Gran had sent her; not that Becky was going to let onto that to the rest of her class. Being thought of as the class druggie gave you infinitely more street cred.)

Becky would never forget the visit she had received, not long after that incident, from her mum and dad. Proud and reserved, they rarely showed their emotions. Unless, that was, they received a phone call from the head of Becky's boarding school telling them that their daughter was under suspicion of possession of class A drugs.

After the ringing in her ears had stopped, Becky decided it was time to get her shit together. Consequently, she finished her A levels with four straight A grades – a matching set for those of her future husband-to-be.

Despite the impressive list of qualifications they held between them, Becky was emphatic in her rebuttal of Jon's claim that private education had worked out okay for the two of them.

'Absolutely no fucking way, over my dead body, no, ever, ever, ever, ever. It didn't fucking well work out for you and me. You were a social pariah, until I took you under my wing and showed you how real people work, and I went totally off the rails, had half the class snorting Elizabeth Arden talcum powder, and slept with so many unsuitable men that I feel like I ought to have some kind of Guinness World Records recognition for it.'

Lovely Jon gulped. He never knew entirely what to say when Becky brought up her somewhat-off-the-rails past. Particularly given he was never completely sure that the off-the-rails element was actually behind her.

Fortunately, a happy compromise was reached. With the new house having an Ofsted outstanding state school within walking distance – which by Becky's estimates had added approximately £250,000 to the house price, meaning they'd actually have *saved* money by paying to privately educate not only their children, but quite possibly half the children in the street – and Lovely Jon having braved a look around and discovered that contrary to the *Daily Mail* reports he had read, state schools didn't all contain brawling feral children brandishing knives while their teachers cowered behind iron bars, and could actually be really rather civilised, a place was obtained in Year 2 for Rosie and everyone breathed a sigh of relief.

The plan had been that they would complete during the previous summer and would be all settled in, ready for Rosie to start school on the first day of the autumn term. Clearly, things had gone somewhat to pot, and now Rosie would be starting at her new school one term and one day into the school year.

'It will be fine,' Lovely Jon had said, when Becky had finally had no alternative but to accept that her daughter would have to be pulled out of the school she was happily settled in after the first term of Year 2. 'So Rosie will have to start school a couple of days after the start of term. She will be absolutely fine.'

Becky, who remembered from bitter personal experience all too well what seven-year-old girls could be like to anyone new joining their class halfway through the year, burst into floods of hysterical tears, and was only eventually placated by the lion's share of the bottle of Bollinger that Lovely Jon's favourite clients had sent him, alongside a promise from Lovely Jon that he would make everything okay.

He had better, Becky thought bitterly to herself, walking up the path to her new home and attempting to prevent Boris – who had totally lost his shit since being released from his car-boot prison – from pissing all over her new neighbours' garden. He had better bloody make everything okay.

Three

The school gates were absolutely heaving. As always, Gemma, Sam and Ava were running terminally late, fighting against the flow of traffic of parents leaving the school grounds in order to get themselves, book bags, PE kits, water bottles and wine-bottle model Shard inside before Mr Cook the caretaker shut the gates and both children (and Gemma) were tarnished with a Late Mark on the first day of term.

On the other side of the gates, Vivienne, whose first day of term outfit seemed to involve an awful lot of extremely tight leather – either she was auditioning for a bondage film or she was deliberately showing off how little she'd overindulged over the Christmas break, in contrast to Gemma, who'd had to actually lift her stomach up with both hands to pour it inside the waistband of her jeans that morning – was standing officiously with a clipboard. Not another sodding clipboard.

Over the hubbub of the crowds and the shrieks of Ava

telling Sam that if he didn't stop breathing the bit of air next to her, on the grounds that it was *her* bit of air ... Gemma heard Vivienne and her entourage barking at each of the Year 2 parents who had the misfortune to catch their eyes that they had better ensure they turned up and were on time for tonight. Vivienne not only had Tartan in Sam's year, but to add insult to injury, her youngest daughter – Satin (of course) – was exactly the same age as Ava, meaning Vivienne seemed to be almost omnipresent in Gemma's school life.

'Don't forget, attendance is mandatory, and I *don't* want anyone letting the side down. Make sure you're there on time, or you'll have me to answer to!' She said it with a rictus grin on her face, but her voice had a steel brittleness to it which made it all too clear that she wasn't fucking joking.

Out of the corner of her eye, Gemma saw Noah Hardcastle's mum arriving in the playground. Sarah Hardcastle was one of the only mothers at the school who could make Gemma feel like she might not be automatically ring-fenced for relegation from the Parenting League Table. With five children in tow – two of whom were in the same year, thanks to Sarah fatefully believing the myth that breastfeeding acted as a natural contraceptive (she now spent much of her time regaling to anyone who would listen how much those pedalling this myth were LYING FUCKING BASTARDS) – Sarah was perpetually late, perpetually harassed and perpetually looked like she might either burst into tears or make a run for it out of the playground shouting 'FREEEEEEEEEEEDOM!' Given how she felt most of the time – and that was with just the two children to deal with – Gemma wouldn't entirely have blamed her if she did.

Gemma raised her hand in a gesture of solidarity to Sarah as the latter attempted to simultaneously tie one child's tie, prevent her youngest from smearing snot onto her older brother (she failed) and forcibly remove the tablet the two oldest were glued to, much to the disapproval of Vivienne and her coven. Now there was a parent after her own heart.

Swerving as far away from Vivienne as she possibly could to avoid being accosted and having all of her failings as a school parent itemised in front of the assembled crowds, Gemma ran frantically through what the woman could be going on about in her head. Tonight ... Tonight ... What the fuck was tonight? Something school-related, presumably. God, could this school not even give them a fighting chance of getting through the first week without adding in a load of extracurricular after-school requirements for parents to attend? This was the trouble with these Ofsted outstanding schools, thought Gemma, grimly. Always trying to fucking outperform themselves. What was wrong with a bit of mediocrity, for goodness' sake?

Sam, now on the KS2 side of the school, was the first to be dropped off. Mutely, he grabbed his book bag, PE kit and water bottle from Gemma, whose primary purpose in the eyes of her children seemed to be that of packhorse, ducked out of the way of her proffered kiss and 'I love you' with a 'Shurrrup, Mum, you're *so embarrassing*' and stomped into school with his wine-bottle model Shard held aloft. Gemma watched him go, already mourning the loss of the brand new school shoes and uniform he was wearing, which would inevitably be shredded and covered in mud – and, if she was really lucky, a spot or two of fox poo – by the end of the day.

One down, one to go. Ava's classroom was on the other side of the school; generally a far more painful drop-off thanks to the propensity of Vivienne and Co. to block the classroom door while they treated the poor, long-suffering Miss Thompson to a dramatic reconstruction of everything their child had done in the eighteen hours since they left her care. Gemma quite often felt like nominating Miss Thompson for a damehood, so patient was she with these horrendous women who systematically leached away her soul whilst itemising every single minutia of their child's bowel movements, so the rest of the (comparatively low-maintenance) parents couldn't even shove their child into the school and make a run for it.

The one advantage of Vivienne taking up her position to harangue everyone as they walked through the gates meant that today Gemma was faced with no such barrier to dropping her daughter off. As Ava deliberated over whether to have the red or green option for lunch, and brightly announced that she was now a vegetarian, 'because it will make up for you killing so many of those poor baby whales, Mummy', Gemma looked around for Miss Thompson. Her no-nonsense Hush Puppies and resigned expression were nowhere to be seen, however, and in her absence Gemma handed Ava across to Miss Harris, the Year 2 classroom assistant. Miss Harris had joined Redcoats Primary fresh out of university and looked progressively more broken and like she wished she'd simply chosen to work at Tesco instead every time Gemma saw her.

Waving her daughter inside, Gemma checked her watch. Two minutes after her first meeting of the day had started.

Marvellous. Hoping that her pelvic floor would keep it together, Gemma braced herself and made a run for the car.

The office was already packed by the time Gemma pulled into the car park at Zero, the offices of which were mercifully only a ten-minute drive away from the kids' school, and dashed inside to try and make it for the first part of the Monday morning management meeting. Dodging the clothing samples and delivery drivers already thronging reception, she walked through the noisy, bustling open-plan office, responding to a series of quick 'hellos' before diving into the glass-fronted capsule which counted as their only meeting room.

'Here she is, at bloody last,' chirped her boss Leroy, whose energy levels were set permanently at that of the Duracell bunny, regardless of the time of day or night. 'What's kept you, Gemma? Too busy salivating over dick pics on Tinder? I told you, you won't find me on there. Don't take this the wrong way, sweets, but you're just not my type. Try Grindr, on the other hand . . . ' He cackled uproariously.

Leroy was a software developer by trade, who fancied himself as the next Mark Zuckerberg and was convinced that creating software which helped people to buy clothes that would actually fit them, even if they were a size eight according to one manufacturer, a size fourteen according to another, and found it impossible to shop in one particular outlet altogether owing to the fact that they were over a size zero, because *clothes sizing is bonkers* . . . was the way to achieve that dream.

To the surprise of everyone – except, perhaps, the effusively optimistic Leroy – Zero had been a hit. In fact, Zero had grown more quickly than anyone had anticipated, and Gemma, who had been employee number four in her first job after finishing her A levels – as a general admin assistant/dogsbody – had found herself having the time of her life. Leroy was mad, occasionally off-the-wall bonkers, and quite impossible to predict, yet also wonderfully generous, and wanted to create a working environment where people loved coming to work every day, and where he could look after the people who were loyal and were helping him transform the business.

Swallowing down rising nausea at the thought of Leroy's dick pics – not to mention her overconsumption of Sauvignon Blanc the previous evening – Gemma shot him the sort of look she employed when Sam attempted to push the boundaries by trying out the latest swear word he'd picked up in the playground. Or from his mother. 'No, I wasn't on sodding Tinder. I was busy delivering my hand-sculpted wine bottle model of the Shard to school without being pulled over by the police wanting to know what the hell I was doing with fourteen empty bottles of wine on the front seat of my car on a Monday morning.'

Natalie, their always immaculately presented sales and marketing director, who was the newest addition to their board team, raised a perfectly arched eyebrow. 'Fuck, I'm never having kids. They make you parents do some utterly mental stuff.'

Understatement of the year, thought Gemma. Understatement of the year.

Sliding into the chair between Leroy and Dave the finance director, a man in his mid fifties who dressed like Sam and smelt alternatively of coffee or Jack Daniel's,

Gemma mentally congratulated herself on successfully getting both herself and her children to their intended destinations without any actual acts of physical violence taking place. Sure, she might be running late – as per – but from the way the team were all crowded around Leroy's laptop laughing she guessed she hadn't missed too much.

The rest of the board meeting passed with the four of them mostly focused on the critical strategic topic of reviewing the photos from the staff Christmas party. Gemma counted twelve nipples, four scrotums and one labial piercing amongst the shots they'd been sent by the guy operating the photo booth they rented. Good to see the pre-party 'Don't get so twatted you end up with your genitals getting photographed' memo had been adhered to.

As they gathered up their stuff and Leroy asked them if there was anything else before they went their separate ways back to their respective teams, Dave vaguely waved a spreadsheet in their faces. 'Just so you know, cash is a bit tight at the moment. I'm chatting to a couple of people to see what we can do to tide ourselves over, but just don't make any crazy purchases in the meantime.'

He was, Gemma thought wryly, almost certainly referring to the time Leroy had decided, fuelled by drink on a Saturday all-nighter, to buy a company yacht. Quite why Zero needed a company yacht, being at least a hundred miles from the nearest coast, was never really made clear. Fortunately for everyone, Dave managed to do some fast talking and the yacht was returned to its vendor, while Leroy muttered bitterly about how Dave had ruined the business's prospects for the year, and how could they possibly be expected to play with the big boys if they didn't even have a company yacht, for goodness' sake?

A company yacht being a critical part of growing a land-locked clothing-sizing business, of course.

Walking back to her desk, Gemma was immediately surrounded by various members of her teams, all wanting to get her input and opinion on matters which varied from how they were going to respond to a major customer complaint that they'd just received to who she thought was going to win *Celebrity Big Brother*.

Frankly, Gemma still thought it was remarkable that anyone valued her opinion at all. Having been fast-tracked by Leroy to success and promoted into her current position three years ago, she still occasionally had to pinch herself to remember that it was true: that she really was Operations Director, with responsibility for more than eighty employees – something she tried not to think about too much, on the grounds that if she did she'd become immediately terrified and probably want to go and hide under her desk with her hands over her face.

Gemma sat down at her desk on her pod and plugged in her laptop. Next to her was her assistant, Siobhan, who'd worked at Zero for almost as long as Gemma had. Siobhan was tiny, feisty and impossibly good at her job; in fact, Gemma often wondered if the only reason she'd held down her own job as long as she had was because she had Siobhan covering her back. The irony was, despite her feistiness, that Siobhan was shockingly lacking in self-confidence, and was just as reliant on Gemma to assure her that yes, she was doing a good job, and no, everyone didn't think she was utterly inept. It had become a standing joke amongst the team that her first words to Gemma every morning, without exception, were always, 'Am I sacked yet?'

'How was your Christmas?' Gemma asked.

'Fucking epic,' responded Siobhan. 'Out every single night, I've not been to bed before four a.m. for the last week and I've likely got pure vodka running through my veins after New Year. What a fucking night.' She paused for a moment, before asking politely, 'You?'

Gemma thought for a moment about her own Christmas break. If you believed everything you read in the media, Christmas with children was just magical. All Gemma could say to that was magical, my arse. Christmas as a single parent had been less about #blessed moments gathered around the Christmas tree unwrapping gifts, and more about a three a.m. Christmas Day wakeup call, both kids descending into meltdown by mid-morning, and covert swigs from the gin bottle she'd secreted in the cereal cupboard while the turkey (that no one would eat anyway) dried out in the oven and she wondered, if she wished hard enough, whether the magic of Christmas might bring Prince Charming to her (old, slightly peeling) front door.

Christmas had been followed by New Year: a Disney movie with the kids and then a Waitrose (she'd upgraded, on account of it being a special occasion) ready meal for one with a bottle of Prosecco that tasted flat and acrid in her mouth. She'd watched Jools Holland welcome in the New Year and had been in bed and asleep by 12.02 a.m.

'Yeah, epic,' she replied sarcastically. 'I think I was probably getting up most days about the same time you were going to bed.'

Siobhan shook her head in disgust and repeated, not for

the first time, what she'd be doing to any man who even so much as thought of getting her up the duff. 'I'd have my hedge clippers out and—' She made a dramatic gesture, accompanied with sound effects which had every man in the vicinity wincing in horror and clutching their genitals protectively.

Laughing out loud, Gemma told them all to pipe down and get on with their work, and that no, Siobhan hadn't brought her hedge clippers with her, so they would not be wasting half of their morning demanding risk assessments for perceived threat against their nether regions.

There were a million and one reasons Gemma loved working at Zero, but the sheer amount of fun she got to have at work was right at the top of the list. She heard all the time from various friends and acquaintances how much they loathed their employment and how they couldn't wait to win the lottery and retire to a beach apartment in Marbella. It was an entirely alien concept to Gemma. Even on the very worst of days, when everyone had lost their shit at home before they'd even opened their eyes, there had never been a time when she hadn't looked forward to going into work. In fact, if she was completely honest, sometimes going into work had been the only thing still joining her to the last vestiges of her sanity.

Her phone buzzed on the desk next to her and Siobhan groaned. 'Don't tell me. It's that bloody school again, isn't it? Honestly, it's like some kind of abusive relationship, the number of times a day they try and contact you.' She shook her head as Gemma picked up her mobile, knowing that her assistant was almost certainly correct.

Gemma had a love/hate relationship with the texting

service provided by the school, direct to your mobile. On the one hand, there was no denying it was useful when it came to remembering to pay overdue invoices for music lessons and the fact that tomorrow was Photosynthesis Day and all children were required to wear green, because it is not fucking hard enough getting everyone washed and dressed and out of the house on a weekday morning anyway, without having to find an elusive item of green clothing as well.

On the other hand, Siobhan wasn't wrong – it could be a little like having a needy ex messaging you at all hours of the day and night. When the texting service had been introduced, parents had been told that it would be used to convey urgent information only, and that standard news and information would continue to be communicated via the school intranet or in letters placed in book bags.

This turned out very much not to be the case.

There had been one particular day when Gemma had been involved in a critical strategy meeting with Leroy and Dave. Keeping her phone at hand, just in case the children needed her, her attention was drawn by a flurry of texts. Apologising, she picked up the phone and scanned through them.

There is NO red option for lunch today. Repeat: NO red option.

Year 2 will need to provide their own recorders for next week's Harvest Festival.

There will be a cake sale after school today. Please bring money! And cakes!

URGENT. URGENT. A blazer has gone missing from
a Year 3 peg. Please check all of your children's uniform URGENTLY.

It was safe to say that the school's definition of what was
urgent and Gemma's differed somewhat.

This time – thank heavens for small mercies – there
was no mention of recorders or missing blazers. Instead,
the series of text messages informed Gemma that all Year
2 parents were required to attend a school meeting that
evening at six p.m. in order to meet the new Year 2 teacher,
who had been drafted in as an emergency replacement
for Miss Thompson. If any parents were unable to attend,
they should call the office so that alternative arrangements
could be made.

Gemma's first thought was to wonder what had happened
to good old Miss Thompson. She had been at the school
as long as Gemma's children had, stalwartly heading up
Year 2 with a look of grim determination on her face. The
kind of teacher Gemma herself had had, she held no truck
with any of this 'modern government nonsense', as she
had once described the National Curriculum to Gemma
and a couple of the other parents, her lips loosened by the
complimentary mulled wine which had been provided at
last year's Nativity play.

Miss Thompson stuck a metaphorical two fingers up at
teaching children grammatical terminology which would
be about as useful to them in day to day life as being
able to write in hieroglyphics, did the bare minimum of
National Curriculum work necessary to scrape her classes
through their SATS and not have hordes of salivating

pushy parents beating down her classroom door, and focused heavily on her great passion of Putting On Plays. A thwarted actress, she had successfully auditioned for RADA, back in the day, but her impoverished parents had been unable to afford the fees. Resigning herself to a career outside of the theatre, Miss Thompson had instead turned to teaching and consoled herself by putting on a play approximately three times a week, to the delight of all of the lucky children she happened to teach.

But now . . . it seemed Miss Thompson had cut her losses and run, leaving Gemma to wonder who would be taking over responsibility for Year 2 for the rest of the academic year. Whoever it was, she didn't envy them. Whereas Sam's class, Year 5, were a generally mild-mannered bunch, Year 2 could be fucking savages. Ava had gleefully told the tale of how one of her classmates had dropped his trousers on the first day of term and taken an actual shit in the playground – 'And George tried to *eat it*.' Gemma didn't know how much teachers were paid, but however much it was, it wasn't enough.

The day passed in a blur of meetings and emails and promises to the guys she worked with that she wouldn't let Siobhan and her hedge clippers anywhere near them. Before she knew it, it was five p.m. and time to make the frantic dash from the office back to after-school club before it closed. When she'd first had kids, Gemma had been terrified about the impact they might have on her career. She'd broached it with Leroy as she'd sat with him planning her maternity leave when she'd first become pregnant with Sam.

To her surprise, Leroy, who was really little more than a

kid himself, had shrugged his shoulders. 'It's not going to be a problem. Why would it be? I don't care what hours you work. You hire the right people to keep the office running, be here when you can be, be with your kids when you need to be with your kids. Or bring them here. Or whatever. Gem, I don't care. I know absolutely nothing about kids, and it's highly unlikely I'll be having any of my own, unless they find a way to change the laws of basic biology so that an egg isn't an essential part of the process . . . but I do know that you keep all of this shit going, and, frankly, if you want to work from a remote island off the coast of Fiji then we'd still make it work. You've got my back, and I've got yours. That's how it works.'

And it had worked. It had worked surprisingly well, despite Gemma's constant juggling of work and home, something that had become even more pronounced after her ex, Nick the Dick, had decided to up and leave without a word. In Leroy, Gemma knew she had a truly supportive boss, and she was grateful for him and his mad little ways every single day.

Now, sitting in traffic, impatiently tapping her bitten nails on the steering wheel, it suddenly hit her like a ton of bricks. Fuck. The after-school meeting. It was too late to phone the school office and tell them that she couldn't be there. She would have to sort something out.

Her mother answered before the phone had even rung twice. 'Hello, love. How was your day?'

'Fine. Mum—'

'Need me to have the kids, do you? Yes, that's no problem. I thought you would, what with all that kerfuffle I saw going on on that Facebook page of yours. Dad and I'll pop over in about twenty minutes, does that give you enough time? No need to rush back, we'll be quite happy catching up on *Midsomer Murders*. Maybe you could go out for a drink with them all afterwards?'

Fighting back the urge to tell her mum exactly what she would say if Vivienne ever, ever asked her out for a drink – not that she would, the very thought was laughable – Gemma thanked her profusely and hung up the hands-free kit. Getting her mum invited to the school Facebook pages had slightly terrified her when her mum had first suggested it, but in actual fact it had turned out to be inspired. This would not be the first time Gemma's mum had known she was in the shit before Gemma herself had even realised it.

The children emerged from after-school club in their usual furious and monosyllabic style. Ava had black whiteboard pen, which Gemma knew from experience would never come out, not even after a combined bleach/boil wash attempt, all down the arms of her white shirt. ('I was drawing my veins.' 'Of course you were.') She also appeared to be sporting black whiteboard pen eyebrows, for absolutely no reason that Gemma could understand.

Sam, meanwhile, had baked beans down his jumper – as a result, no doubt, of his haphazard approach to eating, which was basically to throw all food in the vague direction of his mouth and hope that some of it landed – and Gemma could see one of the soles of his new shoes already starting to flap. Deciding she simply didn't have the time for a full-scale blazing row tonight, she manfully elected to ignore it completely.

Her mum and dad were already there by the time she

arrived home, having let themselves in with their spare key. Disloyal bastards that they were, the children's frowns and noncommittal grunts about what they'd done with their day ('Don't know', 'Can't remember') were immediately wiped off their faces at the sight of their grandparents. As Gemma went upstairs to get changed before heading back out again, she heard Ava telling her mum all about the planets in the solar system which she'd apparently been learning about that day, despite the fact that when Gemma had asked her the exact same question, 'And what's your topic for this term?' she'd received nothing more than a shrugged 'Stuff' in response.

Standing in front of her wardrobe, the inside of which looked more like a junk sale than the perfectly colour-coordinated and streamlined interior she sometimes imagined in her dreams, Gemma debated what items of clothing she possibly owned that could, in front of the heavily judgemental eyes of Vivienne and her Year 2 Mummies' crew, make her look a) thin, b) stylish, and c) like she had her shit together.

A cursory glance showed her that there was absolutely nothing that would tick all three of those boxes, or, indeed, any of them. Not that she'd needed to look in the wardrobe to be sure of that. On the grounds that she really didn't have the energy to polish a turd, she settled for a cursory wash under her arms with a baby wipe, a quick squirt of the Lidl Coco Mademoiselle knock off she'd bought up by the trolley load when it had finally appeared in stock, and a rigorous attempt to run her fingers through her short, curly, and almost as unruly as Sam's, hair. There. She would do. Well, she wouldn't do, she would never do in the eyes of

Vivienne and her crew, even if she turned up at the school gates clad from head to toe in Dolce and Gabbana with her BFF Victoria Beckham on her arm. But who cared what that coven of witches thought about her? Gemma didn't.

Most of the time, that was.

Four

Gemma was running late, as usual, so the Year 2 classroom was packed by the time she had blown a kiss to Sam and Ava, thanked her parents and driven back to the school. Squeezing her arse onto one of the miniature chairs, which had the unfortunate effect of pushing all of her post-baby gut over the top of her jeans, making her feel rather as though she was being strangled from the navel up, she spotted Vivienne and her coven in their traditional school meeting location: right at the front. Twittering around in their ridiculous way – was that a basque that Vivienne was wearing? – they had surrounded some poor, terrified-looking man whom Gemma didn't recognise. Probably one of the dads. Male parents were a rare species at the school gates, most likely because they'd had the common sense to come up with absolutely any excuse they could think of to stay far, far away.

Also at the front of the room was Simon Barnes's mum, Andrea. In stark contrast to Vivienne and her Angels,

Andrea's school run style was best described as Laura Ashley having thrown up all over her. Appearances could be deceiving though, and Andrea was quite as terrifying as Vivienne and Co. in her own special way.

Andrea was absolutely convinced that Simon was an angel sent down from heaven and was determined that every single person – students, teachers and parents alike – should see this too. Unfortunately for her, this perception was somewhat at odds with the reality of Simon Barnes. 'Oh look at him,' she would twitter, as he deliberately and systematically swung his book bag around his head, taking out every small child in the vicinity and leaving them wailing on the ground. 'So spirited!'

Spirited was not the word anyone else would have used to describe Simon Barnes, but Andrea was keen to ensure that this new teacher was fully briefed on her son's genius from day one. Hence sitting in the front row, where she would be able to maximise her opportunities to ask about what activities would be being put on for the Gifted and Talented students that year. Her son hadn't been included in the Gifted and Talented students listing last term, which had clearly been an oversight. Andrea was delighted that they were getting a new teacher, who would surely be better than silly old Miss Thompson at spotting her angel's potential.

About to pull out her phone in order to be able to stare furiously at its screen and thereby avoid having to make awkward small talk – Gemma loathed small talk, which was possibly part of the reason why she'd been so spectacularly unsuccessful at infiltrating any of the friendship groups within the school playground – she was distracted by the sound of another mum crashing down next to her, scraping the legs of her tiny chair across the room as she did so.

'Fuck, I didn't mean to do that. Fuck, I didn't mean to say fuck, either. Fuck, I'm going to be thrown out of this school before Rosie's even got her foot through the door.' Unable to ignore such a dramatic entrance, Gemma unwillingly looked up from her phone, to be confronted by one of the most beautiful women she had ever had the misfortune to meet.

'Hi. I'm Becky. You must be Gemma? We're neighbours! I moved in this morning, well, we all did, me and Lovely Jon – he's my husband, wants to have a look at your car for you – and Rosie – she's the same age as your little girl, it's Ava, isn't it – and The Afterthought, I mean Ella – oh, and Boris the fucking liability, I nearly forgot about him, but don't worry, you'll love him, he's great with kids, and bloody hell, is this thing going to go on for long? I'm absolutely starving.'

Becky said all of this without a breath and Gemma stared at her, absolutely shell-shocked. Who was this whirlwind of energy, how did she know so much about Gemma, and where did she get those *incredible* boots from?

All of these questions would have to wait for the moment as Mrs Goldman, the entirely terrifying headmistress at Redcoats, moved towards the front of the room and commanded silence from the assorted parents in the same way that she did her school of four- to eleven-year-olds in Monday morning assembly: simply by sweeping her gaze around the room. Her lips pursed, she attempted what probably counted as a smile before reverting to her far more customary disapproving frown.

42

'Parents. Thank you very much for attending this evening, and my apologies for the short notice in calling you all to the school. However, I thought it was important that I update you on the situation regarding Miss Thompson.

'As you are all aware, Miss Thompson was due to take your children through their SATS this year. Unfortunately for all of us, it seems that Miss Thompson had something of a . . . moment of madness.' ('Saw the fucking light, more like,' Becky whispered in Gemma's ear, causing her to stifle a giggle which had the head looking over at her furiously.)

'She therefore informed me, on the last day of term, that she would not be returning to Redcoats after the Christmas break, and that she would be –' here Mrs Goldman pursed her lips even tighter, if such a thing were possible '– changing her career path, and moving out of teaching altogether.' There was a gasp from around the room, and Mrs Goldman looked gratified at the clear collective shock from the assembled parents at Miss Thompson's frankly unacceptable behaviour.

'It has therefore left me in the difficult position of having to find a new Year 2 teacher to take over teaching for the remainder of the academic year. Usually, as you will be aware, it requires several terms to secure a teacher of Miss Thompson's calibre. However, I am delighted to be able to tell you –' was it Gemma's imagination, or did she sound rather less than delighted? '– that Mr Jones will be taking over responsibility for Year 2 with immediate effect. Mr Jones.' With a commanding hand, she gestured at the man sitting next to Vivienne to stand up. The man who, Gemma realised with a start, was not a parent, but must be none other than Mr Jones.

'Fuck me.' Becky, again, now practically salivating as she craned her neck to get a better look at Mr Jones. 'That is one beautiful, beautiful man. *Man*, why did I have to get married so young? I might not have rushed into saying those vows quite so quickly if I'd known Idris Elba's even hotter younger brother over there was going to be featuring prominently in my future.'

Mildly appalled though she was by Becky's blatant perving, Gemma was struggling to disagree. The man standing nervously in front of the class – there was surely no way he could do anything so mundane as teaching, was there? This was the kind of man who made a career out of modelling. Or acting. Or stalking around in a sharp-looking suit making millions while he shouted 'BUY! BUY! SELL! SELL!' into his phone and a team of minions ran around him hanging onto his every word.

Tall – but not too tall; young – but not too young; he sported chiselled cheekbones, designer stubble (Gemma gave Mrs Goldman a week, tops, before she had it all shaved off on the grounds that it breached a new school policy which she would be writing specially in Mr Jones's honour), flawless skin, and hair which was not dissimilar to Sam's in the way that it defied gravity and flopped every which way that it wanted. Again, Gemma imagined Mrs Goldman would have him marched down to the barber in town demanding a short back and sides in no time. Mrs Goldman had scant time for floppy, unruly hair.

He wore a navy suit, no tie, with the sleeves rolled up and one hand in his pocket, and Gemma thought she had never seen anyone looking so unlike a teacher in her life.

The parents looked at him expectantly as he nervously

got to his feet and turned to face them. 'Um ... hello. I'm Mr Jones. Tom Jones.' A polite titter ran around the room. 'Yeah, you can blame my parents for that one.

'Um ... so I'll be teaching your children. I'll be starting full time in the classroom from tomorrow. I've got lots of experience from when I taught at ... another school. I'm passionate about helping children to enjoy learning and discover what it is that they're great at. Year 2 can be a difficult year, because we have to get the children through their SATS, but I'll do that in as low-key a manner as possible. Most of them shouldn't even realise that they're taking tests.'

Vivienne raised a disapproving eyebrow and Andrea tutted. Both women wholeheartedly disapproved of the way that schools kept trying to play down tests and league tables. I mean, really, what was the point in having children at all if you weren't going to be able to gloat about their academic prowess and league-table positioning?

'Anyway, you're all busy people and I don't want to keep you here any longer than necessary,' he continued. 'I'm sure you all have things you'd rather be doing, but I'll be here if you have any questions you'd like me to answer, or you're welcome to come and make an appointment to speak with me at the start or end of the school day. I look forward to getting to know you all and, of course, your children. Thanks very much.'

There was a polite ripple of applause as Mr Jones slumped in obvious relief back into his seat. Already, hands were shooting up around the room, with Vivienne and Andrea rather giving the impression of toddlers in desperate need of the toilet, the way they were swivelling around in their seats with their hands high in the air. Gemma zoned out as the two of them began firing questions at the new teacher in quick succession, in the manner of two competing auction bidders. Poor guy; if he could weather this, taking care of thirty six- to seven-year-olds for the rest of the year would likely be child's play by comparison.

With Vivienne and Andrea both in full flow, Gemma had visions of them being stuck there all night. Thankfully Mrs Goldman stepped in, promising the assembled parents that those of them who had further questions for Mr Jones would be able to remain behind to speak to him one to one. From the gleam in the head's eyes, Gemma suspected she was well aware of the baptism of fire she was unleashing upon him.

Seconds later, the throng of mums waiting to interrogate the new teacher was already six deep, those at the back of the pack frantically reapplying their lipstick and primping their hair. Entirely uninterested in joining the queue to interrogate the new teacher – she was just relieved that Mr Jones had turned out to be somewhat less verbose than Miss Thompson, who did like to use these parent/teacher meetings to make up for her thwarted acting ambitions and treat them to a thirty-minute monologue on Teaching Practices Today – Gemma picked up her handbag and prepared to leave. She levered herself out of her tiny chair, tucking her stomach surreptitiously back into her jeans as she did so, and stood up at exactly the same time as Becky, who was looking at her expectantly.

'So, what happens now? Do we go to the pub? Is there somewhere we can get some food? I'm starving! Do you think that actual sex god of a man would like to come with us? God, can you imagine what he'd look like without his clothes on?' She shivered in delicious anticipation.

'Um.' Gemma shook her head to rid it of the disturbingly appealing image of what Mr Jones might look like *sans* clothing. She was somewhat nonplussed by Becky's suggestion that they go to the pub.

In the five years Sam had been at the school, Gemma could count on the fingers of one hand the number of times she'd been asked out socially by another parent, and it had hardly been to desirable locations, either. There had been the trip to the local soft play to drink tepid coffee that tasted like piss while their children entered the Lord of the Flies-style arena and twatted the fuck out of each other (Gemma would never forget Ava triumphantly appearing at the top of the slide into the ball pit and announcing, 'George is crying because he said that boys were better at fighting than girls and now he knows that he is wrong. Also, you need to tell the people who work here that there is blood in the ball pit'). Then there was a horrendous 'Mummies' Night Out' with a couple of the mums who were hovering on the edges of the PTA clique and had invited a handful of similarly out-of-favour parents to the pub in order to increase their social standing and give themselves a fighting chance of getting the nod in the next PTA elections. The seven who had been pressganged into going along had ended up in the local Wetherspoon's, where they'd shared two bottles of unspeakably dreadful wine and then, finding they had absolutely nothing in common other than the fact they'd all had sex minus the contraception to produce their offspring during the same academic year, made their polite excuses and had been home in bed by nine p.m.

The idea that this Becky thought she, Gemma, might be in some way part of the in crowd when it came to the school social scene was, frankly, laughable.

'To be honest, I think I need to get back – my parents are babysitting.' Lying through her teeth, she hoped her extremely unsubtle hint would be taken.

It wasn't. 'That's right – Rose and Tony, isn't it? Met them this afternoon when they popped over. Lovely people. I said to them that I was going up to the school tonight and they suggested we went for a few drinks afterwards, give us a chance to get to know each other. To be honest, it's probably the one chance I'll get all year, what with Jon actually being forced to take a day off for the house move and therefore not in the office until ten o'clock at night. Plus, the longer I stay out, the less unpacking of boxes I'll end up having to do. So what do you reckon?'

Bloody hell, she was persistent. Sighing inwardly, Gemma considered her options. She could put her foot down and say no. She had a ton of work to get through, the house looked like Primark at the end of a busy Saturday, and she could really live without having her Tuesday morning meetings accompanied by a banging hangover.

On the other hand . . . mildly unhinged as she seemed, this Becky was going to be her new neighbour. It made sense to get to know her given they were going to be living within one paper-thin wall of each other; she might be in need of some goodwill when Ava started blasting out 'I'm Sexy And I Know It' through the walls in a faux American accent at five-thirty a.m. And she really was fucking gasping for a drink.

'You're on,' said Gemma decisively. 'Follow me. I know just the place.'

No more than twenty minutes later, Gemma and Becky were safely ensconced in a booth in the nearby George and Dragon. It was one of those pubs which had undergone the now standard early twenty-first-century transformation, from unspeakably grim darkened room with sticky carpet and smelling strongly of urine, to chichi wine bar with uplighters and polished floorboards, serving organic Prosecco and gluten-free bar snacks. A one-time haunt of Gemma's and Nick the Dick's, it was far enough away from the school for Gemma to feel comfortable that none of the other parents were likely to follow them in there.

If Becky was intrigued by the fact that it was just her and Gemma heading off for a drink, she didn't say so. Instead, she followed Gemma's lead to leave her car in the school playground ('It'll annoy the hell out of Mr Cook, but we'll just pretend we had an emergency') and strode down the street at a pace that belied her ferociously high heels on those incredible boots. Gemma had looked on in open-mouthed awe.

Arriving in the almost empty bar – well, it was the first Monday in January – Becky greeted the bar staff like old friends. Gemma stood back as she asked them how they'd been and whether there was anything in particular on the menu that they'd recommend.

'Have you been here before?' Gemma found herself asking curiously.

'Nope! Never seen the place in my life! Just saying hello.' Becky grinned and disappeared to find a table.

They settled in with a shared bottle of Shiraz and, completely ignoring the gluten-free/organic/vegan side of the menu, ordered oversized plates of fish and chips.

Discussions over their dinner choices complete, Gemma had a brief moment of panic when she wondered what the hell they were going to talk about now. It was short lived, as she realised that Becky could talk for Britain, and had enough energy and natural curiosity to keep the conversation going for an entire week.

'So, that Miss Thompson. She's a one, isn't she? You've got to hand it to her, though. Teaching must be an absolute fucking grind. I mean, I only have to spend five minutes reading with Rosie and I want to put her up for adoption and slam my head repeatedly in the oven door whilst screaming for salvation, so goodness knows how teachers keep their shit together. Good for her for finding her toy boy and running off into the sunset.'

Gemma nearly choked on her wine. 'Her ... her what?'

'She finally met the love of her life, didn't she. According to that parents' Facebook page, that is. They've been jabbering on about it all day. Is that Vivienne woman a private investigator or something? She seems to know all about her. Lifelong spinster, surrounded by cats, thought she'd never meet her man ... and then, out of the blue, goes to watch a play one evening, he's in the audience, turns out to be the director – only in his forties - sweeps her off her feet, they have a short and heady romance and the next thing you know she's handing in her notice and running off to live with him in the South of France where he's got a theatre company and she can put on plays all day long, to her heart's content. Ah, it warms the cockles of your heart, doesn't it?'

Gemma was almost too stunned to speak. Miss Thompson ... what? Had run off to the South of France?

50

With a theatre director? Who was about twenty years younger than her? Where the hell had Becky got this ludicrous version of events from?

'Facebook,' said Becky, reading her mind and nodding sagely. 'It's all on there. I knew it would be; Facebook class pages are always where all the gossip is. First thing I did when Rosie was accepted into the school was to wangle myself an invite.'

Blimey. Maybe Gemma should start paying a bit more attention to Facebook. Not only would Sam not end up being the only kid in the class who had to borrow a colander from the school kitchen instead of remembering to bring in his own (she still had not a fucking clue what the colander requirement had been all about), it might mean she wasn't always the last person to find out what was going on.

Becky was still talking. 'And it checks out, too – I looked up this guy, and he does indeed have a theatre company, and she is indeed now listed as guest artistic director. Good for her, I say. And, more's the benefit to us – we get Sexy Mr Jones instead.' She started tunelessly belting out 'Sex Bomb', much to the disapproval of the other punters in the bar.

Well well well. So Miss Thompson had finally met her prince. Good for her. Maybe that meant there was hope for all of them when it came to True Love. Even Gemma.

'Back to the divine Mr Jones, though. Are all the teachers that bloody fit? Actually, strike that: from the look of Mrs Goldman, clearly not.' Becky took an enormous slug of her wine. 'God, I needed that. He's fucking gorgeous. It's a good job he's not teaching me; I'd be sat there totally useless with my tongue hanging out. Ooh, I wonder if he's single.'

Tentatively, Gemma reminded the irrepressible Becky that she did actually have a husband. Becky threw back her beautiful head, laughing uproariously. 'Oh, don't you worry. Lovely Jon and I are sickeningly in love, you'll see. Not bad given we've been married for more than fifteen years.' Before Gemma could blink, Becky had launched into her life story. 'So we met at Oxford – the university. Don't write me off just yet. I'm not one of those toffs, promise. To be honest, I don't remember much about the first time I saw Jon. I was absolutely off my tits and was dressed like I thought I was Lara Croft. I mean, in hindsight, it's no wonder Jon fell for me.' She honked with laughter and swallowed another gulp of wine before flicking through her phone and passing it to Gemma. 'There's me. Quite a sight, no?'

Gemma looked at the slightly blurred photo, clearly scanned in from the days before digital photography was the norm. Neither of her children could quite get their heads around how much technology had moved on since Gemma was their age. 'Did you live in *caves*?' Ava had once asked her, awestruck.

Becky didn't appear to have changed in the slightest between the photo and now. Other than her attire, that was. In the photo she was wearing red sequinned hot pants which Jessica Rabbit would frankly have dismissed as being too risqué, and an item of underwear which was masquerading as a top. She also appeared to be downing a yard of ale. Gemma raised one eyebrow as she passed the phone back.

'Oh, I know. And that was one of my more demure outfits, right? We did tequila slammers after that. Man, student life was the absolute best of times.'

Gemma felt a moment of irrational jealousy. She had never had an opportunity to go to university. Having grown up on a council estate – and not a particularly nice one either – with her brother Craig and her parents, Gemma had always had it drummed into her that she would have to work hard if she wanted to be able to have nice things and live a nice life. Consequently, while all of her friends were heading off to rack up debt on pointless university courses or go and fuck around in Bali on a so-called 'gap year', Gemma was already starting to build her career.

'I don't think Jon had ever seen anyone quite like me in his life,' Becky continued. 'He looked a bit like he wanted to run for the hills. Which was a shame, because I'd already decided that he was going to be my future husband.'

Unused to not having whatever she wanted simply fall into her lap, Becky had found Jon puzzling. 'He avoided me like I had the plague. You see, his parents had drummed it into him that his future wife would be someone who was calm, sensible and knew how to conduct herself when taken home to meet Granny for the first time. Granny, frankly, would have had a coronary arrest if I'd turned up at hers for afternoon tea.'

Becky went on to explain how she and Jon had become friends. 'The only male friend I've ever had who I couldn't coerce into bed. To be honest, I was beginning to doubt myself; I'd thought my seduction skills were infallible. I even considered trying a love spell to get him to fall for me.' She covered her face, laughing. 'I mean, the shame!

'It all ended happily though. Basically, I wormed my way into his – platonic – affections, and then arranged for us to apply for graduate schemes in the same organisation. Oh, and then what do you know? His flat share fell through!' Becky winked at Gemma. 'By sheer good fortune I had a spare room in the place I was renting – and the rest, as they say, is history. He agreed to go out on a date with me, we got engaged to be married, and I even met Granny! After she'd taken her beta blockers, of course.'

Barely pausing for breath, Becky told Gemma how they'd married, had Rosie, and then how she'd gone on to experience what she could only describe as her own midlife crisis. 'There I was, finally getting my life back together after the Actual Circle of Hell which is having a small baby. You remember the days: when you're so exhausted that your eyes permanently burn like you've stubbed cigarettes out in them and even managing to brush your teeth has you feeling like you deserve some kind of Honours from the Queen.' Gemma nodded in pained recognition. 'Eventually, things got gradually less shit, and Rosie turned into an actual walking, talking person with thoughts and opinions of her own, who was just about to start school.

'And then all of a sudden my ovaries start screaming and. Would. Not. Stop.' She put her head in her hands. 'What a fucking idiot, hey?'

'So then you had ...?'

'Ella. Otherwise known as The Afterthought.' She laughed. 'Poor Ella. To be honest, I thought Jon was going to tell me where to go, but he was surprisingly receptive to the idea. My personal opinion is that it was a combination of the opportunity to finally get to have sex again – I'd told him during labour that hell was going to freeze over before he got his bits anywhere near me – plus the knowledge that the vasectomy I kept threatening him with was off the cards. Temporarily, that is.'

'And?' Gemma prompted her.

'I couldn't have got up the stairs fast enough to ceremoniously flush my remaining pills down the toilet. Until, that is, Jon reminded me I wasn't actually on the pill, what with having had a coil fitted and everything. It was okay though. He's such a good husband, he found me some hay-fever tablets to ritually flush down the loo instead. I made an appointment the next morning to get my coil taken out, and ten months later Ella was born!'

'Blimey.' Gemma took another sip of her wine. She felt exhausted after all that.

'So here we are, all these years later, and incredibly, still happily married. Well, still not actually making threats of violence against each other, which I think is about all you can expect fifteen years down the line.'

Gemma grimaced. Fifteen years down the line would have been a pipe dream; Nick the Dick couldn't manage to stick it out for even half of that.

'Anyway, enough about me,' beamed Becky. 'As you've probably already realised, I can talk for ever unless someone has the common decency to tell me to shut up. What about you? Your mum was telling me about your ex. He sounds a right fucking charmer, I must say. Still, though, I imagine you must be inundated with gorgeous hunks queuing up at your door to come and take you out. I'm quite jealous, to be honest. Imagine: someone who wants to spend time with you and romance you and get to know you, as opposed to someone who walks through the front door after a day at the office and whose first words aren't

"Darling, my love of my life, how was your day?" but "Have you washed my green cycling top, because I'm heading out in a moment, and by the way, don't wait up, I'll be back late." I mean, there's a reason why fairy tales end at the moment the prince and princess get married. If they kept going until after he'd watched her squat naked on the floor shitting herself while pushing a baby out and then they'd spent the next five years playing endless games of Competitive Sleep Deprivation ... then the picture might not look quite so pretty, might it?'

Gemma laughed. Bar the cycling – Nick the Dick tended to favour extra-curricular fucking as his workout for the week – Becky had just pretty much described the latter years of her marriage. They had been engaged, married and Gemma pregnant with Sam within a year of having met – far too soon, in hindsight, for the initial lust to have worn off and to have discovered if their relationship really had the strength to go the distance after the marathon sex sessions and seducing each other the moment they walked through the door had worn off.

Nick the Dick had become distant from almost the moment Gemma had pissed on the pregnancy test (having first racked up a grocery bill of almost £72 in Tesco when buying said pregnancy test, because of course there was no way you could just walk into the supermarket and buy a pregnancy test, you had to buy an appropriately camou-flaging amount of baked beans and dried pasta and tinned custard to go alongside it, so that it could pass along the checkout almost unnoticed, without the cashier having any opportunity to cast aspersions on just how much unprotected sex you might have been having) and the life-changing blue line had shown up. He didn't want to read the baby books; he didn't want to touch her stomach and feel the new life moving within it; and he certainly didn't want to go along to NCT classes. (Gemma couldn't entirely blame him for that bit. NCT classes had been every bit as excruciating as she'd imagined; and then a bit worse.)

By the time he'd watched his wife evict something the size of a bowling ball from between her labia, mooing like a cow and crapping in a corner of the overheated birthing suite at the local hospital while she screamed out threats about what she'd be doing to his testicles the moment she got herself out of this predicament, the writing was pretty much on the wall.

Gemma groaned. 'Yeah, Nick was certainly a charmer. Honestly, you'd be better off not knowing.'

Becky leaned across the table expectantly. 'Go on. I promise you I'm pretty unshockable.'

And so Gemma launched into the debacle which had been her ill-thought-out liaison with Nick the Dick. 'I loved him. I really did. But he ... well, it turns out that, when he'd stood in front of me and promised to love me and take care of me "until death do us part", what he actually meant was "or until I get bored with having to be a responsible grown-up and decide that I want to take off on a round-the-world trip with Lucy my secretary who, by the way, I've been fucking for the last two years, and yes, I know we have two children together and I absolutely still want to be involved in their upbringing and care but I'll be doing so from the other side of the world without paying you a penny because round-the-world travel is very expensive don'cha know and anyways *laterrrrrrrrz*."'

'Fucking hell.' Becky was visibly appalled. 'What a tosser.'

'Yes, he was rather.'

'So what did you do?'

Gemma shrugged. 'What everyone does after a messy breakup. Sat on the sofa swigging wine from the bottle and wailing power ballads Bridget Jones-style.'

'For how long?'

'Oh, about twenty minutes, until the neighbours knocked on the door to ask if everything was okay. Then I gave myself a virtual slap around the face, necked a fat Coke and Gregg's sausage roll to deal with the resulting hangover, put on my big girl pants – both literal and metaphorical – and just cracked on with things.'

'Bloody hell.' Becky was in awe. 'Go you. Sounds like you're better off without that prick – Nick the Dick sounds about right – anyway.'

Gemma looked wistfully into the distance for a moment. 'Most of the time, it's absolutely fine.' She paused. 'Other than the times when it's not, that is.'

'Oh, I don't know.' Becky was lost in fantasy land for a moment. 'I can't tell you the number of times I've thought how much easier it would be if it was just me and the children, without Jon to have to worry about. Even Boris the fucking liability is nothing compared to Jon when he finally comes home from work for the approximately two hours a week he actually spends at home, and then fills up my beautiful home with his sodding cycle gear. Apparently he's going to win the Tour de France one day. I wish he'd bloody get on with it.'

'Ah, but that's classic grass is greener syndrome. It always seems like it would be easier in the other person's shoes, until that is you're actually in those shoes. I mean, how would you respond if your son raced into your bedroom one morning and screamed "*Mum!* Look at my *balls*! They're *hairy*!" before bursting into tears. I did everything I could to reassure him and tell him that this was an absolutely normal part of growing up, but he refused to listen to me, on the grounds that "You haven't got any balls, so how would you know?" To which there wasn't really much I could say.'

Becky was killing herself laughing. 'Your kids sound amazing. I'm so pleased I've got girls – no hassle by comparison.'

'You clearly haven't met Ava yet,' Gemma riposted. 'Parenting Sam's a breeze in comparison. Her current obsession is causing actual bodily harm to someone, on the grounds that she would then be able to call an ambulance and claim she'd saved their life, which would mean she could finally get her gold Blue Peter badge.'

The evening flew by. Much to Gemma's surprise, within minutes the two of them had been chatting like old friends. In fact, Gemma couldn't remember the last time she'd felt so comfortable with someone. They finished their first bottle of wine and ordered a second while tucking into their huge plates of fish and chips. For someone so tiny, Becky certainly seemed to have one hell of an appetite.

By the time they were halfway down their second bottle of wine, they'd told each other their life stories and Becky was fully appraised of all of the school goings on, right up to the brilliant end-of-term brawl in the playground just before Christmas, when Vivienne had lost her shit that

Satin hadn't been awarded the lead role of Judas Iscariot (this was Miss Thompson: there were no 'traditional' Nativity plays for KS1 at Redcoats) and had deliberately tripped up Andrea Barnes (whose son, Simon, had), causing her to spill the toffee vodka she'd made for the KS1 teaching staff as end-of-term gifts all over the playground and both Satin and Simon had attempted to lick it up. At this Vivienne had completely lost it and threatened to report Andrea to social services for serving alcohol to minors. Gemma and most of the rest of the Year 2 parents had been almost doubled up in pain, trying to keep a straight face.

In turn, Becky told Gemma all about the events which had led to her moving in next door that morning. Flippant though she was about having to move every few months for Lovely Jon's job, it was clear that it had worn thin.

'I just . . . I don't really know who I am any more. Did you get that? When you had the kids? One day you're a person all of your own, with thoughts and feelings and opinions and choices in life . . . and then suddenly you squeeze a head out of your vadge and it's like all of that goes. You're not even "Becky" any more. I counted a full week when the people I met only ever referred to me as "Rosie's mum". And I love being a mum. Well, some of the time I do. But I also love being me. I used to have a job. I used to have hobbies. I used to have a fucking life. And now . . . look at the fucking state of me. Ella is nearly one and this is the first night out I think I've had since she was born. Lovely Jon is never at home and even when he is, all he's doing is working. Or if not, he's too busy training for the 2024 Olympic cycling squad, and all I can say is *but what about me?*'

For the first time since the start of their evening together, the smile had left Becky's face. All of a sudden she looked tired; her face weary behind her thick black curtain of hair as she sipped her wine and looked down at the table. Then, as though a switch had flicked, she snapped back to life.

'And so? Post Nick the Dick – are you shacked up with someone new, or are you just enjoying the newly single life of copious amounts of no-strings-attached sex? God, how I'd love a bit of no-strings-attached sex, swinging from the chandeliers and taking hours and hours to bring each other to orgasm, as opposed to frantically banging your way through a quickie in the thirty seconds you've got to yourselves before the children spot that you're missing and burst in to interrogate you on why water is wet and other such cockblocking classics.'

'To be honest … since Nick left … there hasn't actually been anyone,' confessed Gemma. 'I've just been a bit … busy.'

'YOU HAVEN'T HAD SEX FOR TWO YEARS?' shrieked Becky, to the evident entertainment of everyone else in the bar; the bar staff were openly smirking. Great. Now Gemma would never be able to show her face in here again.

'Sssssshhhhhhhhhhhhh. It's not as bad as it sounds. I'm still young. Ish. I'm not forty until July.'

'YOU'RE ALMOST FORTY AND YOU HAVEN'T HAD SEX FOR TWO YEARS?' Becky shrieked again. Two beautifully dressed women sitting at a window table tutted, looking over at them, and the bar manager looked like he wanted to throw them out, but was clearly too intimidated by Becky to do anything about it. 'It bloody well is bad; it's fucking dreadful. A beautiful woman like you, single for two years without so much as a decent fuck, or even an indecent fuck, for that matter.' Becky cackled and took an enormous slug of wine. 'Right, we need to get that sorted out for you. And who better to help you than Aunty Becky? You're in luck, girl: your fairy godmother just showed up, and she's going to have you in multiple-orgasm bliss by the time you turn forty, I guarantee it. Ooh, you're going to be my new project!' She pulled out her iPhone, presumably to set up some kind of Project Gemma Gant chart.

Gemma put out a hand to stop her. She wasn't entirely sure she wanted to be Becky's new project. Did she really need a man in her life? The status quo that she, Sam and Ava had was working just fine, and she was reluctant to do anything to rock it. Nick the Dick had done very little to convince her that relationships were a good thing.

On the other hand ... Becky kind of had a point. Two years was a long time to go without sex.

Becky was tapping away on her iPhone, no doubt taking silence as assent. It was on the tip of Gemma's tongue to speak, when a light bulb suddenly came on inside her brain. Becky wasn't the only one who could lead projects; and Gemma happened to be a qualified project management practitioner.

'Right. Hold on just one minute here.' Becky looked up in surprise, and Gemma continued. 'I've known you for all of –' she checked her watch '– three hours, and so far you appear to be absolutely batshit crazy ... but there is also something quite irresistible about you which means that I'm not going to say no. I doubt very much that you'll suc-ceed – I'm fairly certain that by this point I will have been classified as clinically undateable by the male population of the local area – but I'm prepared to give it a go. But – and here's the thing – I'm only going to do it if you agree to let me help you too.

'From everything you've said, you're just as fed up and unfulfilled as I am in your own way. You've lost every shred of your true identity under a sea of nappies and puréed butternut squash and reading diaries. And it's time you got it back. Which I'm going to help you do, starting with finding you the job of your dreams. Lovely Jon's not the only one who can rocket up the career ladder. He's going to need to watch his back, because with me on your side you're going to be overtaking him in no time.

'So what d'you say? Let's make it a joint project. Project Gemma-and-Becky. We've got until my fortieth birthday to get me some sex – and that's sex with someone who doesn't have a hairy back, wear socks and sandals together, or tell me that he can't possibly wear a condom because it would be like going paddling with your wellies on – and you a job. Do we have a deal?'

Becky poured the last of the wine into their glasses and raised hers to Gemma's, her beaming smile showing off her perfect white teeth. 'I like your style. We have a deal. Let's make this shit happen.'

They clinked their glasses together in a shared toast to Project Gemma-and-Becky. They would indeed be making this shit happen.

Five

'Mummy, why don't I have a penis?'

There was silence.

'MUMMY. I said, why don't I have a penis? Sam has a penis, and I don't, and it's really not fair, because how will I ever get to wee standing up?' Ava dissolved into sobs, and Gemma wearily dragged herself out of the drink-induced coma she appeared to be in to attempt to comfort her daughter.

'Sssssshhhh, sssssshhhh, it's okay. Weeing standing up is very overrated. Far too easy to get wee on your feet. Anyway, sweetheart, it's –' she checked the display on the digital clock '– shit, it's seven-thirty already, oh crap, we are going to be late *again*. SAM! TEETH! HAIR! SHOES!' The effort required to shout made the pain in her head intensify, and for one terrible moment she thought she might actually puke undigested Shiraz all over her daughter's head, which would truly be a new parenting low.

Clutching her forehead, she staggered into the bathroom,

leaving Ava still wailing pitifully about her lack of male genitalia, and Sam, entirely unhelpfully, telling his sister that 'if you just tried, Ava, you could probably grow one', which would lead to a whole heap of unravelling that she, frankly, just didn't have the energy for right now.

The hot shower helped what was rapidly descending into a Grade 7 Hangover (head like a herd of wild and untamed yaks are running through it; shitting through the eye of a needle; strong desire to curl up in a ball under your duvet and wail hysterically), but its effects were all too short-lived as she dragged on her jeans and hoody (one of the many advantages of working for a start-up was that you could dress like a teenage boy every day and no one batted an eyelid) and staggered downstairs to corral the children into eating their breakfast and just, please, brushing their fucking teeth.

'Mum?' Sam was pouring himself what appeared to be 90 per cent of a box of Cheerios into a mixing bowl, having rejected the normal cereal bowls which were presumably insufficient to hold a breakfast of such magnitude. Gemma had read multiple accounts of how much teenage boys ate and was mildly terrified as to how she was going to be able to sustain Sam's eating habits as he grew, given he was already more than capable of eating through an entire Tesco shop within one twenty-four-hour period.

'Yes Sam?' God, her head hurt. Drinking an entire bottle of wine on a Monday night had been a terrible idea.

'Have you ever been to an orgy?'

Gemma nearly spat her coffee out all over the table. 'Have I *what?*'

Sam shovelled down another spoon of cereal. 'Have you ever been to an orgy?'

'What's an orgy?' piped up Ava.

'No . . . no . . . absolutely, definitely, no. I have never been to an orgy. And, more to the point, where the hell have you been learning about orgies?'

Sam shrugged, milk falling out of the sides of his mouth and dribbling down onto his school jumper, making him look like some kind of anaemic vampire. 'The Romans. They liked orgies. I just wondered if you'd ever been to one. It seems like the sort of thing you might do.'

Gemma's hangover was getting worse. 'What do you *mean* it seems like the sort of thing I might do? What is it exactly about my entirely pedestrian lifestyle that you think suggests that I regularly invite people into my house to throw their car keys into a bowl and have sex with each other?'

'So is an orgy SEX?' shouted Ava, at a volume which could have been heard several streets away.

'That's swingers, Mum, not an orgy. You don't need car keys in an orgy.'

Gemma put her head in her hands. 'And how do you know about swingers?'

Sam shrugged. 'I just do.'

'SEX SEX SEX, SEX SEX SEX,' sang Ava, to the tune of 'Jingle Bells'.

'Does that mean you have been to an orgy, because there weren't any car keys?'

'I HAVE NOT BEEN TO AN ORGY!' shrieked Gemma. Great – she couldn't wait for this topic of conversation to come up at school.

'I might ask Mrs Willoughby if she's had an orgy,' mused Sam, still spooning cereal into his mouth.

'SEX SEX SEX SEX SEX, HEY!' sang Ava.

Vague recollections of the drunken agreement she'd made with Becky the previous evening filtered back into her throbbing head. Observing the scene which had just unfolded, Gemma realised Project Gemma-and-Becky was completely preposterous. I mean, how the fuck could she bring a man into this asylum? Nice though Becky's idea had been, it was clear it simply wasn't going to work. She would have to tell her that the project was off.

'So, the project's on.' It was later that evening, Gemma had returned home from work, the children from school, and they had been sitting around the dining-room table eating spaghetti bolognese (at least, Gemma and Sam had been eating it. Ava had been sitting and looking at it and picking up the strands of spaghetti and saying to them, 'I won't eat you, don't worry, you poor little worms, you can sleep in my bed instead') when there had been a knock on the door. It was Becky, holding a baby who Gemma immediately identified as Ella, accompanied by a beautiful, dark-haired and bright-eyed little girl who must have been Rosie. She looked at Gemma curiously as she opened the door.

'Hi, neighbour!' Dressed down today, in boyfriend jeans and an All Saints T-shirt, Becky still managed to look as though she'd walked off a catwalk; as opposed to Gemma, who had bolognese sauce down her hoody and whose eyes looked like piss holes in the snow against the pallor of her hungover face. 'Thought we'd see if you guys wanted to come over for a bit. I know it's a school night but ... well, to be honest, Lovely Jon's still at work –' she covered Rosie's ears '– as fucking usual, and I'm just desperate for some company. Bring the kids and we can have a drink?' She caught sight of Gemma's face. 'Or, maybe, coffee?'

'Coffee would be lovely.' Anything to get away from the hell of watching Ava sit endlessly twirling her 'worms' around her plate. Grabbing her house keys, telling Ava she could write her dinner off as a bad job, Gemma and the children followed Becky round to the identical house next door.

Gemma had never actually been next door, the previous occupant being a reclusive elderly gentleman who kept himself to himself. It turned out the physical exteriors of the two houses were where the resemblances ended. Walking across the threshold of Becky's home, Gemma was struck by the sheer ... tidiness. Where were the unopened boxes from moving house? Or the sticky layer of cereal crushed into the parquet flooring? Or the piles of plastic tat which children seemed to carry around with them and deposit absolutely everywhere. Hell, you could even see the surface of Becky's kitchen table.

'Something wrong?' Becky was looking at her curiously.

Gemma let a half smile creep onto her face. 'No ... it's just – I'm not sure we can be friends.' She paused for a beat, just enough to let a modicum of doubt form on Becky's face. 'How can your house be so ridiculously tidy? You've only just moved in and already it looks like a show home. By the time we'd been in our place five minutes there was crap on every surface – some of it literal – and we looked like the move had been sponsored by Lego and Domino's Pizza.'

Becky laughed. 'Oh, I'm a bit of a neat freak. It sounds ridiculous, but with Jon at work all day and Rosie at school, keeping the house tidy has become almost a hobby. I know. I know. I need to get out more.'

'Or you need to come and do mine,' said Gemma, as she sat down at the pristine table and they waited for the kettle to boil. The two girls had already gone off together – Rosie, who was immaculate in her embroidered denim jeans and navy cardigan, looking slightly appalled as Ava, who had tonight dressed for dinner as the Incredible Hulk, had taken her by the hand and demanded to be shown her toys – and Sam was surprisingly enraptured by Ella, who in turn was gazing up at him, besotted, as he told her all about Minecraft and did the best fart noises he could muster, resulting in her rocking with laugher.

'So then, we need to make some plans.' Becky brought two steaming cups of coffee over to the table and opened the biscuit tin. 'We're going to have to get moving if we're going to hit our end of July deadline. Ooh, a summer wedding – wouldn't that be lovely?' She winked at Gemma. 'You never know, you could be swept off your feet.'

'Not going to happen. I've been swept off my feet before, remember? And ended up falling flat on my face, breaking my nose, blacking both eyes and completely losing my dignity.' Becky looked appalled. 'Not literally. Apart from the losing my dignity bit, which definitely happened. To be honest, Becky, I'm not so sure this is a good idea after all. I know I said I'd go for it last night, when I was fuelled by Shiraz, but I woke up this morning and just thought, how the fuck could I possibly bring a man into this chaos?' She recounted the 'orgy' moment to Becky, who had tears of laughter streaming down her cheeks and was threatening to pee herself.

'But that's brilliant! C'mon, Gemma – you can't use your kids as a reason not to go out and live your life. It won't be that long before Sam's a teenager, when, based on my experiences, he's not even going to want to know you. Shortly after that they'll fly the nest altogether, and then where will you be? All by yourself, surrounded by cats and smelling of cooked cabbage. Shit, speaking of cats ...'

She got up, heading for the back door. 'Your two okay with dogs?' Gemma nodded. 'Actually, for dogs, read wild untamed beasts. You're about to meet Boris. He is an absolute fucking liability. You have been warned.'

Opening the door, the coldness of the night streamed in, and so did a flash of golden energy, who shot into the open-plan kitchen/diner barking his head off, ran around the kitchen table several times, bounced around grinning at everyone and generally behaved like a drunk who'd overdosed on Red Bull. Sam was rapt: he'd been begging to have a dog for years. Ella, despite being less than a quarter of the size of the overexcitable Boris, was entirely unfazed and was laughing hysterically as he went over to Rosie's PE kit and started trying to hump it.

'BORIS! Come here.' Boris paused, mid hump. 'COME. HERE.' With a mournful look in his brown eyes, Boris reluctantly left his mating partner and slunk over to Becky. She patted him on the back. 'Calm down. Keep your shit together. We've got guests. At least try and pretend you know how to behave yourself in polite company.'

With a heavy sigh, Boris sat down on Becky's feet and rested his head on his paws. Returning to the room, attracted by the sounds of chaos unfolding, Rosie and Ava went over to him. Rosie was brandishing an object in his

70

direction. Delightedly, he took it in his mouth and chewed on it as he lay there, the girls stroking his flanks.

Gemma looked appalled. 'Is that what I think it is? Surely not?'

'I know. I know. We had an Ann Summers party a couple of years ago and the party host left it behind. He thought it was a dog toy and won't be parted from it. Luckily he's chewed it so much the – shape – has been worn down. Although clearly not that much, if you can still recognise it as a dildo.' She caught Gemma's eye and they both creased over laughing.

'I can't entirely believe it. No, not the dildo. Although that is fucking odd. But Boris . . . he's so, well . . .'

'Fucking insane? Not the type of pet you'd expect me to have in my pristine house and with my verging-on-OCD tendencies?'

Gemma nodded her assent.

'You'd be spot on. Frankly, having a dog with our nomadic lifestyles made no sense whatsoever, but Lovely Jon comes from a long line of aristocracy who insist that a home isn't a home without a dog in it. I quite like dogs, and so I didn't have a problem with it, but I have to be honest, I expected we were more talking on the lines of King Charles spaniels or corgis, as opposed to something like Boris. Lovely Jon got him from a rescue centre. They told him he was "boisterous". What they should have told him was that he was "fucking unhinged, and will destroy your life, home and sanity". He once took against a fur hat that a client of Jon's had worn over to ours and left next to the coat rack. He shagged it, disembowelled it, and then suddenly streaked through the dining room where they were talking, wearing it on his head. Unsurprisingly, Jon never quite managed to close that deal.'

With Boris and his dildo quite happy together, Sam entertaining the baby and Ava and Rosie off doing god knew what, the conversation returned to Project Gemma-and-Becky. It turned out that Gemma's protests were no match for the might of Becky.

'Absolute nonsense. You're just making excuses cos you're scared. So, let's get you set up with a dating profile. I'm guessing you haven't got one already? No, didn't think so. Right, so there're all kinds of options when it comes to dating sites – some more perverse than others – but I say we stick with the classics and go with Tinder. Everyone's using it, it's easy to get started and we're guaranteed to find you Prince Charming in no time. Come on, we can get it downloaded onto your phone now. No time like the present!' She held out her hand for Gemma's somewhat battered phone.

'Nope, absolutely not, no way.' Gemma clutched her phone to her chest. 'I made a terrible mistake agreeing to this last night and I am regretting every single moment of it.' Becky's face fell. 'No, sorry – not every single moment – it was brilliant hanging out with you and I genuinely did enjoy it.' To her surprise, she realised it was true. She couldn't remember the last time she'd had a social encounter with another mother and not come away wanting to shut her head in the fridge. Or a social encounter with anyone, come to think of it.

'But online dating just isn't me. It really isn't. Who knows, maybe I'll meet someone in real life, and that'd be great if it happened. I'm not going out of my way to search on dating apps for some bloke who isn't just going to send me pictures of his skeezy cock, though. I'm really not. Sorry, Becky. I'm going to have to say no.'

Becky sat, watching her closely for a moment. Then she leant back in her chair, easing her perfectly manicured feet onto the edge of the table, folded her arms, and laughed.

'Yeah, whatevs. You're not fooling me. God, you're such a transparent case, even an amateur psychologist like me can see through you. Girl meets boy. Girl falls in love with boy. Girl has kids with boy. Boy is emotionally ill equipped to deal with the sight of a baby coming out of the hole he normally puts his cock in. Boy screws girl over to deal with his feelings of inadequacy. Boy screws his secretary. Boy leaves girl. Girl loses all self-confidence and self-esteem, decides that loving people is too much of a risk and so takes a vow of chastity and sits at home alone until her kids leave home and she's forced to take on fifteen rescue cats, ensuring that her house will smell of cat piss for ever more and Prince Charming won't ever even risk crossing the threshold. End scene. Am I right, or am I right?'

For a moment, Gemma felt furious. Furiously embarrassed. How dare this Becky, who she'd known for less than twenty-four hours, come bursting into her life, start taking over and just assume that she knew everything about her? What she chose to do with her life was absolutely none of Becky's business. She would tell her so and then get the hell out of there before scouring Rightmove for somewhere to move to where her next-door neighbour wouldn't want to run her life for her and manage her into bed with some dodgy bloke.

That said, there was the rather unfortunate fact that

there was no denying that Becky was right. Gemma had played things safe for far too long after Nick the Dick had screwed her over. She was bored, she was lonely, and she really really *really* wanted to have sex.

And, if there was someone out there who wanted to sleep with Miss Thompson . . .

Becky was watching her intently. This was clearly not a woman who was used to being told no.

'Ah, fuck it. Yes, you're absolutely right; yes, the thought of it absolutely terrifies me; but yes, we should go for it. Go on.' She passed Becky her phone before she could change her mind. 'I mean, how bad can it be? Don't answer that question. I don't want to know the answer.'

They sat companionably for a while, Becky tapping into Gemma's phone and asking the occasional question – 'What do you do when you're not working? No, weeing unaccompanied doesn't count as a hobby, although I'd agree it's a fucking treat when it actually happens' – while Gemma transposed Becky's career history onto a LinkedIn page on her laptop; their first step to landing Becky a new job. Gemma attempted to find a photo of Becky from her Facebook albums where she wasn't clutching a glass of alcohol or making a face like a duck; meanwhile Becky searched in vain for a photo of Gemma doing exactly that.

'You need to look accessible. Not terrifying.'

'I am all for looking terrifying if it avoids a slew of crusty scrotum photos hitting my inbox. Least that's one problem you're not going to have with LinkedIn. I mean, I hope you're not.'

Gemma left Becky playing with her newly set-up Tinder profile and went to check on the two girls, who were sitting in the living room, surrounded by what looked like the explosion of a Lego factory.

'Hello Mum,' said Ava. 'Are you a lesbian now?'

Gemma was momentarily rendered speechless. 'Um . . . what?'

Ava shrugged, matter-of-factly. 'You don't live with Dad any more and now you seem to really like Rosie's mum, so we wondered if you were lesbians. A lesbian is a lady who has sex with another lady, did you know?'

'Yes, thank you, Ava, I was aware of that. No, I am not a lesbian.' Gemma stole a look at Rosie who seemed completely unfazed by their topic of discussion. 'Come on. It's time we were getting you home.'

Thanking Becky for her hospitality, Gemma retrieved her phone and gathered up the children, who were most reluctant to leave their new friends. As she paused to kiss Becky goodbye she could hear Ava and Sam chatting as they walked around to theirs about how lesbians could have sex, if they didn't have a penis. 'Maybe one of them grows one, like I am going to do,' mused Ava.

Facepalming, and leaving Becky crying with laughter, Gemma followed them home.

Meanwhile, in his flat over on the other side of town, Tom was lying on the sofa wondering quite what he'd done. Running his hands through his hair, he took a swig from the bottle of beer on the floor next to him and tried to breathe deeply. He had never felt more ill equipped to be a teacher in his life. In fact, never mind Miss Thompson's moment of madness, that paled in comparison when you looked at what he'd decided to do. One minute he'd been ensconced in his high-flying job in the City; the next he had been ... not. A hasty enrolment at teacher training college found him exchanging trading stocks and shares for taking sole responsibility for thirty six- to seven-year-olds who still didn't all have reliable control of their bodily functions. (Mind you, the same could be said for some of his ex-colleagues, particularly after they'd downed a few beers.) Honestly, what had he been thinking?

It's not even like this was his first teaching job, either. Tom had learnt his trade in the terrifying training ground of an inner-city school in Tower Hamlets, where he genuinely felt like he should have been paid danger money. Most of the kids were amazing, the boys particularly, the novelty of having a male teacher – and a non-white male teacher at that – drawing them to him like magnets, finally finding a role model with whom they could identify. But there was a small minority who were definitely not, who were there for nothing more than to cause trouble and create danger for teachers and pupils alike. Despite the fact it was a primary school, Tom had had cause to remove a knife from a student on more than one occasion. It broke his heart.

It hadn't been Tom's choice to leave Tower Hamlets. He would have stayed on, but the school had been put into special measures, funding had been cut and there simply weren't enough students to justify the number of staff. Tears in her eyes, the young head had clasped his hands in hers as they said goodbye and had told him how lucky his next school was going to be to have him. 'Plus, after Tower Hamlets ... anything else should be a breeze, right?'

You would have thought so, but Tom was starting to have

a rather nasty feeling that this was going to be a case of out of the frying pan, into the fire.

It had been almost ten o'clock the previous evening by the time he'd finally been able to escape the clutches of Vivienne and the rest of the Year 2 PTA. His Tower Hamlets school had never been able to drum up sufficient parental support to establish a PTA. At the time, he'd thought what a shame it had been. Now, he wasn't so sure that having a load of indifferent parents wasn't actually the better option.

Vivienne, leaning as close to him as she could, had whispered how she was so looking forward to working alongside him, and that perhaps they could arrange a regular weekly catch up to ensure that 'our paths are aligning'. Tom thought that the only way he could see their paths aligning was if Vivienne was chasing him as he desperately ran away from her, but he smiled and nodded non-committedly, fascinated by the way her entire forehead stayed in one homogenous lump as she spoke, no amount of attempted facial expressions shifting it even slightly.

He'd answered question after question about SATS and league tables, somehow managing to resist the urge to jump onto the table and scream that it was all a load of bollocks anyway and quite why any of them gave a shit about the results their six- and seven-year-olds got in a pointless test that the government had made up solely to put schools and teachers and pupils alike under more pressure and would have no bearing on their later life options whatsoever was frankly beyond him. Finally, even Vivienne had run out of questions to ask, and with it now being more than four hours after the time her poor, desperately-searching-for-new-employment nanny's shift usually ended, she decided reluctantly to take her leave and allow him to escape.

If he'd thought he was past the worst of it, he was sadly mistaken. He'd arrived at work shortly after seven a.m. that morning, desperate to make a good first impression and start to get his lesson plans in place. He'd met his TA, Miss Harris, who seemed charming and competent, if they could just get over the little tiny matter of her turning the colour of a lobster and staring at the floor whenever she spoke to him. By eight forty-five a.m., when the gates opened, he was ready to greet his class.

He wasn't expecting the mob of mothers outside the door, who appeared to have dressed more as though they were going out clubbing than on the school run. Where were the patterned anoraks and greying sportswear which were the norm amongst the parents at Tower Hamlets? Vivienne in their midst, they had pushed and crushed into the classroom entrance until he had actually become concerned for the children and had pulled rank, telling them all sternly that he did not have time to answer their questions that morning, that they would need to make an appointment if they wanted to come and see him, and could they please step to one side and allow the children to come in.

Mutinously, they did so, and Year 2 filed into the classroom, which was at once filled with the excited shrieks and laughter of thirty children. His last pupil through the door, he was able to close it behind him, not without relief. To be on the safe side, he double-locked it. He wouldn't put it past Vivienne to manage to evade Mr Cook, on the grounds that she was carrying out unspecified PTA duties, and somehow infiltrate his classroom, materialising behind him like a member of the SAS as he attempted to explain to the child whose entire family were strictly vegan why they wouldn't be able to choose roast chicken at lunchtime.

The teaching, on the other hand … in comparison to the parents, that had been the easy bit. Mrs Goldman had described Year 2 as 'spirited' – and Tom had met quite enough so-called 'spirited' children in his teaching career thus far to know exactly what that meant. 'Monstrous' was a reasonable translation.

The class had treated him to something of a baptism of fire, when the moment he introduced himself to them all, a flurry of hands went up, and he answered questions ranging from 'Do you have pubes, Mr Jones?' to 'Do you like Mrs Goldman?' to 'Can you guess which person in this class has eaten Actual Poo?' He'd had Oscar Abbott glue his finger to the inside of his own nose, necessitating extensive scrubbing by Miss Harris with hot soapy water, and Joseph Taylor had been discovered to have secreted a load of tampons into his trouser pockets which he'd taken out of their wrappers, thrown onto the ground and then screamed 'MICE AND RATS! HELP!' which had the entire class running around histrionically (including Miss Harris) and screaming like banshees.

By the time they reached lunchtime, things had got slightly more under control, and he actually felt like he was finding his stride. Of course, it wouldn't last; that was the nature of children, they lured you into a false sense of security, and then all hell would break loose. But it certainly felt like he was getting somewhere.

Now, though, he was back in his clean yet horrendously

impersonal flat, with its upstairs neighbours who appeared to have graduated from the School of Noisy Shagging. Did they not understand that it was possible to reach orgasm without announcing it to the entire street? He groaned and put his head under one of the sofa cushions. It did absolutely nothing to block out the sound of the female member of the partnership screaming to her lover how much she loved it when he put his finger up her bottom.

Short of immediately putting the flat up for sale and getting back onto Rightmove, the only way to survive this, Tom decided, would be to ensure his social life was so stellar that he'd only ever have to come back here to shower and sleep. And possibly to change his wireless router name – which should easily be picked up upstairs – to ICANHEARYOUHAVINGSEX.

There was just one problem.

Not only was his social life not stellar, it was pretty much non-existent.

He would usually look to make friends at work, but right now, the chances of him finding anyone in the staffroom who would want to join him as he headed out partying seemed slim. Mrs Goldman tended to hire her teaching staff in her own image, presumably to avoid any risk whatsoever that they'd end up shagging their way around the staffroom. The average age of the teachers and TAs at Redcoats was almost fifty – and that was heavily dragged down by Tom and Miss Harris. He suspected if he wanted to find a group of mates, he was going to need to look elsewhere.

Where, though? That was the question. This was a small community and there was a serious danger that anyone he met was going to be in some way connected with the school. The one thing Tom had quickly learnt was that he did not want to find himself socialising with anyone whose child he was teaching. There had been a memorable party at Tower Hamlets when he'd found himself suddenly next to the parents of Zak, one of the brightest children in his class. Zak, aged seven, had come into class one morning to tell Tom very seriously that 'Mr Jones, last night Mummy and Daddy were playing trains, because I went into their bedroom in the middle of the night when they thought I was asleep and Mummy was making a puff huff puff noise and Daddy was rocking on top of her because he was riding the train.' After Tom had bitten his lip so hard to stop himself from laughing that he'd actually drawn blood, he had promised a worried-looking Zak that he would mention to his mummy that he didn't like it when she and Daddy played trains when he wasn't allowed to join in. He had indeed made Zak's mum aware when she'd arrived to pick her son up, and she'd studiously avoided coming into contact with him ever since, until now, when apparently they were going to be invited guests at the same intimate house party. Tom had made his excuses and left soon afterwards.

Perhaps he should start dating again. His mum kept suggesting it, every time they spoke, which meant the gaps between their calls had got longer and longer as he'd made excuses not to ring her. He didn't want to be alone, but he'd learnt the hard way that there were far worse things in life than being single. Finally, he felt like he was starting to find his feet. And the thought of bringing someone else into his life ... no. No, the more he thought about it, that really didn't seem like a very good idea at all.

Absent-mindedly, as the TV blazed in the background, and 'Mr Hubba Hubba' (according to the screams of desire which could probably be heard from space) rhythmically slammed his way inside his girlfriend with a vigour that had the entire first floor shaking, Tom reached for his mobile phone. He'd downloaded Tinder when he'd moved, as part of his plan to reinvent his life.

But wouldn't reinventing his life be so much easier without a girlfriend in tow? Decisively, Tom selected the app and deleted it.

Six

'So, what are our options?' They had been sitting around the small boardroom table for the past two hours and Leroy was visibly losing interest.

'It's very simple. We either have to expand our product range and bring in an additional revenue flow, or we have to seek funding and find someone who's willing to put an injection of cash into the business ... or we have to make efficiencies.' Dave, thankfully smelling of coffee rather than whisky today, spoke abruptly. He needed to get Leroy to understand.

'When you say efficiencies ... what do you mean by efficiencies? Work harder? Work faster? Stop being cryptic with me. Tell me what we need to do, and we'll do it.' Leroy, his trademark grin unusually absent from his face, tapped fretfully with his biro on the table.

Dave sighed. 'Leroy, you know what we need to do. We need to restructure. Put very simply, we're spending more money than we're making. Which means ... '

'Redundancies. We need to make redundancies.' Gemma spoke with a quiet certainty. 'That's what you're saying, isn't it? This line here on the P&L – it stands out like a sore thumb. Basically, you're saying that if Zero wants to make it through to the end of this financial year, we need to sack people.'

There was a short pause. Natalie was tapping frantically on a calculator. Leroy was still messing around with his biro, seemingly ignoring her. Dave nodded, shortly.

'That's right.'

'Oh *bollocks*, Dave.' Leroy suddenly sprang up from the table, slamming his hands down onto it. 'You keep coming out with this shite, and it's just bollocks. We're not going to run out of money. It's going to be fine. I've got all kinds of plans. You'll see. Honestly, everyone, stop panicking.'

He looked at them all, sitting around the table, drawn and concerned. Suddenly, it was like a switch had flicked. The frustration disappeared in an instant, to be replaced by a beaming smile. Dave and Natalie seemed convinced, both visibly relaxing, but Gemma wasn't. Leroy's smile reached nowhere near his eyes.

'Dave, man, chill the fuck out. You got us all worried there. Yes, we get it. No more yachts. I promise not to buy any luxury cruise liners, okay? That help?' He clapped his hand on Dave's back enthusiastically, Dave wincing as Leroy's signet ring made contact with his spine. 'We've got enough money to get us through to the summer, yes?' Dave nodded. 'Well, that's fine! That's months away! Almost six whole months, to be precise! Anything can happen in that time. Stop fretting. I'll work something out. Right, that's quite enough of that. Everyone back to work!' He clapped his hands and strode out of the office, a tiny figure in his charcoal skinny jeans with turquoise zips and gold lamé tee.

Dave, Natalie and Gemma looked at each other. 'Will he actually work something out?' asked Natalie, the newest of the team, still trying to get her head around Leroy's peculiarities and unusual spin on life.

'I bloody well hope so,' said Dave, frowning and rubbing his chin. 'I bloody well hope so.'

'Have you seen this one?' Passing her phone to Becky as they waited for the school gates to open one morning in the drizzling rain – Gemma having, in what was quite possibly a world first, made it to school not only on time, but actually early (it would later transpire that the only reason she'd managed it was because Ava was still wearing her pyjama top under her school jumper, and Sam had come out of the house minus his shoes) – she watched her neighbour scan through the Tinder messages she'd received.

'Blimey. That's, um ... I don't even know what that is. And I thought I'd done it all. I mean, I'm sure he's got the best of intentions, but ... that's not the sort of thing you ask for on a first date, is it? Or even a second!'

'Sssssshhhh.' Gemma was only too conscious of Andrea Barnes in the vicinity, blatantly eavesdropping under the cover of her Laura Ashley umbrella. She'd have to run for the school defibrillator if Andrea caught sight of this particular message. 'I'm not sure it's the kind of thing you ask for, ever. Outside of a torture chamber, that is.' Gemma felt the heat rising in her cheeks as she took the phone back and looked again at what 'Magnus' was suggesting they do. Whilst the exact ... *manoeuvre* was not one she'd ever heard of before, his intention was clear. 'I'm not sure this app's working, to be honest. I thought you could only message people if you'd both swiped right on each other's profile, but this pervert's been able to send this, and I've never seen him before in my life.'

'Ah.' Becky looked guilt-stricken. 'I may possibly have had a little play around when I set your profile up. I feel like I might have got a bit trigger-happy.'

Gemma covered her eyes with her hand at the thought of the horrendously unsuitable men Becky would inevitably have swiped right on. This would explain the guy who appeared to have dressed as Dracula for his profile photo – complete with fangs – and the bloke with the terrifying eyebrows who was a dead ringer for someone she'd seen on the news the other day being investigated by Operation Yewtree.

Mr Cook was opening the school gates and parents and children streamed through. All of a sudden Gemma caught sight of Sam's mouth. It was absolutely covered in small black particles.

'Sam, what the hell is going on with your mouth? What have you been doing?'

Andrea Barnes caught sight of Sam and gave a little gasp; no doubt the rumour would be round the school in a heartbeat that he had some kind of terribly infectious disease and had been foaming at the mouth.

Her son looked sheepish. 'Um.'

'What do you mean, um?'

'Um ... Ava made me eat a teabag.'

There were times in parenting, Gemma had discovered over the years, when you just had no words.

While Gemma was distracted, Becky managed to grab her phone back off her and start flicking through profiles. 'Ooh, I like him . . . urrrggghhh, not him . . . hmmm, this one could be good. Honestly, online dating is brilliant, isn't it? I wish I was single.' Gemma stared at her friend. 'Um, obviously . . . I don't. Maybe don't mention that to Jon, yeah?'

The slightly awkward silence was broken as they arrived at Ava and Rosie's classroom, where Mr Jones was waiting.

'Mummy?' said Ava, in a voice as clear as a bell, which echoed across the playground, ricocheting off the KS2 building to land in the ears of every single waiting parent. 'What's a pervert? Can I have one?'

Mr Jones was professional to a fault, but Gemma was fairly certain she saw him snigger.

Much to Gemma's surprise, at some point in between the offers from Magnus to perform a sexual manoeuvre that was probably illegal in most of Europe, and the suggestion from a gentleman called Jake that she could come and join him and his wife for a threesome, because he'd 'always wanted to do it with a fat bird' – god, Becky had picked some charmers for her – there was a series of messages from a man called Andy. Andy seemed normal enough on the face of it – he had brown eyes, brown hair, wasn't posing topless and hadn't started his message with 'Fancy a Fuck?', so he was practically marriage material in Gemma's eyes. They had got chatting and now he was suggesting meeting up. Gemma thought she might actually vomit at the thought of a Real Life Date.

'I just don't think I can do it,' she confessed to Becky as the children ate dinner round hers that night, Becky's being off limits after Boris the fucking liability had decided to bring a live pigeon into the house. Sensibly, Becky decided her best approach was to lock Boris in his kennel, close the door on the once-live-now-dead pigeon situation in the kitchen for Lovely Jon to deal with when he got home, and head over to Gemma's with the children and a bottle of wine, which she proposed drinking very quickly, quite possibly with a straw, to blank out what Boris and the pigeon had done to her beautiful home.

'Why not?' Becky was halfway through her red wine and looked like Ava had done her lipstick for her. 'A deal's a deal.'

'But ... look at me. Just look at me.' For the first time, Gemma voiced the fears she'd been keeping inside. 'Andy – you've seen his photo. He's a good-looking guy. And me – I'm a mess.'

'She is a mess,' said Sam, showing his usual level of maternal devotion, and clearly getting his own back for the somewhat cremated pizza Gemma had allowed Becky to serve up to them, Becky reassuring the children that 'the burnt bits will put hairs on your chest.' Ava was delighted and was now sitting in her pants, waiting for her hairy chest to grow.

'Yeah, and when she bent over the other day when she was all nudey, I saw up her butt-butt and it was all *hairy*.' Ava laughed so much Gemma had to remove her pizza crust from her for fear she would choke.

'You see?' Gemma threw her hands up in despair. 'Even my children agree, and they both style themselves like they got dressed in the dark whilst drinking tequila every day. I'm a mess. I don't know what's in and what's out when it comes to clothes. My hair last got cut in around 1982 and my – apparently hairy – arse has raged so out of control that it got stuck in the fridge of its own volition yesterday. My nipples – as drawn by Ava for the lovely Mr Jones; oh god, I'd forgotten he'll have seen that, yet another parenting moment to cherish – hang down to my knees and I have to tuck my stomach overhang into my pants. The only make-up I own is a Heather Shimmer lipstick, which was probably last fashionable when my arse was still hair free. This man is going to turn up to meet me and he is going to mistake me for his elderly mother and he'll have me booked into a care home and be back off out to find some young nubile twenty-something whose tits are so pert she can probably balance sodding turnips on them. That will be my date. How can you put me through this?'

'Who wants to balance turnips on their tits? That sounds like a fetish too far even for the charming Magnus. And a care home doesn't sound all that bad.' Becky had picked up a slice of the children's discarded burnt pizza and was attempting to chew through it. 'They just sit around and get drunk all day while they shout abuse at each other, don't they? You'll be fine. It's a date; there's no obligation to immediately strip off and show him your labia, you know. We'll give you a makeover, Pretty Woman style. Message Andy and tell him you're free to meet up tomorrow night. I'll babysit. Job done.'

'You're not making me over as a hooker,' Gemma muttered, but without conviction. Frankly, if Becky managed to get her looking even a tenth as hot as Julia Roberts in that film then she'd have no issue if Andy wanted to offer her cash in return for sex.

Via a series of messages, a date was set. Andy was indeed available to meet tomorrow, and Becky would be round with her 'magic brushes', as she referred to them, just after four p.m. Gemma *would* go to the ball.

True to her word, Becky knocked on the door just after four the next day. Gemma's parents had kindly offered to have the children for a sleepover, meaning Gemma could have her meltdown over how she was going to camouflage her out-of-control arse in peace.

By the time Becky arrived on her doorstep, Gemma was in despair. She'd tried on every single item of clothing she owned in an attempt to find something that made her look like Julia Roberts. Drawing a blank, she was currently running around the house in the biggest pair of Spanx it was possible to buy, and an underwired bra which was more akin to two crash helmets strapped on with gaffer tape than it was an erotic item of lingerie. Ava had once insisted upon wearing it to the supermarket as a hat.

Becky took it all in her stride. Soothing Gemma instantly with a large slug of the homemade sloe gin she'd brought over for this very eventuality, Becky soon had her trying on new combinations of clothing, which looked so much more glamorous the moment they were accessorised with a pair of Becky's high heels. Gemma was unlikely ever to be able to share any other item of clothing with her new neighbour, what with being able to squeeze approximately half of one ankle into Becky's skinny jeans, but shoe sizes never discriminated, and Becky and Gemma both happened to be a perfect size five.

In a surprisingly short space of time she was dressed in

navy jeggings teamed with a simple black top and blazer, one of Becky's statement necklaces and a pair of zebra stripe heels. She sat, grinning and sipping sloe gin, as Becky pinned her curls in a style she'd never have had the patience or the coordination to try herself, and then carefully smoothed creams and serums onto her face until her skin was smooth and even, her eyebrows were perfectly plucked, her lips highlighted with a shimmering swoosh of lip gloss and her eyes made up until they looked three times their normal size.

'Ta-da!' Becky turned her around and did the grand reveal in her full-length mirror. 'Don't you look beautiful?'

It might have been the sloe gin, or it might have been the fact that Becky was the first person who had referred to her as beautiful since – actually, probably ever, Nick the Dick not being big on compliments – but Gemma felt tears spring to her eyes. 'Becky, thank you *so* much. This is incredible. You are incredible. I can't believe you would do something so kind for me.'

Becky raised one eyebrow as she stacked her brushes back into their vanity case. 'Of course I'd do something kind for you. You're my friend.'

Her friend? Gemma was taken aback. She didn't think she'd ever had anyone refer to themselves as her friend before, not since school, when her best friend Caroline had stayed up with her all night while she chundered – two bottles of White Lightning on an empty stomach not having been their greatest idea ever – because 'your mum'll kill me if you die. And, you know, you are my best mate and everything.' She had muttered the last bit awkwardly; they had never been ones for overt displays of affection.

Gemma wondered what had happened to Caroline. Their promises to be 'best friends for EVER' had lasted about as long as the school shirts they'd graffitied all over on their last day. These days, all that she knew about Caroline came from her Facebook page, which portrayed her with her perfect husband and her perfect children and her perfect life.

Caroline's irritating perfection aside, that night she had stayed up with Gemma had honestly been one of the nicest things anyone had ever done for her. Until now.

At the thought of her and Becky's embryonic friendship; a huge beam lit up her face and Becky looked at her in bemusement. 'What on earth's the matter with you? You look hysterical. Come on, let's go and have a drink before you have to go.'

The key word in Becky's sentence should, Gemma would later come to realise, have been 'a'. 'Let's go and have *a* drink.' Not 'two'. Not 'several'. Not 'most of the rest of the bottle of sloe gin.' 'A.'

By the time her pre-booked taxi arrived to take her to meet Andy, at the bar where Becky had got her into this mess just a couple of weeks ago, the sloe gin bottle was two-thirds empty and Becky was beginning to have her doubts.

'Gemma . . . are you sure you're okay?'

''f course 'm okay. 'm a meeting Andy. Lov'ly Andy. Love Andy.'

'Oh, crap. How much of that stuff have you drunk?' Becky was well versed in the potency of her sloe gin, having once thrown up into her own cleavage as a result of it, and had therefore just sipped slowly on a small tumbler, meaning that Gemma had drunk the lion's share.

And it was showing.

Ignoring Becky's protests that maybe she should call Andy and suggest to him they meet up next week, Gemma, with the slow carefulness of a drunk, picked up Becky's D&G bag, which she had promised on pain of death not to lose – or vomit into – staggered towards the door on her zebra print heels, and turned to wave at Becky.

'Bye, lov'ly Becks. Iloveyoooooooou. I see you later. Kiss kiss.' And she turned to get into the waiting taxi, leaving the front door wide open and with one leg of her Spanx already working its way in a bulge up her thigh under the skinny jeans.

'Fucking hell.' Mildly concerned though she was for what the hell was going to happen to Gemma, Becky couldn't help laughing. 'Good luck, Andy.'

Andy had been nervously waiting at a table in a corner of the bar for the last twenty minutes; since he'd been a small boy, he had had a pathological fear of being late. He looked around, wondering which one of the many punters filling the room would turn out to be Gemma. Having been on a number of online dates before, Andy knew only too well that the relationship between someone's Tinder photo and what they turned out to look like in real life could be tenuous at best. He'd once agreed to meet up with a girl he would have sworn could have been a double for J-Law, only to have her arrive looking like his Aunty Marge after one too many Baileys at Christmas.

There was a girl standing in the doorway, but she didn't look anything like Gemma, who in Andy's head was the kind of comfortable, reliable person you could take home to meet your parents without having to worry that she might suddenly turn up for dinner wearing a translucent top which you could see her nipples through, resulting in his dad nearly needing a defibrillator (Andy's last date), or that she might suddenly decide that, actually, guys weren't her thing after all, and make a move on his little sister instead (Andy's last but one date).

She was coming towards him. Unconsciously, Andy pulled in his stomach muscles and attempted to hold his pint in a cool, insouciant manner. He looked more like he was modelling for a Littlewoods catalogue, but the girl didn't seem to mind, as she swayed towards him and held out her arms like they were old friends.

'Andy! Y'mus be Andy! 'm Gemma. You can call me Gem. Ooh, drinkies. Shall we have some little drinkies? 'n then we can go home 'n have wild sex cos I've shaved my legs spesssshhul . . . spessshhhull . . . 'nyway? Drinkies?'

She was, Andy realised with horror, really quite cata-strophically pissed.

He would have liked to have made his excuses and left, but by that point Gemma was sitting down next to him, waving jauntily at the furious-looking bar staff and encour-aging them to bring her over 'a tin and jonic! I'mean, gin and tonic. Jus' a teeny weeny one. Maybe a double. Or a triple.' He assumed they would ignore her, but one of the girls poured one and brought it over to her.

'You're the one who hasn't had sex for two years, aren't you?' said the girl as she placed Gemma's drink on the table and winked at Andy. Fortunately for Gemma, she was too drunk to care that this horrific fact had just been announced to the man she was meant to be spending the evening with.

'Tha's right. No sex, for *two* years. Two. Whole. Years. My hole's prob'ly closed back up again. Shall we go back to mine and find out?' She leant over to Andy in what she imagined was an erotic fashion, breathing gin fumes into his face.

'Um.' Andy couldn't remember the last time he'd felt this awkward, ever. Which was quite something, given his last but one date had clocked the kippers over breakfast and explained to his appalled parents why going down on a girl was absolutely nothing like licking a mackerel. 'Why don't we ... get to know each other a bit, first. Would you like something to eat?'

Gemma would. She had a vague notion that the helicopters were starting – always a bad sign – but she dismissed them with a wave of her hand and encouraged Andy to order pretty much everything on the menu. Lovely lovely food. What a brilliant idea.

'So,' said Andy, desperately trying to edge further away from the drunk lady. 'Tell me about yourself.'

Gemma needed no further invitation. As Andy wondered if it would be possible for him to feign his own death, she took him right back through her childhood, including the day of her first period ('the blood ... it's jus' ... *everywhere*'), and then onto her marriage to Nick the Dick ('such a teeny weeny penis, like a little prawn'), and finally onto the birth of her two children ('their heads, they jus' ... *split* you open, your front bottom looks like there've been ... *crabs*! Crabs with *knitting needles*! Fighting with it! 'N' then you get blood clots the size of *hamsters* falling out of it for the next six weeks. Miracle of new life, my fuckin' arse').

Andy turned green and took a surreptitious look at his

watch. Christ, it was only eight p.m. His only hope was that she got so drunk she passed out.

Gemma went one better than that. Having devoured with gusto the artisan breads with oils, the ostrich burger with spinach relish, and the additional sides of halloumi and sweet potato hash, she suddenly felt an uneasy sensation in the pit of her stomach.

Andy took advantage of the fact she'd finally, *finally* stopped talking about blood clots the size of small mammals emerging from her nether regions and rapidly changed the subject to the current political landscape and who she thought would triumph at the next general election. Not Gemma's strong point at the best of times, she willingly zoned out of the conversation in order to focus every bit of her efforts on not puking on the table.

'I mean, you've got to admire what they've done with the environmental policies, but their proposals for Trident are just ludicrous, don't you think?' Andy looked encouragingly at Gemma.

Gemma thought only one thing right at that moment, which was that she needed to get out of the bar as soon as humanly possible.

'I'm … actually feeling … little bit tired. Taxi?' Gemma attempted a winsome smile, oblivious to the fact that she had spinach stuck in her teeth, clashing attractively with her face, which had turned the colour of a slightly rotten lemon.

Andy had been around enough drunken women over the years to know that time was of the essence here. Sweeping Gemma, her jacket and Becky's prized D&G bag up with one arm, he propelled her towards the entrance at the speed of a young Usain Bolt.

They were in luck. A taxi was just dropping off a young, smartly dressed couple, who stepped out of their way in disdain as they saw the state of Gemma. 'Honestly, these mums,' Gemma heard the girl – who was wearing a backless halterneck dress *with no bra*, the pert-breasted hussy – whisper to her partner. 'Let themselves go, have one night out, and then look at the state of them. Don't worry. I'll never be like that.' They smiled smugly at each other, and if Gemma hadn't been fighting so fiercely to stem the rising tide of vomit in her throat she would have shouted after her, 'You bloody will, *and* your nipples will hang down to your knees, you smug, tight-fannied bitch.'

Waving, in the manner of a desperate man (which, indeed, he was), Andy frantically signalled for the taxi to stay put. The driver, a stocky chap in his fifties or sixties, got out and looked at Gemma suspiciously. 'She going to be sick in my cab?'

'No, no, absolutely not . . . she's just got a touch of . . . man flu! Haven't you, Gemma?'

Gemma didn't dare to move. She had a very nasty feeling about what was about to happen.

'All right, but I'm warning you, it's a £250 valet charge if you puke in the back, okay love?' The driver opened the back door and gestured for Gemma to jump in.

Andy visibly exhaled with relief. He'd hoped it might be third time a charm, but it seemed that was patently not going to be the case. Maybe he should just give up on this dating malarkey altogether. He might join a different dating website. Or the priesthood.

'So, it's been lovely,' he lied through gritted teeth. He didn't bother to add that maybe they'd see each other again.

They both knew that, should they have the misfortune to cross paths again, they would actively walk to the other side of the road to avoid each other.

Niceties dictated that he should offer up a kiss. Tentatively, with about as much enthusiasm as if he were puckering up to snog an electric eel, he aimed his lips in the general direction of her cheek.

At which point the pent-up nausea which Gemma had been attempting to hold back just became too much and, with a level of violence that the girl from *The Exorcist* would frankly have been proud of, she vomited profusely right down the side of his face, onto his shirt and into his shoes.

The taxi driver was the first to speak. 'Better out than in, that's what I say. Come on then, love, I'll give you a lift now you've got all that up – but you'd better grab my emergency bucket from the boot, just to be on the safe side.'

It was small consolation, Gemma would think afterwards, that at least she had kept her promise to Becky and managed not to throw up in her D&G bag.

Seven

When she woke up the next morning, at first Gemma couldn't remember what day it was or where she'd been the previous night. She felt surprisingly well given the amount of sloe gin she'd consumed with Becky. She remembered – just about – saying goodbye to Becky and leaving the house ... but then there was a complete blank. Had she gone to the bar to meet Andy? She presumed so, but when she wracked her brain to try and work out what had happened there was just an enormous empty space.

Picking up her mobile phone from her bedside table she saw that she had a series of WhatsApp messages from Becky. Scanning through them, she found to her surprise that they started last night – midway through the evening, in fact. Becky was reminding her to sleep on her side and drink plenty of water. But the time stamp seemed to suggest that she'd sent this at about 8.45 p.m., little more than an hour after Gemma had left the house. What the hell had happened?

Groggily, she staggered into the bathroom, wincing as she stepped on half of Sam's Lego that he'd generously chosen to leave all over the floor for her, and bending over to pick out Lego Spider-Man's web from where it was embedded in the sole of her big toe. Sitting on the toilet she tapped out a quick message to Becky.

Have just woken up. WTF happened?

A reply came back within seconds.

Thank god you're awake! Had visions all night of you choking on your own vomit, was going to bring you back to mine and make you sleep in the spare room where I could keep an eye on you! Give me five, will come over.

Clearly, whatever she'd been up to, it hadn't been pretty. She brushed her teeth quickly to get the taste of bile out of her mouth and looked at her mascara-stained face and reddened eyes in the mirror. She looked a little bit like the love child of Mick Jagger and Jabba the Hutt.

The doorbell rang and Gemma wrapped her striped towelling dressing gown around her before heading down the stairs to open the door. The taste of bile hadn't entirely left her and she had a nasty feeling that the dull ache in her right temple was going to turn into rather a pounding headache. So much for her being unaffected by her antics the night before. She was clearly only not hungover because she was still fucking hammered.

Becky, wearing workout gear and with her thick black hair looped into a high ponytail, bouncing around on the doorstep in a manner which made Gemma frankly want to vomit, was positively glowing with energy and couldn't have formed more of a contrast to her friend if she'd tried.

'Fucking hell, you look absolutely dreadful.' Becky didn't believe in social pleasantries. 'Here, let me.' Wrapping her arms around herself, Gemma allowed Becky to lead her to the kitchen sofa where she slumped as Becky bustled around the kitchen, making black coffee and toast smeared thickly with butter. Gemma attempted to control her dry heaves.

'Don't spare me the details. It's like a plaster: it's best if you get it over with all in one go. Tell me – what the fuck happened to me?'

And so Becky told her, from the moment the taxi driver had knocked on her front door to tell her he had a 'lady who's indisposed, love, so you'd better come and look after her, because I can't leave her on her own. Oh, and she can keep the bucket, but it's an extra fiver on the fare.' Becky had duly paid the fare (plus bucket surcharge) and got a brief summary of events from the driver from the point at which he'd arrived outside the bar, before hauling a vomiting Gemma out of the hydrangeas she'd collapsed into, and sitting with her while she wailed that she'd made a total cock up of the whole evening and there was 'no way, just no way, that anyone is ever going to want to shag me, let alone marry me, ever again'.

'Oh good god.' Gemma had turned even paler, something she hadn't thought was possible. 'Tell me I didn't throw up over poor Andy.'

'It sounds like you did, in quite some style too. Has he not messaged you?'

Frantically, Gemma grabbed her mobile phone and

checked Tinder. There was a message from Andy! Despite herself, she felt her spirits rise. Maybe she'd actually been amazing company, and the evening hadn't been such a write-off after all.

Hey Gemma. Hope you got home okay. I just wanted to check that you're alright and that the taxi driver got you home safely. Let me know, but after that ... I mean, don't take this the wrong way, but I'm not sure you're the girl for me. In fact, I'm not sure I'm going to be dating again, ever. I think maybe the bachelor lifestyle is what I was meant for. I'll be deleting my Tinder account today, so if you don't get a reply, that's why. Um, bye.

Wordlessly, Gemma passed her phone over to Becky. As she did so, a hot flush of shame ran up her back, as all of a sudden she was hit with a rush of memories from the previous evening.

'Oh god. I think I told him about giving birth. No, I definitely told him about giving birth. And the clots. The hamster-sized clots. I talked a lot about those. And ... oh my god. I told him about Nick's penis. I talked to my date about my ex-husband's penis. Oh god. Oh god. Oh god.'

Becky was shaking with suppressed laughter. With an effort, she managed to assume a straight face.

'But that's not that bad. You could have done loads worse things than that.'

'Like throw up all over him, you mean?' Gemma said dully. 'Fuck this shit. I'm going back to bed, and I'm never going on a date ever again. Or leaving the house, for that matter. Oh, the shame.'

Leaving Gemma to sleep off both her hangover and her utter mortification, Becky let herself out and wandered back to hers. It was a rare morning when Jon was actually at home and not either in the office or out cycling. He'd been getting his bike ready when Becky had left, so she didn't hold out large amounts of hope for the lovely family day she occasionally imagined they might have together, but at least he'd agreed to babysit the kids while she went and checked on Gemma. His words, not hers. Honestly. 'Babysit.' Like he was some kind of hired help she'd brought in to childmind, as opposed to being the biological father of Rosie and Ella.

If she was honest, things between herself and her husband seemed to be at an all-time low. Becky had hoped that moving into this house together would be a new start for them. If it had been a new start, all she could say was that it was going very much in the wrong direction.

Friday had been fairly typical of a Day in the Life of Becky and Jon. It had been ten p.m. on the Thursday evening before Jon had got home from work, only to be faced with a kitchen full of feathers thanks to Boris's ritual sacrifice of the pigeon. Not a man for extremes of emotion, he had remained tight-lipped as Becky had explained the situation to him, before peeling off his designer suit and systematically cleaning up the kitchen – feathers, bloodied carcass and all.

Becky had honestly meant to stay up, to show emotional if not actual physical support, bird carcasses really really *really* not being her thing, but when Ella had cried out she had gone upstairs and brought her into their bed, lying down next to her. The next thing she knew the birds were singing outside and Jon, a feather still sticking to his left ear, was snoring softly in bed with her. Ella formed a human shield between them, and Rosie – who never wanted to be left out when they co-slept with Ella – had crept in at some point during the night and was currently lying fast asleep on their feet like a loyal hound.

She had intended to thank him that morning for the clear-up job he'd done the previous evening, but had forgotten that their sum total of contact time in the mornings was usually around two and a half minutes. When his alarm went off Jon jumped out of bed like he'd been shot, was into the bathroom and showered, shaved and suited inside six and a half minutes.

Hovering around the bathroom door, a fractious Ella in her arms – Rosie was already downstairs glued to those sociopaths Topsy and Tim and their clearly-on-prescription-drugs mother on CBeebies – Becky had made the mistake of saying that it was a shame they were still seeing so little of each other, now that they'd made the move to live here.

Jon never really lost his temper, but by Jon standards he positively exploded. Which is to say that his brow furrowed and he actually swore. 'And when the fuck do you expect to see me, when I work every waking hour to allow you to swan around at home with the children? I would love to spend time with you and the girls, but I have to be in the office in –' he checked his watch '– less than thirty minutes, and do you have any idea what the Circle line is like at this time of the morning?'

Becky didn't have any idea what the Circle line was like at that time of the morning, what with her commute every day involving rather less public transport than it did a swift jog down the stairs to respond to whichever one of her children had decided to make the first of a series of incessant demands which would be repeated in one continual loop all day. She bloody wished she did know what the Circle line was like at that time of the morning. Whilst it would undoubtedly be packed with sweaty commuters – and she had never entirely managed to master the Circle line without first going in completely the wrong direction – she was still betting a trip on the Circle line involved substantially fewer bodily fluids than she would normally find herself hands on with by eight a.m.

Becky frequently wished that NCT classes had focused less on the process of birthing your baby, and more on the life skills you would need to acquire once they were here. Getting A Good Night's Sleep When You Only Have Twelve Square Inches of Mattress To Call Your Own and How To Still Maintain Some Kind Of Romantic Relationship With Your Husband When You Have Two Child-Shaped Cock-Blockers Insistent On Ruining Your Lives being just a couple of those she was yet to master.

It was time, Becky decided, to shake things up. The news of her impending employment – not that she'd been offered a job yet, or even so much as attended an interview, but Becky was nothing if not an eternal optimist – seemed like the perfect driver to spend some quality time with her husband and reignite her marriage.

But it was difficult, Becky mused to herself. The fairy tale one got sold of marriage was really not what it turned out to be like. At all. Becky and Lovely Jon's wedding day had been the stuff that dreams were made of. Passionately in love with each other, they had spent the entire day gazing into each other's eyes, holding hands and exchanging kisses, whilst surrounded by their family and friends in the beautiful surroundings of a stately home in the Sussex countryside, which happened conveniently to belong to Jon's uncle.

Becky couldn't remember the exact moment things started to change. Certainly, throughout her pregnancy with Rosie, they had been as loved up as ever. Jon had come along to every single scan and had even given up alcohol alongside her. Truly, greater love hath no man.

Even at the birth itself, her husband had shown no signs of being fazed as she screamed obscenities at the midwife and lost control of all of her bodily functions. Hell, he'd even offered to man the sieve. The baby books she'd purchased whilst pregnant had glossed over the downsides of water births. Your husband having to extract floating pieces of your shit from the water, using a sieve which looked disturbingly like the one you'd strained the pasta through in your kitchen sink only forty-eight hours earlier, was most definitely one of them.

Perhaps it was when they'd got home from the hospital, to discover Becky had given birth to The Baby Who Never Went To Sleep, Ever. Very quickly things had deteriorated from Jon sending her flowers and telling her how much he loved her, that he couldn't believe she'd brought their child into the world, to them finding themselves caught in round after round of Competitive Sleep Deprivation and only communicating with each other in four-letter obscenities via the medium of their non-sleeping daughter. 'Oh dear, looks like Mummy is going to be an unreasonable bitch again.' 'Well, Mummy wouldn't have to be an unreasonable bitch, would she, if Daddy didn't spend all his time telling her how tired he was, despite being the person who was snoring for the entire night last night like a FUCKING WANKER.' That kind of thing.

Yes, things had certainly gone downhill rapidly after Rosie was born, and while they'd managed to improve the situation for long enough to conceive Ella, it struck Becky that they were still quite some way off the newly married bliss she remembered from their wedding day.

It was time for things to change.

Becky planned her approach carefully. It was essential that she found a night when Lovely Jon was going to actually leave the office before midnight, for a start. Picking up the phone, she called his secretary Janet, who had become Becky's close confidante over the years. Having explained her plan, Janet immediately identified the perfect slot. 'He was due to have dinner with Mr Matthews this Thursday evening, but Mr Matthews' PA has just called me to cancel. I'll keep it in the diary, so he can't book anything else in, and then at the appointed time I'll break the good news to him. He'll be back with you by seven p.m., I promise.' Thanking Janet profusely, Becky hung up the phone.

With just forty-eight hours to go, she needed to decide on a menu. Cooking, it was fair to say, was not Becky's forte. She could manage beans on toast or the occasional pesto pasta (although she had once managed to somehow burn the pasta, despite it being cooked fully immersed in water. She had almost felt proud), but beyond that it was ready meals all the way.

A microwaved macaroni cheese didn't quite feel like it was going to cut the mustard on this occasion, though. What was Jon's favourite food? Of course! Predictable to the last, it was steak. This possibly dated back to the time Becky had made the mistake of telling him about the alternative Valentine's Day on 14 March: Steak and Blowjob Day. Lovely Jon had been so enamoured by the concept that he'd ended up sporting a rather embarrassing erection the next few times they'd walked down the meat aisle in Tesco.

I'll keep it simple, Becky decided. Steak and chips. Perfect.

Thursday duly rolled around. Jon had headed off to work that morning in his usual rush, dropping a perfunctory kiss on the top of her head and reminding her how lucky she was to get to stay at home and relax while he dealt with that pestilent Circle line. Conscious of her planned romantic liaison for them that evening, Becky chose not to spoil the moment by loudly shouting 'FUCKWIT' out of the door after him, and instead muttered it under her breath whilst dealing with shitty nappies and attempting to find the fourteenth water bottle Rosie had lost since she'd started at her new school.

With Rosie (and water bottle) safely at school, Becky spent most of the day teaching Ella about the art of beautifying oneself. Her daughter looked on in fascination as Becky waxed her top lip, her bikini line and her toes. Honestly, being a woman really was absolutely fucking ridiculous.

By the time seven p.m. came, she was ready. The children were in bed. Barry White was playing on the stereo, because Becky thought that subtlety was, frankly, overrated. She was dressed to kill in her LBD and Jimmy Choos. Jon wasn't going to know what had hit him when he walked through the door.

In the end, what hit Jon when he walked through the

door was very nearly Becky's fist. This is because, by the time Jon walked through the door, it was five minutes to midnight.

To say Becky's evening had not gone to plan would be an understatement. And it had started so promisingly, too. The children had gone to bed and actually stayed there. By googling, she'd discovered that you couldn't cook steak in the microwave and so had put the frying pan on the hob to get warm. The red wine had been decanted and Becky had poured herself an enormous glass, just to check it tasted okay.

Perhaps it was the wine that had addled her judgement. When the steak had started to smoke slightly as it had cooked, she'd opened the back door to let the smoke out, forgetting entirely the very good reason that she had left the back door firmly shut. Instead of the smoke going out, therefore, Boris the fucking liability had come rushing in and had made a beeline for the steaks sizzling in the pan. Jumping up to grab one of them, he had knocked the pan handle as he did so. The pan had tipped, resulting in the remaining steak (the one which wasn't now in Boris's mouth) falling directly onto the flames of the gas hob, which spat globules of burning fat dangerously close to Boris's shaggy coat. Swearing profusely, Becky had dragged the dog, still clutching his prize, by his collar and out of the back door before he set himself alight. She had then grabbed the fire blanket they kept in the kitchen for just such occurrences, putting out the smouldering steak but setting alight a tea towel in the process.

Finally, having hurled water from the washing-up bowl across the cooker and up the walls in an attempt to put both the steak and the tea towel out, she thought she had the situation back under control.

At which point Rosie ran down the stairs and said, 'Mummy, I smelled the smoke and so I called the fire brigade, like they told us to in school.'

She wasn't joking, either. The firemen who had attended had been very nice about the situation but Becky had been mortified at wasting their time, and even more mortified at the thought of what Jon was going to say if he walked in and found her surrounded by firemen whilst looking like she was going out on the pull.

The only saving grace was that Jon didn't walk in and find her like that. In fact, by the time Jon did walk in, not only had the smoke cleared and the kitchen dried out, but Becky had found time to repaint the singed ceiling with some paint from the garage, and was now sitting at the kitchen table, absolutely apoplectic, working her way through a plate of cold chips and the rest of the red wine.

She heard the key in the door and took another large slug of wine, steeling herself. Clearly surprised to see her still up, Jon popped his head around the door.

'I thought you'd be in bed?' He looked tired and dishevelled, with his tie hanging loosely around his neck, and smelt vaguely of booze and cigarettes.

'I've been waiting for you.' Becky didn't entirely trust herself to speak, for fear of what might come out of her mouth.

'Really?' He looked surprised. 'Why were you waiting for me?'

'You were meant to be back early. Janet told me she'd make sure you were back early.'

'Janet . . . what? I had a dinner tonight. A dinner with Mr Matthews. Janet must have got the day wrong.'

She hadn't; Mr Matthews had cancelled, but Becky was too exhausted and close to tears to let him know that she knew that. Quite where her husband had spent his evening was an argument for another day.

'Everything okay? Kids okay?'

'They are now, now that the fire brigade have gone.' She took another enormous gulp of her wine and stifled a sob.

'The fire brigade were here? What . . . what's happened?' He looked frantically around, as though expecting burning chunks of wood to fall from the ceiling at any moment.

'Oh, it's fine. It's nothing.' Becky felt her voice start to waver and tears building up in her eyes which she made no effort to stop from overflowing. 'Except, no, it isn't nothing, because tonight I made a real effort, and you weren't here to appreciate any of it. I bought steak and chips and red wine, even though it isn't Steak and Blowjob Day, and I got the children into bed, and I got myself all tarted up, and I was going to cook you a lovely meal so that we could rekindle our relationship and you could fall in love with me all over again, except that didn't happen, I burnt the dinner, and Rosie called the fire brigade, and they all turned up and laughed at me, and then it took another hour and a half to calm Rosie down enough for her to go to sleep, and you still weren't here, so I microwaved the chips, which taste like shit, and drank the red wine and now here you are, and I am very drunk, so I'm going to go to bed, and I suggest you sleep in the spare room, and by the way, I'm going to get a job, so your nights out with the imaginary Mr Matthews, who I know you didn't spend the evening with, because

111

when I spoke to Janet she told me Mr Matthews' PA had cancelled, so you can start thinking up excuses as to where you've actually been right now ... anyway, those nights out are going to be coming to an end. I am going back to work, and things are going to be changing round here on Walton's Mountain.'

Leaving an open-mouthed Jon standing motionless, Becky swayed her way across the room, the effect only marginally spoiled by her poise momentarily deserting her as she slammed into the side of the door frame and ricocheted back off again.

'You're getting a job?' He sounded shell-shocked.

'You better believe it.' She stared back at him, defiantly, arms crossed.

Her husband raised one eyebrow. 'I'm hoping it's not in catering.'

Becky went to bed.

Eight

Tom whistled cheerfully to himself as he chained his bike to the railings outside the school playground and headed into the school to prepare for the day. He'd been at Redcoats for almost two months now and was finally starting to feel like he'd found his feet.

Today was going to be a test, though; it was his first school trip since he'd taken up post here. Buoyed by his success of the early weeks, when Mrs Goldman had asked him whether he thought he'd be up to running the usual Year 2 spring term trip to the local farm, he had agreed before she'd even finished her sentence.

The problem, as usual, wasn't going to be the kids; it was the parents. With thirty children to keep a watchful eye on, additional DBS-checked volunteers had to be drafted in, and this inevitably included some of the parents of the kids in his class. Unsurprisingly, Vivienne, closely followed by Andrea Barnes, had been at the head of the queue.

He scanned down the list of parent helpers. Most of

the names he recognised; they belonged to the mums who joined Vivienne at his classroom door every morning and insisted on giving him a blow by blow account of everything their child had done since they'd left his care the previous afternoon. One of these days he was going to forget all of his professional training and scream back at them, 'Please, try telling someone who gives a shit.' He just hoped it wouldn't be while Mrs Goldman was watching.

One name caught his eye: it was Rosie Barrington's mum – Becky, he thought her name was. Out of all of the children in his class, Rosie was the only one giving him real cause for concern. She'd joined Redcoats at the same time as him, having moved schools when her mum and dad had moved into the local area. When he'd first assessed her he'd been impressed: she was bright, inquisitive and clearly academic. Since then, though, she'd become gradually more withdrawn; not participating in class discussions, unwilling to put her hand up, and often seeming to be in something of an unhappy daze. He'd been meaning to speak to her parents about her; today would clearly give him the perfect opportunity.

For her part, Becky had signed up for the trip because she too had started to have concerns about Rosie. Even at home, her usual seven-year-old enthusiasm had become tempered, and although she never confessed to anything worrying her, Becky wasn't so sure. In her heart of hearts she was pretty certain she knew what the problem was. There was no way of escaping how things had deteriorated between her and Jon since The Night of the Fire Brigade, as she'd subsequently described it to Gemma. ('But were the firemen fit?' 'Of course they were, but that's not the point!') Jon had been at home even less since then, if such a thing were possible, and the few interactions they had had with each other had been icily cold. Rosie had clearly picked up on the tensions at home, and Becky was hoping to observe her with her school friends to see if it was also affecting her at school.

The other reason Becky had signed up, which she shared openly with Gemma, was her desire to find out more about Mr Jones. 'Something just doesn't add up,' she had told her friend. 'He had some high-flying job in the City – I mean, you should *see* his LinkedIn profile. He must be worth mega bucks. And then he jacks it all in to come and teach primary school children. Either he's a covert paedophile, or there's something we're missing.' The school trip, she convinced Gemma, was her perfect opportunity to find out what.

The downside of this particular plan was that now Becky actually had to go on the trip. Large groups of small children were not really her forte; far too many uncontrolled bodily fluids for her liking. Arriving with Rosie, she reported in to Mr Jones and was allocated her 'group', four children, including Ava, Gemma's daughter.

'Right then, children!' Becky clapped her hands brightly to instil confidence; like dogs, she suspected they could smell her fear. 'I'm Mrs Barrington and I'm going to be in charge of your group today.'

'Her name is Becky and she likes getting drunk with my mummy,' Ava told the other three children cheerfully, all of whom laughed. Excellent. Marvellous.

After asking everyone multiple times if they needed the toilet, including, mortifyingly, Mr Jones, Becky and her group filed onto the coach. Vivienne had of course got there first with her group – which included her daughter Satin and also Rosie, who looked terrified – and had taken over the front seat, kneeling on it to conduct a chorus of 'Ging Gang Goolie', which Satin and her chums sang along to with gusto. Rosie stayed mute, and failed to crack a smile even when Becky pulled a ridiculous face at her. Becky felt her heart sink. Something was definitely up.

Frantically counting heads onto the coach, Tom assured himself that everyone was present and correct, and indicated to the coach driver that they were ready to start. Having been warned by every single member of the teaching staff at Redcoats, who were personally delighting in the *Schadenfreude* of it being some other poor bastard in the firing line that day, what to expect on school trips with KS1, he had the sick bucket primed and was sprinting up the aisle with it just in time to reach Simon Barnes, who'd eaten his entire packed lunch in the toilets prior to leaving, before the coach had even made its way out the end of the school road.

The farm was only a ten-minute coach journey away. In that time, in between Andrea Barnes appropriating the seat next to Tom and telling him in strident tones exactly what she thought of the coach driver, whose driving had clearly had such a disastrous effect on her darling's delicate stomach, two other children had been sick, one had threatened to poo himself (Simon Barnes, again, the effects of tuna sandwiches at eight-thirty a.m. clearly being too much for him), and Becky had endured a terrifying interrogation from Ava, who had appropriated the seat next to her and was delighted to have Becky all to herself.

'So are you and Jon going to get divorced?' she asked in a very matter-of-fact tone. 'It doesn't matter if you do, because you will still get to keep your children. Or just one of them, if you only like one of them. Would you keep both of your children or just one? I would probably keep Rosie if I was you, because Ella is quite annoying, and also Rosie poos in the toilet and not in nappies, and then Jon can deal with all of Ella's stinky poos all by himself.'

Slightly aghast, Becky assured Ava that she would indeed be keeping both of her children, not that that was going to be an issue, because her and Jon were not going to be getting divorced.

From the look on Ava's face, she clearly didn't believe her. 'I think you probably need to try a bit harder, because I don't see Jon in your house very much. My daddy wasn't in our house very much and then he and Mummy got divorced, because he was having sex with some slut called Lucy. Do you think Jon is having sex with some slut called Lucy?'

Fuck, why had she ever agreed to come on this trip?

Thoroughly distracted by Ava's interrogation – the girl was clearly going to walk out of school straight into a job with MI5 – Becky had forgotten to keep an eye out for Rosie. She had been marched off the coach by Vivienne and was now over standing in a little circle in her group on the other side of the car park. Becky attempted a wave but was flat out ignored by her daughter, who had her hands shoved in the pockets of her school coat and was pulling the classic My Mum Is Mortifying Me facial expression, recognisable the world over. In fact, Becky still found herself doing it occasionally when her own mum decided to summon her to her home to have a little chat about quite what she was doing with her life.

Tom checked his itinerary for the day for what felt like the five hundredth time. In theory, it seemed so simple. They'd be watching the cows being milked first; then off for a tractor ride; followed by a tour around the farm and then ending the day feeding the newborn piglets. In reality, the concept of getting thirty six- and seven-year-olds around a farmyard for the day without disaster unfolding seemed vanishingly unlikely. He really wished he'd thought to bring his hip flask.

However, defying his wildest expectations, the trip went surprisingly smoothly. Health and safety regulations being what they were, every element of it had been risk assessed up to the eyeballs. Even Becky started to relax into things, not least because it seemed like Ava was far too enchanted by farmyard life to commence another round of interrogation.

At lunchtime, she found five minutes to collar the divine Mr Jones, who was looking really quite devastatingly attractive in his dress-down vibe of soft navy cords and a cornflower-blue polo shirt. Something which had not gone unnoticed by Vivienne, who was hovering just inches from where he stood, no doubt just waiting to pretend to trip – 'Whoops, silly me!' – straight into his waiting arms.

'So I just wondered whether you'd be able to keep an eye out for me?' finished Becky, having brought Tom up to speed with her concerns about Rosie.

'Absolutely, of course I will,' promised Tom, who, whilst genuinely interested in Rosie's well-being, was at that precise moment far more concerned about the fact that

Simon Barnes – it was always Simon Barnes – appeared to be attempting to insert his water bottle up his bottom. Andrea was standing nearby, an indulgent look on her face. 'Always pushing boundaries, that's my Simon. He's just so spirited!'

'She does seem quite happy today, though,' Tom continued. 'Seems to be making friends; that's bound to help.'

'Um,' said Becky, looking over at her daughter. She was sitting on a picnic bench next to Satin, who whispered something in her ear, then giggled. Rosie's face didn't change; her mouth stayed grimly set. What the hell was Satin saying? 'Let's hope so.'

Tom looked around again, doing another frantic headcount of the children. He could feel beads of sweat forming in the small of his back. He'd clearly been kidding himself when he'd told himself that a school trip would be just like another day in the classroom. At least at school the kids were contained. Here, they could be anywhere: on a tractor; in the duck pond; running out of the farm and across the nearby dual carriageway. His stomach churned at the very thought. God, imagine having to go back and tell Mrs Goldman that he'd lost one of the children. It didn't even bear thinking about.

Becky was watching him closely. 'This your first time?' As he turned to respond, she continued: 'It's just the way you're looking absolutely terrified and like you might want to cry, that's all. I'm guessing you haven't done this before?'

Good to see his poker face was doing its job. There was a reason that, unlike Miss Thompson, he'd never considered a career on the stage. Briefly, he weighed up in his own mind whether to attempt to feign being completely on top of things, but the need for someone to share the burden with won out. 'Yep – this is my first time in sole charge of a school trip. I mean, so far, so good: we haven't lost any of the children yet. Right? Right?' Horrified that he might have tempted fate, he did another count up. Nope, all present and correct, once he'd identified Isaac Williams, who appeared to be attempting to copulate with a picnic bench.

Becky latched onto this new bit of information like a dog with a bone. 'So, you've not been doing this teaching thing all that long?'

He shook his head. 'This is only my first full-time teaching role after my placement. Don't worry though, I've got plenty of experience of preventing the shit from hitting the fan from my previous job. Turns out there are a lot of transferrable skills from working in financial services which are all too useful when it comes to teaching.'

Now they were getting somewhere! Delighted by his apparent willingness to open up, Becky was about to pose her killer question, 'So what made you change career?', when she was interrupted by none other than a furious Vivienne, who had been most aggrieved at the amount of one to one time Becky had been having with the object of her affections.

'Mr Jones, were you aware that one of your charges is excreting in the middle of the farmyard?'

Horrified, Tom made a dash for George Smith, who had indeed dropped his trousers and was squatting with intent, leaving Vivienne to sneer nastily at Becky and stalk off in her spike heels and black leather catsuit. Which was of course totally sensible attire for a school trip to a farm.

With George Smith successfully persuaded to use the toilet prior to the actual point of evacuation, Tom finally allowed himself to start to relax. It looked like they'd made it. There was just one more activity before they got back on the coach to go home: feeding the baby pigs. Ava had been waiting for this all day and was beside herself with excitement, jumping up and down next to Becky, desperate to get there first.

Typically, Vivienne's group had made it before they had and so Ava was relegated to the second row. Vivienne was now charming the farmhand, a terrified-looking youth whom Becky reckoned was probably young enough to be her son. Thrusting her leather-clad breasts in his general direction, she persuaded him to hand her over the bottle of milk with which he was giving top-up feeds to the piglets. Passing her iPhone to Satin, she encouraged her to photograph her mother feeding the piglets. This would make the perfect shot for the cover of the annual PTA calendar!

Ava looked on mutinously as Vivienne held the teat of the bottle out towards the piglets and the class oohed and aahed. Ava had wanted to be the first one to feed the baby pigs.

Ava also really wanted her gold Blue Peter badge.

After the event, no one was able to say exactly what had happened. All that was known was that, by the time Tom came rushing towards the sound of the shrieks, all of Year 2 was in hysterics, Ava was proudly announcing that she would be calling an ambulance, and Vivienne was somehow on the other side of the low wall between them and the piglets, face down on the ground, her leather jumpsuit covered in slurry and her head in an enormous pile of pig shit.

Becky just wished she'd filmed it.

If she was honest, the school trip had been a welcome distraction from the misery which had been her job search. She'd been so excited to get started. With Gemma having set up her LinkedIn profile for her, she'd added details of the marketing graduate programme she'd been fast-tracked through at Jon's firm and her subsequent career progression to deputy marketing director, prior to jacking it all in to go and wreck her vagina with the miracle of childbirth, included her seriously impressive set of academic achievements – and then she'd waited. With experience like hers, surely recruiters were going to be knocking down her door to sign her up?

It seemed not. After a week, with not a single approach in her inbox, she'd realised she was going to have to be more proactive than this. Trawling the job boards, she started to search for a job. She was looking for something vaguely marketing-related, which would allow her to use her previous experience, was open to flexible working hours around school runs and where she could work a two- or three-day week.

She was about to be very disappointed.

'I just don't understand,' she complained to Gemma at the weekend, over a sandwich lunch in her kitchen. Jon had curtly informed her that he was heading out on a hundred-mile bike ride and would be back around teatime. When, Becky wondered, had they changed from being a couple who politely enquired with the other if they would mind if they committed to a particular activity, to one that had apparently stopped caring about each other's opinion and just announced that that was how things were going to be? It was not an encouraging development.

'I'm not asking for the moon on a stick here. All I want is a vaguely interesting job which will allow me to still see my children. Is that really so unreasonable?'

At that moment Ava appeared in the doorway. 'Mummy, Becky, did you know that my wardrobe is absolutely *full* of hookers?'

Having spent a good ten minutes attempting to explain to her daughter the difference between hangers and hookers – which had clearly been pointless given she'd then left the room announcing that she couldn't wait to tell Mr Jones on Monday how many hookers she had at home (Gemma couldn't wait to take that particular phone call from the school) – Gemma returned to the topic in hand. 'Becky, what you've described just there is the holy grail of working parents everywhere. We all have to work to pay the bills, or we want to work, to keep ourselves sane, but we also need a job that fits around school hours and means that we don't have to be in the office until ten o'clock every night. With so many people wanting that, you'd think employers would have cottoned on, but unfortunately most of them haven't, which is why, on the off chance you are lucky enough to find a job like you've described, you'll have to beat off about three thousand other applicants in order to land it.' She sighed. 'It shouldn't be like that – and it isn't like that everywhere, at Zero, for example, we ensure all of our jobs can be worked flexibly – but most of the time it is.'

'Any jobs going at Zero?' Becky looked up, expectantly, until Gemma shook her head sadly and her shoulders slumped back down again. Jobs at Zero – ha, that was a good one! At the rate things were going, Gemma would be joining Becky on her job search before very much longer.

'But that's ridiculous.' Becky, bouncing Ella on her knee, couldn't get her head round it. 'Are you basically saying that anyone with children isn't able to get a job?'

'They're going to struggle to find a job that's interesting, and intellectually stimulating, and pays more than the minimum wage, and still allows them to make it to the occasional assembly and sports day, that's for sure. Don't look at me like that: I think it's totally wrong, but it is what it is, and I'm afraid that's the backdrop we're working against.'

Becky was shaking her head. 'It's ridiculous. We need to change it. Right, first of all I'm going to get a job, and then I'm going to work out a way to make sure every other parent who wants to get a job and still see their children can do.'

Gemma would have laughed, but her friend's face was so determined that she thought better of it. 'Okay, maybe we should start small and build up. Let's get you a job first. Here, pass me your iPad and we'll get you registered with some agencies.'

A week later, during which time Gemma had been called out of a board meeting in order to reassure Mr Jones that, no, she was not running a brothel at home, thanks to Ava having raced into class to tell him all about her many 'hookers', a miracle happened. Becky was called to her first interview, which sent her into a flat spin, because, as she reminded Gemma, 'I've not had an interview since I was twenty-one, and that was after I'd been on a three-day bender so to be honest, I can't remember anything about it because I was still so completely off my tits.'

'Well, turning up to interview sober will already put you ahead of probably fifty per cent of the candidates. Come on, you're going to be fine. Let's work out what you're going to wear, and then I'll run you through some sample interview questions. You're going to ace this.'

Nine

The next morning, bright and early, Becky was outside the firm of solicitors where she'd been shortlisted for a general administration role, 'working hours flexible for the right candidate'. Sure, it wasn't marketing, but as Gemma had reminded her, she was in no position to be choosy.

Nervously pacing until her allocated interview slot, she found time to admire her reflection in a shop window. After much debate on quite what to wear, she'd elected to go for a classic skirt suit: black, well tailored and figure hugging, with a pair of canary-yellow heels to contrast. With her hair neatly lacquered back in a chignon, she was dressed to kick interview butt. Which was just as well, really, because inside she was a fucking nervous wreck and really *really* wanted to go home and hide in a ball under her duvet. However, Becky's expensive private education had not been for nothing. Pulling herself together and adopting her best 'finishing school pose', she threw back her head, grasped the strap of her lucky handbag and stalked into reception on her yellow heels.

The waiting area was cold, grey and impersonal, and Becky felt her heart start to sink. In the excitement of finding a job which would provide some kind of intellectual stimulation greater than that required to purée butternut squash and create space rockets out of empty Tampax boxes, she'd forgotten the often drab reality of corporate life. Bland, blandy blandness. Even her yellow shoes seemed to have lost their shine in the blur of grey officiousness.

To her surprise, when she introduced herself at reception, she found a number of other interview candidates also waiting. Her heart rate started to increase. Surely this wasn't going to be one of those horrific group interviews she'd heard about, that she knew they sometimes did at Jon's place? Gemma's interview preparation with her had all been on the assumption that this would be a straightforward, one-to-one interview, not the recruitment equivalent of *The Hunger Games*. She wondered if she had time to go outside and phone Gemma for tips. Either that or strap on a crossbow.

All five candidates were female and appeared to be a similar age to Becky, apart from one lady who was clearly much older. She was adeptly flicking through a file of papers and exuded confidence. Damn, should she have brought a file with her? Gemma hadn't mentioned any need for a file. Taking a seat, Becky smiled confidently around at the others, even though inside she was anything but.

Before long the door to the reception area opened and a young girl – she could have been no older than her early twenties – came in, wearing one of the shortest skirts Becky had ever seen. And Becky was no stranger to short skirts, having been thrown out of multiple lectures at university for wearing items of clothing which 'fail to adequately cover your underwear', in the words of her lecturers. This skirt looked like it had come straight out of university-Becky's wardrobe.

Introducing herself as Alicia, the girl tottered over on her vertiginous platform heels, and showed the candidates into what was presumably the boardroom. At the board table were seated two men, who stood up and greeted the candidates. This, it seemed, was where the fight to the death for the one available job would take place.

'Right then.' The younger of the two men cast his eyes swiftly up and down the group of interviewees. 'You –' he pointed at the older lady '– and you –' the girl Becky had been sitting next to, who wore a trouser suit instead of the skirt suits favoured by the rest of the group, and was wearing flats instead of heels '– thank you very much for coming. Alicia will show you out.'

Smiling, Alicia held the door open and gestured to the two women that they should follow her out. Mutely, they followed her. The door closed silently behind them, and the younger man encouraged the remaining three candidates to sit.

'Good morning, and congratulations on making it through to the final stage of our selection process. I am Mr Hammond, and this gentleman here is my father, Mr Hammond Senior. We are the two partners of this firm, and we are looking ... yes?' Rather crossly, he cut his speech short, as Becky had raised her hand, nerves now completely dissipated in her complete and utter outrage at what she perceived to have just happened.

'I'm sorry to interrupt, but I just wanted to ask. Those two candidates who you just showed out – what's happened to them?'

Mr Hammond looked at his father. A small smile passed between them.

'They haven't been successful.'

'What do you mean, they haven't been successful?'

His smile had left his face and he sounded impatient. 'I mean, they have not succeeded in passing that particular stage of the recruitment process. Now, unless you wish to be asked to leave too, I suggest you stop asking questions.'

'But why have they been asked to leave the recruitment process? You haven't even asked us any questions yet. How can they have been deselected?' Becky knew that she was quite possibly talking herself out of a job here, but decided she didn't care.

The younger Mr Hammond turned puce and, for a moment, looked like he wanted to scream at her. Then, in response to a hand on his shoulder from his father, and a couple of whispered exchanges between the two men, he stood and motioned to her to follow him. Presumably to show her out.

Grabbing her handbag, Becky followed him. The two remaining candidates gave her looks – whether of sympathy or pity, she couldn't tell. They exited the boardroom through a door to the right, which Becky hadn't noticed when she came in. It led to a small anteroom, carpeted in the same plush wool carpet that she'd seen throughout the building. These guys clearly had money.

'It's Becky, yes?' Mr Hammond stood facing her, his left hand on the door handle. He smiled, a charming smile which showed off his gleaming white teeth to their best advantage, yet didn't quite reach his eyes. Becky curtly nodded her assent.

'Becky, you seem to be under some misconceptions about our recruitment process, so let me just explain it to you. To be honest, if you'd been any other candidate, you'd have been shown the door off the back of such blatant backchat, but my father and I see great ... potential, in you. You see, the thing is, Becky, Hammonds is a major player in the legal world.' It seemed unlikely – she'd never heard of them before this job had come up. 'We have a brand to uphold. And this role ... this will become one of the faces of the Hammond brand. What I'm trying to say is that we can't consider anyone who doesn't fit with our corporate image. You're a bright girl, clearly. Do you get what I'm saying?'

Oh, she got what he was saying all right, though she was struggling to believe it. So, basically, all of Gemma's detailed interview practice with her had been entirely pointless. In this particular firm, if you were female, it didn't matter what your greatest strengths were or where you hoped to be in five years' time. No, all that was relevant was how good you looked in a mini skirt and whether you were willing to risk permanent damage to your spine by wearing four-inch heels to work every day.

Becky's theory was then proved beyond all doubt when Mr Hammond Junior leant over her, breathed wolfishly in her face, and suggested to her he would easily be able to fast track her to the final stage if she'd just consider dropping to her knees to make up for her minor indiscretion out there in the boardroom.

'And that's when I kneed him in the balls,' Becky recounted to Gemma, much later that evening, while the older kids were glued to an episode of *Horrid Henry* (and god, that child really was fucking horrid) and she was sinking a much-needed glass of chilled white wine in Gemma's kitchen.

Gemma put her hand to her mouth. 'Oh my god. You didn't?'

'No, I didn't. I wanted to, though. Decided that all things considered though, I didn't really want my first LinkedIn endorsement to be for GBH, so settled for telling him exactly what I thought of him and that I looked forward to bringing my employment tribunal claim against his firm very shortly.'

'And are you going to? Bring a claim, I mean?'

Becky stretched back in her chair. 'No. What's the point?'

Gemma sipped at her wine, feeling strangely let down. How could Becky say that she wouldn't be bringing a claim? What happened to the Becky of last week who was hell bent on campaigning for flexible working opportunities for everyone? Where had she gone?

'You're not?'

'Nope. A tribunal claim would fly far too under the radar. I'm going straight to the press. Jon's got a contact at the *Guardian*; I'm going to meet him for lunch tomorrow. Mr Hammonds Junior and Senior are going to wish they'd never fucking met me. It's appalling, that this kind of thing is still happening. Put it this way: I don't reckon it's flat shoes and midi-length skirts that are going to be the primary things damaging the Hammonds brand for very much longer.'

Sam wandered into the kitchen. 'Mum. Have you got my stuff for my trip tomorrow?'

Gemma felt her blood run cold. 'What trip?'

'You know. I told you. My trip to the outdoor centre. We're going to be gone all day and I need a packed lunch and waterproof trousers. Oh, and you need to make sure you've paid online, otherwise they might tell me that I can't go. You have paid, haven't you?' He looked worried, biting his lip and shifting uneasily from foot to foot.

'Sam, *what* trip?' Gemma knew her organisational skills were hardly in the running for any awards any time soon, but she was fairly certain she'd have remembered if Sam had mentioned a trip requiring waterproof trousers. *Waterproof trousers?* Who the fuck owned waterproof trousers? Not for the first time, Gemma wondered if she'd missed some kind of Parenting Fundamentals class which informed you of the various items of equipment you would need to ensure you had in your armoury at all times as your children grew up. Waterproof trousers – which, if she was honest, she hadn't even known were a thing that existed – being top of that list.

'Um, we're going to go. Thanks very much for the wine.' Becky had been a spectator on misunderstandings between Sam and his mum before, and it wasn't pretty. With Rosie having started to flinch every time she or Jon raised their voices, she didn't imagine exposing her to a full-blown row over here was going to do much for her state of mind.

Gemma attempted to keep her cool as she said goodbye to Becky, Rosie and Ella and went to load the tea things into the dishwasher. Sam stood next to her, hopping from foot to foot.

'I told you, Mum. We've got a trip tomorrow, and I need a packed lunch, and waterproof trousers, and you have to pay on the internet, and if you don't then I can't go.' He sounded like he might cry.

'Yeah, and if he doesn't go, then he'll have no friends at school, and he'll have to do lessons with KS1, and all his friends will laugh at him, and he'll be so embarrassed he'll never be able to go back to school ever again and will probably *die*.' Ava; helpful as ever.

Gemma took a deep breath. 'Sam, has there been a letter about this trip?' She honestly couldn't remember seeing one, but then, with the amount of permission forms she was constantly sending back for things – she'd counted sixteen, *sixteen*, the other Tuesday – it was entirely possible that it had just slipped her memory.

Sam looked miserable. 'Um, yes. I think so. Probably.' Poor Sam. He was as rubbish as his mum when it came to remembering things. Since Ava had started school, they'd got into quite a good system whereby Ava gave Gemma all of the letters from school and Sam's were able to fester grimly in his book bag until the end of term. Unfortunately for Sam and Gemma, this only worked so long as the letters were sent out to the whole school and not solely to Year 5.

'Right, well, why don't we have a look in your book bag.' Sam was always reluctant for Gemma to go anywhere near his book bag, and when she got it open she realised why. On top of all of his sodding rocks, there was also Ava's reading diary that she'd completely lost her shit over when it disappeared the other week, and Sam had sworn he'd never seen it in his life and wouldn't have touched it even if he had; plus the remains of a cream cheese sandwich, which was smeared all over his book bag, rocks, and a series of almost illegible letters, so crumpled and covered with cream cheese were they.

It had been an unseasonably warm week and the cream cheese had clearly been there for some time. Gagging, Gemma dumped the contents of the book bag in the sink and began pouring hot water and bleach over them.

'Not my reading diary!' Ava was hysterical, so much so that Gemma capitulated and handed her the cheese-mould encrusted book. On balance, she would probably rather her house smelt of rotting dairy products than she would have Ava descend into meltdown. Ava's tantrums had gone down into folklore amongst Gemma's family and friends. The one where she screamed so loudly and made herself go so rigid in the frozen veg aisle in Tesco – because Gemma selfishly refused to shrink the trolley to a size that would enable Ava to pick it up and hold it in the palm of her hand – that Gemma, having exhausted all options open to her, had lifted her up and placed her into the chest freezer, alongside the frozen peas (it had silenced her instantly and had left Gemma thinking that more parenting books really ought to recommend more unorthodox methods for keeping control of your children), had been particularly memorable.

Carefully, unpeeling the letters, Gemma happened upon the one which referenced Sam's trip. Based on the date of it, it had been handed out two weeks previously. Gemma was tired, she was cross, and she was covered in mouldy cream cheese and bleach. She lost the plot.

'Two weeks ago, you got this. Why didn't you give it to me?'

'*Do you want me to phone Childline for you?*' Ava stage whispered at her brother, before Gemma gave her The Look and she sashayed out of the room loudly singing Michael Jackson's 'Bad'.

'I thought I did, but I didn't, okay?' Sam, who could be as stubborn as Ava in his own way, was standing there, arms folded, glaring at her as she held out the soggy, smelly letter between them.

'So if you don't hand me the letters, how do you think I'm going to know you need your trip paying for? I'm good, Sam, but I'm not Mystic Sodding Meg.' Looking at the letter, she caught sight of the price. 'Bloody hell, twenty-six pounds to sit on a coach and go and run around in a field for the day? What do they think I am, made of money? Tell you what: you can give me a fiver and run around all day in the back garden instead. What d'you reckon?'

She'd attempted to lighten the mood, but it hadn't worked. Sam's bottom lip started to tremble, a sure sign that tears were on the way. He rarely cried these days, assuming his position of 'man of the house'. At not yet ten he was already not far off shoulder height on Gemma, and she knew there were times when she forgot that he was still really just a child. Times like this. She needed to go easier on him.

On the other hand, how hard could it be to remember to hand her a letter, when all you had to think about all day was whether you were going to choose the red option or the green option for lunch at school, and then decide which of the various inane YouTube stars you were going to spend the evening staring aimlessly at.

135

'I'm just asking for a bit of help here, Sam, that's all. I run this house by myself as well as working full time. Your dad's not here any more, and you guys are getting older. All I need is for you to help me out with the basics. I don't mind spending twenty-six pounds on a school trip, and I don't even mind buying a ridiculous pair of waterproof trousers that you will wear once, lose, and I'll never see again. All I'm asking is that you just take a few minutes out of your day to stop staring at DanTDM downloading his latest Minecraft mod, and help me know what you need. Is that too much to ask?'

From the look on Sam's face, it was.

'Why does it all have to be up to me, though? I'm the kid. You're the grown-up, you're meant to be helping me remember stuff. You should have checked my bag for letters, or reminded me that I needed to. Or, if you ever bothered to come and pick me and Ava up from school on time, rather than making us go to after-school club, then you'd see all the other mums chatting about the trip and then you'd know that it was happening. You're never here, Mum. You're never here when I need you. And even when you are here, basically all you're doing is looking at your mobile phone and sending work emails or trying to find some random man to have sex with.' Gemma gulped; she hadn't realised he'd heard that bit. 'You might tell me I'm rubbish for forgetting that letter, but I'm not as rubbish as you. You're a RUBBISH MUM.' And, tears streaming down his face, he stormed up to his bedroom, leaving Gemma shattered.

The water and bleach combo overflowed from the sink behind her onto the floor and she didn't even notice. Sam probably knew that he'd gone too far, but it didn't matter; those words couldn't be unsaid. Was she really a rubbish mum? Yes, she probably was. Sam was right. She wasn't there for school pick ups; she was always late for school drop offs; she lost her patience far too easily when he asked her to explain yet another archaic grammatical concept that apparently the government had now decided was essential for all primary school children to be taught, yet she had never heard of; and the last time he'd asked her to help him make the pizza he'd devised the recipe for, she'd only half supervised him while she'd fielded a stream of emails from Leroy and the pizza had ended up uncooked in the middle and had given them all a nasty tummy ache.

Fuck, she was a *terrible* mum. Overcome with mortification, Gemma put her head down on the kitchen table and wept.

Curious, Ava put her head round the door, now dressed as half Spider-Man, half Incredible Hulk. 'Why are you sad, Mummy? Are you going to die soon? When you do, can I have all your stuff?' Oh, and now she'd flooded the kitchen. Marvellous. Just marvellous.

Much later, as she lay in bed, staring into the darkness, Gemma made a plan. Only slightly distracted by the sight of Spider-Man/Hulk snoring on the pillow next to her – Ava had a very 'what's yours is mine' approach to beds, and rarely stayed the entire night in her own, usually materialising in either Sam's or Gemma's at some point after midnight, where she would lie diagonally, taking up a surprisingly large amount of space for such a small person, and kick Gemma repeatedly in the vagina – she decided that something was going to have to give.

And it was going to have to be her job.

Gemma loved her job, but her working full time clearly just wasn't working for the children. And, given they were her number-one priority, her number-two priority was going to have to take a back seat. She gulped when she imagined Leroy's face when she told him that she was going to need to reduce her hours; hell, that she might even need to take a less demanding position altogether. She knew that Leroy saw her as his right-hand woman: they had grown the business together from practically Day One. But her kids came first. And she was going to prove to them both – Sam, in particular – that they did.

Spider-Man/Hulk stretched out and smashed into her mother's episiotomy scar with the sole of one foot, as Gemma's mind raced. It was going to be a long, sleepless night.

Ten

Sam spent the next morning studiously ignoring Gemma, despite the fact that guilt had compelled her to make the best packed lunch any of them had ever seen. Having given up on sleep entirely thanks to Ava appearing to be practising penalty kicks as she snored, she'd scoured the contents of the kitchen cupboards, fridge and freezer and made a rare foray onto Pinterest to see what the non-rubbish mums were doing with lunch boxes these days. Fuck, it was terrifying. Sandwiches cut into the shape of Pixar characters and fruit and vegetable crudités lined up to form a rainbow. Okay, so that was going to be out of her league, but she still managed to cook up some miniature Yorkshire puddings which, with chipolata sausages, would create the perfect lunchbox version of toad in the hole – Sam's favourite meal.

Such was her guilt that she even cracked into her emergency stash of Twiglets to wrap some up into a little foil parcel, which she packed into his lunchbox alongside the cold toad in the hole and some Frubes. A handful of Jammie

Dodgers, and she was done. She'd probably get struck off by the school sugar police, but it would be worth it if it made Sam smile.

He didn't smile, not even when she announced to him that she'd performed an overnight miracle and procured a pair of waterproof trousers – Heidi turning out to apparently have previously untapped supermum qualities, possessing not just a pair of waterproof trousers for her son Jacob, who was almost exactly the same size as Sam, but also a *spare* pair. Gemma would have felt even worse about her parenting abilities, were she not so relieved that this would mean Sam could go on his trip after all.

Dropping the children off at school – Ava attempting to reduce the palpable tension between her mother and brother in her own unique way, by singing a composition of her own creation which appeared to consist solely of the word 'LABIA! LABIA! LABIA!' sung on repeat (Gemma stood by her decision not to ever keep information from her children and to tell them the honest answer to questions at whatever age they asked them, but hadn't fully appreciated how her daughter's resulting encyclopaedic knowledge of the names of parts of the human anatomy could come to backfire on her) – she kissed Sam on the top of his head and held him close for a moment, despite his protests.

'I'm going to talk to Leroy today and see about reducing my hours so I can spend some more time with you. I promise.'

Sam shrugged. 'Whatever. You don't need to. I'm fine. I'm used to it now.'

He still wouldn't smile, or meet her eyes, and so she

settled for a final, tight squeeze before she set him free to join his friends.

They didn't mention this bit in the parenting books. Mind you, there was an awful lot they didn't mention in the parenting books. Gemma was fairly certain the human race would die out within a couple of years if they told you the truth about having children before you actually had them. I mean, an honest description of the first post-birth poo alone would be enough to put you off. Gemma had genuinely thought she'd just gone and birthed another baby when she'd first used the toilet after having Sam.

Waving Ava off at her classroom door, her mind was in such a spin that she barely noticed Mr Jones looking as though he wanted to speak to her. She was back out of the gates and into her car before he could say anything, and it only later crossed her mind that he might have been trying to attract her attention.

The office was heaving by the time she made it in. It was the first Tuesday of the month, which meant that the sales team were having their monthly meeting to discuss what new business they'd brought in, and the finance team were shoulder-deep in month end. On the operations side, all Gemma really needed to do was to keep business running as usual, but today she had her work cut out to keep the rumours at bay that were running rife around the office.

There were times when Zero reminded her more of a university halls or a school common room than a business, and today was one of those times. From the moment she walked through the main reception she could hear there was something up. Excited conversations were hushed as she walked past – Gemma, as a board member, was seen to be simultaneously In The Know and Not To Be Trusted – and the whole place seemed to be in a frenzy of excitement.

Siobhan was alternately swigging strong black coffee from a Starbucks cup and typing furiously when Gemma arrived. Gemma knew the signs: Siobhan was stressed, which meant that in all likelihood, something really was up. Siobhan had been around long enough to be able to differentiate fake news from something big that was genuinely happening.

'No, you're not sacked,' Gemma began, almost reflexively, pre-empting the first words that usually came out of her assistant's mouth. 'But what's going on? The entire place seems to be in uproar?'

Siobhan paused in her typing to stare at her through manic, red-ringed eyes. 'Bigwigs in suits are in, meeting Leroy and Dave.' She lowered her voice. 'Rumour has it they're going to close us down.'

'Oh bollocks are they,' laughed Gemma. Honestly, did Siobhan not think she'd be in on it if the company was about to be put into administration? All the same, a small dart of concern shot through her. Neither Leroy nor Dave had mentioned anything about anyone coming in at the weekly management meeting yesterday. On the contrary, it had been all bonhomie and *joie de vivre*, as Natalie told them about her latest fuck-buddy, who went like a train, apparently – clearly, if you managed to spend at least the first hour on a date not physically vomiting over them, you might actually make it to the bedroom – and Dave gently rapped Leroy over the knuckles for his abject failure to curb his spending like he'd promised. Although he'd not purchased any more yachts, so that was progress, at least.

With Gemma now in situ at her desk, the noise in the office calmed down and gradually things got back to normal. At least, as normal as they ever got at Zero. With Leroy's love of the madcap – he'd once had a week where he'd issued everyone in the office with a pogo stick, on the grounds that it would be a creative way of improving their cardiovascular health as they pogoed from desk to meeting to photocopier (he only finally agreed to acquiesce that there might perhaps be one or two downsides to his great plan when they'd clocked up their third broken limb of the morning) – the collection of individuals he'd recruited to run his business were far from your typical corporate beings. It meant every day at work had the potential to be batshit crazy; but that suited Gemma down to the ground.

The morning shot by in a blur of meetings and emails, and before she knew it it was lunchtime and Paula, Leroy's PA/general office dogsbody had arrived at her desk to see if she wanted her to pick up a sandwich when she went out to fetch lunch for Leroy, Dave and the men in grey suits.

'I'm fine thanks, Paula, but listen, what's going on? Who are the guys who Leroy and Dave are in with? What are they talking about?'

Paula could be maddeningly inscrutable at times. Tapping the side of her nose – with fingers whose nails were so perfectly polished in a rose pink gel, Gemma found herself sitting on her hands to hide her own, which were bitten down to the quick – the PA made it clear that she would be giving nothing away. Honestly. Like Gemma and Leroy had secrets from each other. It wasn't like he wouldn't be bouncing out to tell her, the moment his meeting had finished.

But he didn't. In fact, when, mid-afternoon, the meeting finally finished, Leroy stayed in the meeting room alone for quite some time after Dave had seen the two men out, and when he did finally emerge, it was like someone had deflated him. He managed his usual smile and entirely inappropriate suggestion involving three burly men and a goat at the team manning their software support desk, but by the time he reached his desk at the pod next to Gemma's the smile had left his face and he looked utterly dejected. Gemma couldn't remember ever seeing him like this.

She had hoped to get to speak to him, but her afternoon was filled with meetings, and by the time five p.m. rolled around they'd not even exchanged two words. On an impulse, she went out into the lobby and phoned her mum, who was more than happy to pick Sam and Ava up from after-school club that day. It didn't occur to Gemma for a moment that she'd faithfully promised Sam she'd be there that evening to hear all about how his trip had gone.

The office slowly started to empty. With the eclectic working patterns they all adopted at Zero, you could never be entirely sure when people would be in, but the vast majority stuck to something close to a standard working day. Before long the open-plan office was deserted, with just a couple of the developers (who would likely be there until three in the morning, based on the usual hours they kept) plugged into their headphones in a corner of the room, Gemma and Leroy.

Gemma took her wheelie chair and spun it over to where Leroy was sitting, headphones on, deep in concentration. He was so deep in thought he didn't even notice she was sitting centimetres away from him, until she reached out and took the photo he kept of him and his boyfriend on his desk to take a closer look at it. They were sitting on a beach somewhere hot and expensive and were clearly sickeningly in love.

Finally noticing her for the first time, Leroy took off his headphones and gave her a weak smile.

'I love this photo. How is Jeremy? I haven't seen him for ages.'

Leroy shrugged. 'He's fine. No, he's good. We're just going through a bit of a tough time at the moment. He says he never gets to see me. He's probably right, but I don't know what he expects me to do about it. His line of work is so flaky, it's me who pays the mortgage. If I don't make Zero work, we could be in big trouble.'

He took the photo from Gemma and stared at it sadly. 'That was only last year. We were so happy and carefree. Now look at the state of us.'

It was the in Gemma needed. She swung him round to face her. 'Leroy, what's going on? Who were those guys you and Dave had in with you earlier? Why didn't you tell me they were coming in?'

He looked her straight in the eyes. 'I didn't know they were coming in. Dave grabbed me last night and explained he had a couple of the finance people from the bank coming in. He told me I should probably clear my diary to meet with them. I assumed it was just to do with the filing of our end of year accounts, but when I got into the room they explained they didn't believe we were capable of operating as a going concern.' Gemma raised her eyebrows. 'It's basically what Dave said. We're running out of cash. We're spending more than we're bringing in, and there doesn't seem to be any way to turn it around, not without bringing in a new revenue stream, which we can't do, because it's a total chicken and egg situation. We need new revenue if we're not going to fail, but to set up that new revenue stream is going to take capital, which we don't have. So they made it very clear to me what our options were.'

Gemma felt her heart starting to pump faster. 'And what are our options?'

Leroy looked down at the photo of him and Jeremy. 'We have two months to see if a minor miracle occurs. After that, we either have to cut headcount. Dramatically. We'd probably have to make about half of the people who work here redundant.

'Or the business folds.'

There was a silence. Gemma looked at her boss and saw, for the first time since she'd known him, that he was fighting back tears. She couldn't blame him. Zero had been his baby. It had been the only work he had ever known. For so long, everything had gone so right. How was it possible that now, all of their hard work might have turned out to be in vain?

Gemma looked around. The developers were lost in their own little world; even if they hadn't been, they'd have run a mile from any sign of human emotion. There was no chance of them being overheard.

'But it can't have got that bad, that quickly, surely? What about the cash we were due to get in from Vanity?' Vanity – one of their largest corporate accounts – paid annually, and their annual March cash injection had historically secured Zero's future for the rest of the year.

Leroy shook his head. 'I thought you knew. Dave told me he'd spoken to you. We're in dispute with Vanity. They're claiming the latest release of the software compromised functionality. At the moment they're refusing to pay, until we rectify the errors.'

'And are there errors? Can we rectify them?' Gemma was frantic. Why were they wasting away their weekly management meetings reviewing the sodding Christmas party photos and Natalie's latest shag, for fuck's sake, when all of their futures were at stake?

Leroy ran his hands down his face. 'Some, yes. They seem to have gone unnoticed by most of the other accounts, but you know what Vanity are like. As for whether we can fix them . . . that's what I'm working on now. It should be simple, but for whatever reason, I can't get it to hold together.'

For the second time that evening, tears threatened to overflow down his cheeks. Gemma was tempted to pull him over for a hug, but that would a) frighten the developers out of their wits, Actual Human Contact being a definite no go in their world, and b) no doubt lead to yet another rumour that she and Leroy were an item. These had popped up at regular intervals over the years, the concept that a woman could rise to a senior position within an organisation without having to bang her boss – even one who openly batted for the other team – seemingly alien to certain staff members.

'C'mon, Leroy.' She spoke softly to him, like she would one of her children – when she wasn't busy screaming 'TEETH! HAIR! SHOES!' at them, that was. 'We've been in worse scrapes than this. We can get out of this. You know we can.'

Leroy shook his head. 'I know we have, Gem, but this time ... I'm honestly not sure. I've got so many ideas that could save us. We could diversify, branch out from just looking at clothing. What about all the times you've got home with a piece of flat pack furniture which ends up looking absolutely nothing like the assembled version you saw in the shop? Or you buy a lipstick which promises to make your teeth look whiter and instead makes you look like you're auditioning for the musical remake of *The Addams Family*? I lie awake every night, thinking of where the product could go next. But to do any of that we've got to have funding. And we haven't got any. It's as simple as that.'

He crossed his arms defensively and looked at Gemma, who looked back at him. There was nothing more that either of them could say. Leroy was right. It was as simple as that.

There was an outside chance that Vanity might still pay, Leroy told her. If they paid even a fraction of the outstanding invoice, they would be able to make it through past the summer, when another large corporate client was due to be billed. There was a chance they might even stagger through the rest of the year. Beyond that, though, the future looked very bleak indeed.

Saying goodnight to Leroy, Gemma gathered her stuff and walked out to her car. The evenings were lighter now, and she could hear some birds singing in the trees overhead as the sky turned from blue to gold. On any other day she would have been struck by its beauty, but today all she could think about was what was going to happen to Zero. And what was going to happen to her.

Gemma had always known, when she'd committed to a

career working for Leroy, that the highs would be incredibly high, and the lows incredibly low. It was a reflection of Leroy's personality, and the way he did business in general. Other competitors of theirs had taken a far more risk-averse approach. Their businesses had grown steadily, but had seen nothing like the meteoric success that Zero had to date. That high-risk strategy, though, came with a price.

She drove home in silence, her thoughts entirely on work. For the first time, she wondered whether this was the end of the line for her at Zero. Never mind whether or not she was made redundant. Even if she wasn't – and she knew that Leroy would fight tooth and nail to keep her – could she honestly live with this constant insecurity? It wasn't just herself she had to think of, it was the children, too.

Fuck, the children. As she pulled up outside her house, it suddenly hit her like a ton of bricks. Today was supposed to have been all about her speaking to Leroy about reducing her hours. Not only that, but she'd promised – *promised* – Sam that she would be back to collect him from his trip. Oh fuck, fuck, bollocking arse.

She let herself in, to find Ava performing an interpretative dance version of the facts of life, which George in her class had apparently kindly been teaching her, to the background beat of 'My Milkshake Brings All The Boys To The Yard'. Gemma's parents, looking bemused, were sat there clapping along in response to Ava's gyrations ('This is the bit when the sperm comes out of the PENIS'). Sam was nowhere to be seen.

Apologising profusely, Gemma dropped a quick kiss on each of her parents' cheeks as they rushed out of the door

149

to get off to the bowling club, where they were president and secretary respectively. Not for the first time, it struck her that their social life was better than hers. God, Becky would be nagging her about getting another date soon. One on which she would be steering clear of anything with a percentage proof. And maybe taking a bucket with her, just to be on the safe side.

First though: Sam. Leaving Ava writhing on the floor ('It's getting to the egg, Mummy'), she took the stairs two at a time and pushed open the door to his darkened bedroom.

Sam was, as she had predicted, sitting in the darkness staring raptly at a man called DanTDM, who had made his millions from sitting in front of a computer screen exactly as Sam was doing now, playing a game Gemma found completely baffling called Minecraft (it was like Lego, only shitter), and causing small children the world over to hero-worship him as he did so. Gemma knew that if only she made a living from posting videos of her playing computer games onto YouTube, she would be able to do no wrong in Sam's eyes.

Tentatively, she stroked the back of her son's hair, relishing the unusual physical contact with him and fighting the urge to plunge her nose towards him and sniff the back of his neck, smelling his lovely, Sammish smell, which would probably have him locking the door on her and phoning the police. 'You just wait,' she'd tell him when he looked at her shaking his head as she grabbed Ava, who would still just about tolerate it, and take in great lungfuls of the smell of her daughter's head. 'When you have kids of your own, you'll understand the head-smelling thing.'

Sam sprang round like he'd been shot, pulling his

headphones off his ears as he did so. His face relaxed as he saw it was only Gemma. 'Oh. Hello, Mum.'

'Hello, sweetheart.' She sat down on the end of his bed. 'How was your day?'

He shrugged. 'It was okay.'

'What about the trip?'

He looked blankly at her. 'What trip?'

'You know, the trip you were going on today, the one you went on and on at me about last night over? That trip?'

'Oh. Yeah.' He had the good grace to smile. 'Yeah. It was all right. It was quite good, actually. We waited until Mrs Willoughby got on the coach and then all of the boys let out the farts we had been saving up all at once and Mrs Willoughby had to make the coach driver stop because she said she might be sick, and then Jacob shouted out "Mrs Willoughby's got a vagina as big as a *fridge*!", and then he got into masses of trouble and he has to go and see Mrs Goldman tomorrow and it's going to be *brilliant*.' He sniggered to himself, no doubt at the thought of vaginas as big as a fridge. Gemma thought of poor Mrs Willoughby. She couldn't imagine how much gin she would need to get through an experience like that.

Gemma decided to level with her son. 'Listen, Sam, sweetheart, I'm really sorry I got cross with you last night. I was just worried, because I wanted you to be able to go on your trip, and if you'd told me when you'd first got the letter, we would have been able to have got everything sorted out in time and we wouldn't have had to have a big panic at the last minute.'

Sam looked at her. 'No we wouldn't. We always have a big panic at the last minute. We've always forgotten something, or you're late because you have to do stupid work, or Ava is being mad and shouting at the postman that she loves him and that she thinks he might be her daddy and has he ever had a paternity test like they have on Jeremy Kyle, and so we end up not being ready in time. That's how it always is.'

Gemma was about to rebut this accusation, when she realised she couldn't, because it was true. Sam was right. No matter how well thought out her plans were, something always went wrong and they always had a big panic at the last minute. It was like she'd missed the class at parenting school when they told you how to avoid Big Panics. Another epic parenting fail on her part.

What could she say? 'I'm sorry sweetheart. I will try and get better.'

'Maybe it will be better now you're going to work less. Did your work say it would be okay?'

Fuck. Fuck, fuck, fuck. She considered lying to him, but decided she wasn't going to go there. Honesty and transparency were traits she valued in the relationship between her and her children more than any other.

'I didn't get a chance to ask today, love. Leroy was in meetings. But I'll ask him tomorrow, I promise I will.'

She would have missed it if she hadn't been watching him closely, but she saw a light go out in Sam's eyes. Once again, she'd let him down.

'Whatever. It doesn't matter. I knew you wouldn't.' His headphones were already back on; she was dismissed.

When she finally got the children into bed, after Ava had played approximately thirty rounds of 'I Can't Go To Sleep Because . . . ' her winning attempt being ' . . . because my legs are looking at me, and I do not like it', Gemma's phone beeped with a message from Siobhan. It was their traditional evening interchange.

GEM! How was your day? How was Leroy? Am I sacked yet?

For the first time since she'd started working with Siobhan, Gemma couldn't find it in her to answer.

Eleven

Half-term had come and gone almost before Tom had realised it. One of the great draws when he'd first considered moving into teaching was the sheer amount of holiday you seemed to get. When he'd been with his ex, they'd had a mutual friend who was a teacher, and Tom never tired of ribbing her about how stressful her job must have been, what with all those weeks of the year when you just got to lie around doing nothing. Now, in a teaching position himself, Tom frequently wished he could go back in time and slap his former self repeatedly around the face for being such an utter fucking dick.

His so-called 'week off' had consisted of frantically planning lessons, SATS preparation and trying to come up with a series of polite yet insightful statements about every single child in his class, ahead of Parents' Evening. Far from lying around doing nothing, the only time it seemed he had a moment to lie still was in bed at night, when he lay there prone, frantically staring at the ceiling and wondering how the hell he would manage to get everything done before he went back at the start of term.

He was dreading Parents' Evening. If you'd told him, five years ago, that the most terrifying part of the school year would be having to sit around and make small talk with the parents of the children he was teaching, he would have laughed at you. Polite small talk had been Tom's forte; he could always be called upon to calm the most fretful of clients, or smooth over the most difficult of inter-office political situations.

What had happened had changed all of that, and these days Tom found himself far more comfortable in the company of under-tens than he was with their parents. Vivienne, in particular. His heart sank at the very thought of what she'd be like with unfettered access to him. Maybe she'd have the decency to bring along some poor, hen-pecked husband who might ensure Tom was safe from her seduction techniques for the evening.

Unfortunately for Tom, Vivienne had sent her husband packing a number of years ago, on exactly the same day that his business failed and the promised millions that had so enticed her were lost for ever. She'd had a suitcase of his belongings packed by the time he got back through the front door, having met with his bank manager, and had suggested it was probably time for them to go their separate ways.

'But don't you love me?' he'd asked her. 'I thought we promised to stay together, in sickness and in health?'

That was the point when Vivienne, crocodile tears in her eyes, confessed to him that she'd never actually loved him, and now that he was penniless, to be honest, there was really nothing keeping them together. Oh, but before he left, could he just confirm whether the recent purchases on her Selfridges account would be paid off, or if she'd need to return them?

In hindsight, it was the best thing that had ever happened to him. He now owned a tiny shepherd's hut in the middle of the Highlands and lived on the land around him. Being off grid was a small price to pay for knowing that there was not a chance of Vivienne venturing this far out into the wilderness.

All of this consequently meant that when Vivienne did arrive for Parents' Evening, resplendent in an outfit which looked like she'd stepped straight down from a podium in Stringfellows, there was absolutely no one and nobody holding her back as she made a beeline for the table Tom was sitting behind, turned the chair which was set out for her a full 180 degrees, and sat down provocatively on it with her breasts protruding over the back and her legs spread in a manner which he presumed she thought was erotic, but actually made her look as though she was squatting to go to the toilet. Tom had never felt more relieved to have a table to hide behind.

'So, Mrs . . . Avery, isn't it?' he mumbled, rifling through his papers until he saw Satin's name.

'Oh, Vivienne, please,' she purred throatily, taking a strand of her auburn hair and curling it around her finger. 'Come on, Tom. We know each other well enough by now. Let's not stand on ceremony here.'

Mrs Willoughby looked over curiously from the next table at the woman's overfamiliar tone, and Tom prayed devoutly that Vivienne bloody well would stand on ceremony. He could see Mrs Goldman eyeing him from the side of the hall and knew that she would be wondering quite how he was managing to so successfully charm the woman whom an unnamed member of his class – Tom had given nothing away when he'd returned from the disastrous trip – had hurled directly into a pile of pig dung. The dressing down the head had given Tom when they'd returned and Vivienne, caked in muck and stinking to high heavens, had told her exactly what had happened, had reminded him of being back in his old job for a moment. He had shuddered and fought to block out the memories. That was a long time ago now, and however irritated Mrs Goldman might have been that her primary fundraiser for the school had been publicly humiliated and covered in shit, it was small fry by comparison.

To be honest, one silver lining from the trip would have been if it had put Vivienne off him, but unfortunately, if anything, it had only fanned her ardour. She'd been the talk of the playground, and hadn't held back in telling everyone how Tom had come to her rescue, 'like my knight in shining armour, vaulting the wall and throwing me over his shoulder to get me out of there'. The fact that it had been the farmhand, not Tom, who had led the rescue, and that he'd not so much as thrown Vivienne over his shoulder as dragged her by her feet, while she screeched like a banshee and flung her arms around as though being attacked by a swarm of bees, didn't seem to bother her in the slightest. Why let facts get in the way of a perfectly good dramatic reconstruction?

Even more unfortunately, it was something that Vivienne now had over him, and she knew it. Not only would she be using it in an attempt to spin up a non-existent relationship between them ('such a bonding experience, these near-death moments'), she also had every intention of making sure that such an indiscretion guaranteed Satin every position of responsibility and part in the school play that she'd ever wanted.

'So, Satin.' He struggled to bring the conversation back on track. 'Let's have a look and see how she's doing. She's ... I would say that so far she's exactly where she needs to be at this point in the academic year. Her literacy is slightly better than her maths, but generally speaking I would say that she's slap bang in the middle of the class, right where she should be.'

Vivienne dropped her seduction technique in a nanosecond, and looked absolutely appalled. 'What do you mean she's in the middle of the class? How has she managed to end up there? Satin's not a child who is average at anything. She's always been gifted and talented; I'm not sure if you're aware, but at last year's prize-giving she won every prize for excellence it's possible to win. Are you telling me that she's no longer at the top of the class?'

Tom bit his lip nervously. 'Um. That's right. Myself and Miss Harris have assessed all of the children since the start of the year, and Satin has consistently scored round about in the middle, academically.'

Vivienne stared at him, furiously. 'All I can say, Mr Jones, is that your inferior teaching methods must be to blame. How long is it that you've been qualified? I can assure you, that when Miss Thompson – a very experienced teacher – was in charge, Satin never slipped down below second place.'

He bet she hadn't. Miss Harris, in an unguarded moment one evening when they'd found themselves stuck behind to create a wall display, had confessed to him that Miss Thompson had automatically added an additional 25 per cent on to anything Satin did. 'Anything for an easy life, darling,' she'd told the classroom assistant. 'I can't be doing with that frightful woman coming in here, thrusting her mammaries around like she's Pamela bloody Anderson and telling me that I don't know anything about teaching. Much easier to just bump her daughter's scores up and keep her out of my hair.'

While Tom had been appalled at this blatant fiddling of the records, he had to say that part of him wished he'd been sensible enough to take the same stance. For a moment, he thought Vivienne was going to grab him by the collar and pull him across the desk in order to better stare him down until he agreed to put Satin back in her rightful place at the top of the class.

Then, suddenly, something clicked behind her eyes, and her face softened. 'But of course. How thoughtless of me. You're still getting up to speed with things here. Maybe what Satin needs is some additional tuition. How would you feel, I wonder, about giving her some private tuition . . . at my home? Perhaps if we scheduled it for a Saturday afternoon, then after you'd finished I could pack the children off to their rooms and you and I could enjoy a meal and a glass of wine together. What do you reckon –' here she lowered her voice even more seductively and leaned right across the desk to him '– *darling*?'

Tom physically recoiled, sending his chair skittering back across the parquet floor. Mrs Goldman looked over at him and audibly tutted. Oh god, that was all he needed, another dressing down from the head. He looked at his watch. Vivienne's allotted ten minutes were more than up, and in the background he could see an increasing queue of impatient parents waiting for him. He hoped one of them would come and rescue him.

With Vivienne showing absolutely no signs of leaving, but rather settling in for the long haul, no one could have been more grateful than Tom when his longed-for rescue did actually happen. It came in the form of Becky, who, with Lovely Jon working late – *again* – had been forced to bring both children with her. Rosie sat quietly on a chair on the other side of the hall, seemingly uninterested in joining her classmates who were running around maniacally on the stage, Satin in the thick of them. Becky bounced Ella on her hip as she strode over to Tom's table and placed her hand firmly down on it.

'Mr Jones. Vivienne. Hi. I am *so* sorry to interrupt, but you've now run twenty minutes over your appointment time, Vivienne, and there's a whole queue of us waiting. I've got the baby to get home to bed, and I'm sure Mr Jones has got places he'd much rather be too, so if you don't mind, Vivienne, are you okay if I take your place?' She placed her hand on Vivienne's chair, almost as though she was considering tipping her out of it.

Vivienne was unmoving. 'I don't know who you are, or why you have so rudely interrupted me like this, but this is my Parents' Evening appointment, and I would therefore ask you to mind your own business and wait until I have finished.' She gave Becky a glare which would have sent most parents scuttling to the safety of the other side of the room, but Becky was made of much sterner stuff than that.

'I've just seen Satin playing with Leticia from Year 4. Her mother's been telling me she's got the most awful boils. Incredibly contagious, so I've heard.'

The thought of Leticia's – entirely fictitious – boils did what the combined might of Tom and Becky had been unable to do. With a horrified gasp, Vivienne was up in a flash and screeching across the hall 'SATIN! SATIN DARLING! COME TO MUMMY! COME AWAY FROM THE NASTY, DIRTY CHILDREN!'

'God, she's vile.' Becky turned the chair around, dropping into the seat vacated by Vivienne and handed Ella a rice cake to distract her. 'Sorry, I hope I didn't interrupt anything?'

Tom sighed with relief. 'Only her attempts to hire me as a sex slave, from the sounds of what she was proposing.' He looked over nervously at Mrs Goldman, but she was no longer watching his table and had her entire attention fixed on Satin, who was screaming her little lungs out as her mother attempted to march her out of the hall. 'Thank you so much for saving me. I've never met anyone quite like Vivienne in all my life.'

Becky was dismissive. 'Ah, mothers like that are two a penny if you have the misfortune to be privately educated.' She paused. 'I'm so sorry, for all I know you were.'

He smiled at her. 'Don't worry, you're fine. No, I wasn't privately educated. It was the local comp all the way for me. It served me pretty well ... other than when it came to knowing how to deal with women like Vivienne, that is.'

'The only way to deal with women like Vivienne is to

keep on telling them to fuck off until they get the bloody hint,' Becky quipped. 'God, my language is appalling. There's something about being back at school that brings out the worst in me and makes me want to run around defying authority and selling drugs to all the students.' Tom looked horrified. 'Oh, don't worry, it wasn't really cocaine, it was Elizabeth Arden talcum powder.' Now he just looked bemused. 'Ignore me. It's a long story.'

Having established that Becky wasn't actually the resident drug dealer, they moved onto the subject of Rosie. Things hadn't improved; if anything, she'd withdrawn even further into herself. Becky had tried every trick she knew to get her to open up, but all she got was a shake of the head and an 'I'm fine, Mummy.' It broke her heart.

'I just don't know what to do. She's clearly unhappy, but I don't know what's causing it, and if I don't know the cause, then I can't solve it for her. Have you seen anything going on at school? Who does she play with?'

Tom racked his brains for anything he'd seen which might be contributing to Rosie's unhappiness, but drew a blank. 'To be honest, she's working well. Consistently at the top of the class; she's clearly very bright. Socially, I would say that she's still settling in, but she's rarely on her own at break times. Satin seems to be taking her under her wing a lot of the time, to be honest. Not that that's a relationship I would necessarily encourage.'

'God, no.' Becky looked appalled. 'Can you imagine it? Playdates around Vivienne's? I'd rather spend three hours in soft play, and I've always considered soft play on a par with the inner circle of hell.'

In the absence of any clues to the cause of Rosie's

unhappiness, Tom agreed that he would spend some one to one time with her and see if she might be willing to open up to him. Thanking him, Becky removed Ella before the baby followed through on her threat to eat Tom's carefully drawn-up Parents' Evening notes and collected Rosie so that they could head home. Morosely, the little girl clutched onto her mum's hand and they wandered out into the chill breeze of the evening.

Looking down at Rosie, Becky felt a stab of sadness. All of the parenting books and articles she'd ever read had concentrated on how tough the early years of having a child were, and they were quite right: in fact, 'tough' was an understatement. But, in many ways, having to purée up fifteen different types of organic vegetables or the moment when your potty training child placed an actual Real Life Shit which they'd just produced into your hand in the middle of a packed restaurant (true story) was child's play compared to this. What kind of a mother was she, if she couldn't even work out what was breaking her baby's heart?

She squeezed Rosie's hand. 'Dad will be back late tonight. Why don't I put Ella to bed and you and me can stay up and get Domino's and watch a movie, just the two of us? What do you reckon?'

'Okay,' said Rosie, but still she didn't crack a smile.

Gemma was running late. Again. To be honest, 'late' was now so much her new normal that it would have been more noteworthy to say that she was running on time. Leroy had collared her when she'd been about to leave for Parents' Evening, and had ended up breaking down in floods of tears and asking her what she thought he should do about the business. A renowned problem solver, Gemma was rarely lost for ideas, but she felt totally out of her depth on this one. From what she could see, their best option was to cross their fingers and pray. Either that, or polish up their CVs and get themselves down to the Job Centre. She tactfully elected not to mention that particular scenario to Leroy.

As she turned to leave, it hit her: her working hours. She had faithfully promised Sam that she would speak to Leroy about cutting down her hours. There was no way she could let her son down again. But looking at Leroy's desolate face, it was clear that Gemma asking to reduce her hours now would be the worst possible timing. How could she possibly add to her boss's woes and give him yet another thing to worry about? Her loyalties to home and work impossibly divided, she decided to deal with the problem by doing absolutely nothing about it and hoping it would somehow go away.

By the time she got into the car it was already ten minutes after her allotted appointment time. She would just have to hope that Sam and Ava's teachers were running late. Using her hands-free kit, she called home, where her parents were babysitting. Everything was fine, her mum reassured her, although Ava had told her she was going to be getting a tattoo of Lionel Messi on her face, and was that actually true, because so far as her mum was aware, it wasn't yet legal to tattoo seven-year-olds, and a tattoo of a world-famous footballer on Ava's face was almost certainly going to violate the strict school uniform policy.

Setting the score straight, Gemma promised she'd be home as soon as she finished at the school. Based on that little snippet of conversation, goodness knows what her children's teachers would have to tell her that evening.

Mr Cook was already starting to lock up as Gemma turned in through the school gates. He raised his eyebrows at her as she jumped out of the car and started to run towards the hall. 'Cutting it a bit fine, aren't you? Those gates'll be locked at seven p.m. sharp, so don't be back late if you want to get your car back tonight.' Promising him she wouldn't, she raced inside.

Sam's teacher, the formidable Mrs Willoughby, was already packing up as Gemma went over to her, apologising profusely for her tardiness. Mrs Willoughby, who had never yet seen Sam's mum turn up on time for any school event – or, indeed, turn up at all, most of the time – accepted her apologies and ran through a brief precis of Sam's progress at school. He was essentially a bright lad, who would be doing far better academically than he was if he didn't treat school 'like a youth club. I get the impression that me teaching him is almost an inconvenience as it interrupts the fun he's having with his friends.' Yep: that was her son.

His work usually looked as though it had been run over by a truck, if she had to ask him once to tuck in his shirt, she'd had to ask him a thousand times, and could Gemma *please* do something about his hair … but in between the complaints, Gemma got the impression that Mrs Willoughby had something of a soft spot for her son, and was actually quite pleased with how he was coming along. Thanking the teacher for staying late, and making a mental note that she really must track down a local barber to keep Sam's hair in check, she left the Year 5 area and walked over to where Mr Jones was just finishing speaking with Kristin, one of Vivienne's coven.

He looked exhausted, a slightly broken man whose facial

expression said that all he wanted to do right now was to get the hell out of there and do nothing more taxing than drink a nice cold beer. Gemma felt terrible that she was about to completely ruin his evening – even more than interrogation by twenty-nine different sets of parents had already ruined it for him, that was.

Nervously, she raised a hand in his direction. 'Hi. I'm—'

'Ava's mum. I know,' Tom said tiredly. 'Sorry . . . do you have an appointment?'

'I did. Thirty minutes ago. I'm so sorry. Work was absolutely manic, and I've only just managed to get here. Listen, though, if you'd rather I arranged to come back and see you another time, I would totally understand. All I really want to know is whether Ava's behaving herself, or rather, whether she's managing to curb her lunatic tendencies long enough to not completely disrupt your classroom.'

Tom cracked a smile; a weak one, but a smile nonetheless. 'She's certainly unique, that's for sure! You're fine. Here, have a seat.' He proffered her the plastic chair, but before she could sit down, an ominous rattle of keys and a clearing of the throat came from across the other side of the room.

'Time's up, I'm afraid,' announced Mr Cook. 'I've got to get to bingo, so you can all clear off. Go on. Scram. Lights are going off in thirty seconds.'

'That man has really missed his calling,' said Tom. 'He should have been a bouncer.'

'He really should,' agreed Gemma. 'So, that's that, I guess. I'll phone the office and make an appointment to come and speak with you. Unless . . .' A thought had occurred to her. A most un-Gemma-like thought. It was as though Becky had suddenly infiltrated her mind.

'Unless?' Tom looked at her expectantly as they walked out of the hall together.

'I was just wondering . . . did you fancy going and getting something to eat? I haven't had a lunch break and I'm absolutely starving, and you must be the same. There's a great pub around the corner which does food, and then you could tell me how Ava's doing, and we could kill two birds with one stone. What do you reckon?' I am definitely having an out of body experience, thought Gemma to herself, as she waited for his answer.

Tom weighed up his options. On the one hand, he was absolutely exhausted and just wanted to go home and collapse into bed. On the other hand . . . he was pretty hungry. And while he knew he'd made a pact never to socialise with any of the parents from the school, Gemma was so rarely at the school gate that she might as well not have been a parent at all. In fact, now he came to think about it, he was genuinely quite intrigued to find out more about her.

'Sure.' The word was out before his brain even knew he'd agreed to it. 'I'd love to.'

Twelve

The pub was crowded by the time they got there, but they managed to find themselves a table at the back of the room, away from the raucous quiz night, which was clearly the entertainment for the evening. Tom went to the bar to get drinks and returned with a bottle of white and two glasses.

'Cheers.' He took a gulp of the wine he'd just poured them and drank it down like a man who'd been starved of water for days. 'I honestly cannot tell you how much I needed that.'

'You're not the only one.' Gemma mirrored him. 'What a day. What a bloody day.'

'You too?' He looked concerned. 'Forgive me ... I don't actually know what it is you do.'

Gemma told him, omitting the fact that the only job she'd ever known might be about to disappear from under her, leaving her unemployed and at the mercy of the Job Centre. It struck her, not for the first time, how fragile the line between financial stability and losing everything really was.

'Blimey. That sounds pretty full on.'

She was about to deny it, to say that it wasn't full on at all, that it was just a job. But it wasn't, was it? Zero had become so much more than just a job to her; it was her livelihood, her vocation, her family. Which didn't make it easy, when both her family at work and her family at home needed her, all at the same time. How could she possibly prioritise? How could she ever win?

'You're right. It is. I mean, most of the time, I don't really think about it. You just do what you have to do, don't you? And I absolutely love my job; I can't imagine not working. But I absolutely love my kids as well . . . and now, more and more, those two things seem to be in conflict with each other.' She took another sip of her wine, before telling him about the altercation she'd had with Sam the other evening. 'And it's only going to get worse, I know it is. In another year and a bit he'll be off to secondary school. I thought things would get easier as he got older, but I know parents who've had to completely give up work to ensure they can be there after school to help their kids with their homework to get them through their GCSEs. I can't even identify a fronted adverbial, for fuck's sake. What hope have I possibly got of getting him through GCSE maths?'

To her horror, she felt tears pricking her eyes, and gulped down the remains of her wine to hide them. Tactfully, Tom had left her to go over to the bar, where he ordered burgers and fat chips for both of them.

'I'm so sorry,' said Gemma as he came back, looking at her with concern. She dried her eyes as she apologised. 'I don't know what's wrong with me. God, you probably wish you'd gone home for that Tesco microwave meal for one after all. Or two … I mean, you must have a girlfriend, right? Or a boyfriend?'

Tom smiled, both at her incredibly awkward efforts to be politically correct and also at her blatant attempts to find out more about his personal life. Unlike Vivienne, though, he felt that opening up a little would be okay. Despite her perpetual air of being slightly manic, there was something about Gemma that inspired confidence – and a strange sense that he'd known her for a lot longer than he actually had.

'Nope.' He shook his head. 'Wrong on both counts. No girlfriend, and certainly no boyfriend. Not even a cat to cement my bachelor status. Just me and my Tesco microwave meal for one … which is why having company for dinner makes such a pleasant change.'

Blimey. A man this good-looking, who thus far hadn't revealed any major personality flaws, and was actually legitimately single, as opposed to claiming he was single and then revealing that what he actually meant was that he was married but liked to pretend in his head that he was single – why the hell couldn't she find someone like Tom on Tinder? She sighed.

'Everything okay?' He cleared a space on the table as their burgers and chips arrived.

'Yes. Sorry. I was just thinking about dating.' She realised to her horror what she'd just said and felt her face flame crimson with utter mortification. 'Not dating you, I mean. Dating in general. I think I might be the world's worst at dating. I mean, first I married a man who turned out to be a total penis. Even though he was a total penis he decided he was too good for me, and so he left me. And then I had a date. A bad date. A very *very* bad date. I basically got pissed out of my head and threw up all over him. And not even in a manner which could be construed as kinky. I think it must have been a sign, and basically I am destined never to ever have sex ever again. It's been more than two years. Oh god. I can't believe I've just told you that. In fact, I can't believe I've just told you any of that. I am a disaster. One great big fucking disaster. And now I am going to shove this burger into my mouth to physically prevent any more incriminatory confessions from coming out.'

And she did, immediately regretting it as the size of the bite she'd taken threatened to choke her. Marvellous: the last man she'd gone out for dinner with had had her vomit all over him, now the next one was going to end up needing to give her CPR. She really was quite the catch.

Concentrating hard on chewing her burger without restricting her airway, Gemma completely missed the way Tom was looking at her. Far from being appalled, he looked positively smitten. It was probably just as well she'd been focusing on her burger: she would definitely have needed CPR if she'd seen that.

'Gemma, you're so down on yourself. You're a single parent, holding down a full-time job that most people would struggle with if they had no kids and someone else to share the household chores with, let alone with everything else you have on your plate. And your kids are amazing: they really are. They're a credit to you. Sam's an absolute gent – I wish I'd had the chance to teach him – and Ava is … okay, slightly bonkers, but she's one of the brightest children I've ever taught, and sticks two fingers up to conforming in a way that I'm still not sure I have the confidence to do now. They're stars, both of them ... and that's all down to you. Stop beating yourself up. You're absolutely smashing it.'

Was she absolutely smashing it? It didn't feel like it, most of the time. Quite often it felt like she could go through an entire day letting down everyone she came into contact with. But somehow, sitting here, listening to Tom, a man she'd only properly met for the first time a couple of hours ago, Gemma could feel like she almost believed him.

It was a novel sensation.

Back home after Parents' Evening, Becky and Rosie had indeed had their promised Domino's. They'd sat together and watched *The Parent Trap*, which Becky had hoped might give her an opportunity to quiz Rosie on whether it was the tensions at home between herself and Lovely Jon that were causing her concerns. Full of pizza though, and tired out, Rosie had fallen asleep before the film was even twenty minutes in, so that was the end of that. Leaving her sleeping on the sofa, Becky had pulled a throw over her, warned Boris the absolute fucking liability that he was on no account to wake her up, and had gone to check on Ella, who was sleeping peacefully on her tummy ignoring all safe sleeping guidelines, bottom stuck firmly up in the air.

A noise from downstairs startled Becky. Boris, presumably. Probably trying to mate with the television again. He'd taken a liking to it after they'd made the mistake of allowing him to watch *Crufts*. She took the stairs two at a time in her hurry to ensure he didn't wake Rosie.

To her surprise, when she reached the hallway, there was not just a bounding, panting Boris, but Jon too. Home by – she checked her watch – eight-thirty p.m. This was an occurrence of such rarity that she practically felt like taking out an advert in the local paper to announce it. What the hell was he doing home so early? He must have been sacked.

'Fuck, you've been sacked, haven't you?' she blurted out, fear making the pizza churn uncomfortably in her stomach.

He unfolded himself from where he'd been kneeling, patting a delighted Boris, who had covered his black suit with pale gold hairs and dog drool. 'And hello to you, too, darling. How was your day?' Despite the Cold War which had been unfolding between them, the gleam in his eyes told her he wasn't really irritated. Lovely Jon could never stay annoyed with anyone for very long. Even her.

'No, I haven't been sacked.' He crossed the hall and for a moment looked as though he was going to pull her into his arms, but thought better of it. With things between them recently being as they had, any kind of physical contact had been off the menu. He wasn't entirely sure how Becky would respond if he attempted to hug her right now. The risk that an affectionate embrace could turn into a slap round the face or a knee in the balls was enough to keep him at arm's length. 'I'm conscious of everything you've been telling me about how I'm not at home enough for the girls at the moment – or for you – and so I'm trying to change that.'

'And arriving home at eight-thirty at night is you being at home more, is it?' quipped Becky. 'I'm joking. It's lovely to see you.' To her surprise, after weeks of fantasising about Jon's imminent demise, and the incredible outfit she'd don for his funeral, she realised she actually meant it. 'Now, can I tempt you with some cold pizza served from the box for dinner?'

With Rosie still snoring on the sofa, they sat companionably in the kitchen, Jon working his way through the remains of his daughter's Hawaiian – which had been going down so well, right until the moment Rosie remembered that she didn't like pineapple and that eating ham was basically like eating Peppa Pig. (Becky would gladly have dined out on that squeaky fucking porcine brat. There were many children's television programmes she loathed and abhorred, but *Peppa Pig* was definitely right up at the top of the list.)

They discussed Parents' Evening and Becky, for the first time, raised her concerns about Rosie. Jon didn't disagree, which all of a sudden made them so much more real and actually quite frightening. *Something* was going on with her daughter, and she was going to have to find out what.

Jon told her all about how his cycling training was going (apparently there was a big race coming up which he was planning on entering), which she managed to feign polite interest in by reminding herself she had promised to love him in sickness and in health. And this was definitely his sickness.

In turn, she updated him on how her job hunting was going. She'd contacted various press outlets with the story of her horrendous experience at the solicitors', but had heard nothing back. Even Jon's contact at the *Guardian*, though polite, had clearly been uninterested. Jon ventured to suggest that perhaps it was because such behaviours had become so normalised that they no longer even counted as news. It was the same conclusion Becky herself had come to. God, how utterly depressing.

She'd had various interviews since, all of which had come to nothing. It was like the moment you mentioned you had had the audacity to breed – you know, to prevent the human race from dying out – the interviewers' eyes would glaze over and they lost interest. Mention that you were ideally looking for two or three days a week, school hours only, and you might as well have been asking for the moon on a stick. Never mind that she was bright, had had an amazing career prior to having children and had plenty to offer a business. Unless she was able to do it sitting at a desk for a minimum of thirty-five hours a week, it seemed no one was interested.

Once again, Jon suggested that she didn't need to put herself through this. He earned plenty enough to support the both of them. Why didn't she stop stressing herself out with trying to find work that she didn't need to do, and concentrate on being at home for their girls?

It was quite possibly the worst thing he could have said. Becky exploded, so much so that Boris the fucking liability ran from his vantage point under the table where he was waiting for pizza scraps, chewing on his favourite dildo, and hid under the throw with Rosie, who miraculously remained asleep.

'Oh, it's easy for you to say that, isn't it? You, who've been able to live out every single one of your dreams since you left university. Obtain graduate placement in your dream industry. Check. Be consistently promoted to bigger and better roles within the organisation that thinks you're the best thing since sliced bread. Check. Marry hot girl and get her to squeeze the heads of your offspring out of her once-intact vagina and housekeep for you while you spend

175

all day every day either in the office or fucking around looking like an utter TWAT in Lycra on a bike. Check. But what happened to what I want? When did that stop being important?'

Becky was crying by now, and Jon looked at her, impotent to know how to make things better. Both of them found a moment to wonder quite when the fairy tale had descended into this.

He attempted to make amends. 'Listen, Becks. I'm sorry, really, I am. Of course I'm supportive of you getting a job, if that's what you want to do. It just seemed like it was causing you more stress, that's all. Come on.' He reached out an arm and pulled her into him, and she didn't pull away. 'What can I do to help?'

'Educate business leaders the world over that having given birth doesn't mean that you no longer understand how to turn a computer on or find your way to the office?' They both laughed, and she snuggled into him, feeling more at peace than she had done for weeks. 'Actually, there is something you can do. I've been asked to go for an interview next Thursday, for an office manager job. It sounds pretty perfect, actually. Gemma's parents have been looking after Ella for me, but they can't do Thursday.'

The words were out of his mouth before she'd even finished speaking. 'Done. I'll book it as annual leave. You're going to go along to this interview, and you're going to absolutely nail it. How could anyone not want to hire my super wife?'

They went to bed, and while their relationship hadn't rekindled to the extent that Becky was actually willing to have sex with him, she went to sleep holding his hand and without fantasising about cutting off his balls and feeding them to Boris. Which was definite progress.

The day of Becky's interview dawned bright and sunny; Easter would be upon them before they knew it. Becky had been up since five a.m., practising her now polished interview routine. This mostly involved running through a few sample interview questions in her head and then attempting to find an interview outfit which simultane-ously conveyed professional competence and made it clear to any male interviewers that no, she would not be letting them grab her arse or stare blatantly at her breasts, regardless of whether or not that was the interview suc-cess criteria.

Downstairs, Jon had been true to his promise and was up spooning baby porridge into a delighted Ella while Rosie snuggled up next to him eating toast and watching CBeebies in her school uniform. For the forty-sixth time, Becky checked with him that he knew the way to the school and remembered what time Rosie had to be there.

'We're all good. I've got this. You go off and smash that interview. Doesn't Mummy look amazing, girls?' Rosie agreed that she did, and Ella enthusiastically hurled por-ridge across the room, narrowly missing Becky's suit, which they all decided was a definite sign of support.

It was eight a.m., and her interview started at eight-thirty. The office was only a ten-minute walk away, but Becky wasn't going to risk being late. Kissing her daughters goodbye, she put on her shoes and grabbed her handbag, at precisely the moment Jon's mobile rang.

Out in the hallway, one hand on the front door handle,

she was about to walk out when she heard Jon's voice becoming increasingly agitated. 'No ... no ... I understand ... yes ... yes ... absolutely ... of course ... no problem at all ... just give me five minutes. Be with you shortly.' Becky felt a horrible sinking feeling in the pit of her stomach as Jon, having put the phone down, crossed the kitchen at the speed of light and burst out into the hallway.

'Becky ... darling. I am so sorry. I am so, so sorry. That was the office. The Moriz deal is back on, at the eleventh hour. One of our competitors screwed them over and now we're back in pole position, but only if we pull something truly incredible out of the bag by close of play today. I've got to go into the office. It's be there or be fired. I'm so sorry. Will you be okay to reschedule your interview?'

Becky stood in the hallway, her handbag between them like a shield, and was startled by the strength of vitriol she felt towards her husband. She knew it. She just fucking knew it. Of course he couldn't actually follow through on any promises he made, because work would trump them all, every single time. There had been no suggestion that he tell his boss that no, he wouldn't be able to come into the office, because his wife had an interview. Not even a consideration for the fact that he would need to sort out alternative childcare. No, as usual, it was all dumped squarely at the feet of Becky, while he swanned off to the office like nothing had ever happened.

She was about to unleash a stream of venom in his direction, when her attention was caught by a terrified-looking Rosie, peering round the door of the kitchen, her face pale against the dark cloud of her hair. Oh god: she'd been right. It wasn't school that was causing Rosie to be so withdrawn;

it was things at home that were upsetting her. Not only was her daughter unhappy, but it was Becky herself who was the cause of it. What a mess. What a fucking mess.

Pasting a smile on her face for her daughter, and telling her to go and find her book bag, Becky straightened up and stared Jon straight in the face.

'Go. Just go.'

He went.

Careful not to show Rosie a single bit of the sheer blind panic she was now feeling, Becky frantically ran through options in her head. Gemma would take Rosie to school with her. Maybe she would be able to have Ella as well. Grabbing the baby, with Rosie in tow, she rushed next door, where the door was answered by a suspicious-looking Ava, wearing nothing but a single wellington boot.

'Hello, Ava. Shouldn't you be ready for school by now?'

Ava shrugged. 'It's still early. Me and Sam don't get ready until Mum has said the F word at least three times and screamed about teeth and hair and shoes so many times that her voice goes all funny and croaky.' She cackled uproariously, presumably at the thought of her mum's funny croaky voice, before grabbing Rosie's hand and streaking – in all senses – through the house.

Gemma came to the door, mobile phone in one hand, laptop in the other, and curls stuck up in a halo around her head. 'Becky! Hi! Forgive the chaos. It's ... well, it's just a standard morning round ours, really. Everything okay?'

Becky swiftly filled her in. 'So, any chance you could take Rosie into school for me. And ... I know it's a massive ask, but I don't suppose you could have Ella for a couple of hours as well?'

Gemma's face fell. 'I'm so sorry. I only wish I could, but Leroy's called an urgent management meeting and I've absolutely got to be there. Rosie's no problem, but I just can't get out of it to have Ella.'

'Don't worry, it's not your fault. It'll be fine, I'll work something out. Thanks so much for taking Rosie.' Kissing her daughter goodbye, who had reappeared with Ava (now sporting both wellington boots and one of Gemma's bras hanging around her waist, but still not an item of school uniform in sight), she hoisted Ella further up onto her hip and considered her options.

She supposed she should just call the place she was meant to be having her interview at and give her apologies, explain that something had come up and she couldn't be there after all.

But she really wanted this job. Really *really* wanted this job. Particularly given – for the first time she allowed her-self to think the thought she had been battling to keep far away from her mind – that maybe sometime soon, Gemma wasn't going to be the only single parent around here. That actually, given the state of her and Jon's marriage, having her own income might suddenly have become more impor-tant than ever.

Resolved, Becky held Ella high in the air above her head until she chuckled and bicycled her chubby legs with glee. 'Right then, Ella-bella. Time for you and me to go get a job.'

Despite her unscheduled delay, by walking briskly she made it to the offices with plenty of time to spare. No hell-ish group selection process this time: she'd made sure of that when they'd called her to offer her an interview. With any luck, this time they'd be more interested in her skill set than her bra size.

There was just the minor issue of the fact she had a baby in tow to get around.

Walking into reception, which was already buzzing and full of people, Becky kept her head held high as she nonchalantly held Ella on one hip like she was nothing more than the latest fashion accessory. 'All of the best candidates are taking babies to interviews these days,' Becky told Ella, who gabbled in response and smeared god knew what down her mother's arm.

The receptionist was looking at her enquiringly from behind her Perspex desk. 'Can I help you?'

'Hi!' Becky was at her most charming: she'd heard interview decisions were quite often made based not on what happened in the interview room itself, but on how you treated the other members of staff you came into contact with before and after you met the panel. 'Rebecca Barrington. I'm here for an interview today.'

If the girl was somewhat startled by the sight of Ella, she had the good grace not to mention it. Smiling warmly at Becky, she walked around the desk and took her straight through to a meeting room at the end of the corridor, empty apart from a large, polished oak table and four tumblers of water.

'Please do take a seat and make yourself comfortable.' She gestured at the single seat on one side of the huge table. 'The panel will be with you shortly.' She left, closing the door softly behind her.

'So far so good,' Becky said to Ella, who slammed her fists into the polished table and attempted to get her teething gums into the side of it. 'No, no. No eating the table. I'm fairly sure the official interview guides would tell you that consuming any of the furniture while being interviewed is definitely not advised.'

The door clicked open behind her, and three people walked into the room; a man and two women. They were chatting and laughing, already making Becky feel that this interview would likely be a million miles away from the first miserable experience that she'd had. Rounding the table, they made to sit down opposite her and then simultaneously paused in surprise.

'Goodness,' said the man wearing jeans and a polo shirt, who appeared to have recovered himself first. 'This is a surprise. We don't get many babies in interviews these days.'

'Though we did have a dog, don't forget,' said the woman next to him, brushing her mass of golden curls back from her face and reaching across to shake Becky's hand. 'Hello, it's lovely to meet you. I'm Alison, the HR Manager here. This is Jason, the MD –' the polo-shirted man shook her hand and smiled at her '– and Victoria, his PA.'

'Thank you so much for meeting with me.' Becky was on the full charm offensive, as she beamed around at them and tried to ignore the fact that Ella had dug her nails into her right nipple so fiercely she could currently see stars. 'Can I start by apologising for the fact that I have my daughter with me today? I really hope it's okay, I appreciate that it's not usually the done thing. My husband had to go into the office to deal with an emergency today, and there was nobody else I could ask to have her at such short notice. Do you mind?' For a brief moment, she imagined what Messrs Hammond would have thought if she'd turned up with Ella there. They probably would have had her forcibly removed from the premises.

'Of course we don't mind,' said the lady called Alison, who was making exaggerated gestures and smiling at Ella, who in turn was waving her fists for all she was worth. 'I remember when my two were little; it can be a nightmare to try and juggle work and babies. I'm sure she'll be good as gold.' The other two panel members nodded, although with slightly less conviction.

How Becky wished that Alison had been correct. Unfortunately, it seemed that a formal interview setting turned Ella – who was usually the most chilled-out baby – into some kind of satanic hell demon. Over the course of the next forty-five minutes, she alternated between attempts to bite through the table top, punch Becky in the face, slice her mother's nipple from her breast using only her fingernails, imitate the sound of a steam train and produce a turd in her nappy which was so offensive that Jason made his excuses to leave the room and Victoria ran to get the emergency air circulation system turned on. Alison and Becky were left sitting in the stench, as Becky realised that, in the rush to leave the house, she'd totally forgotten to bring the changing bag, and therefore had no means of alleviating the situation. Even assuming, that was, that the offices had changing facilities, which of course they wouldn't, because there was no other moron who was stupid enough to think that bringing their baby to work was a good idea.

Alison, bless her, attempted to continue to ask Becky questions about her experience, but by this point Ella was screaming so loudly that nothing either of them said could be heard.

Becky felt tears sting her eyes and decided she was going to be better off leaving and cutting her losses before things got any worse. Thanking Alison profusely for her time and for being so understanding, she walked as quickly as she could back through reception and out into the blissfully fresh air.

She hadn't even made it back home when she received a lovely note via email from Alison, thanking her so much for coming in, but explaining that they had decided in the end to give the role to an internal candidate.

Becky rested her head gently onto Ella's – who was now fast asleep, oblivious to the problems she'd caused – and wept.

Thirteen

'Oh my god. So you actually leaked breast milk at them?' Gemma looked simultaneously amused and appalled.

'Don't.' Becky put her head in her hands. It was two weeks after her most recent Interview From Hell: The Baby Edition – and she could now just about laugh at the experience. Just. 'It was awful. Like the kind of bad dream that you'd have as part of your pre-interview nerves … except mine was real life. Honestly, sometimes I swear the hashtag FML was created just for me.'

'Oh, you and me both,' agreed Gemma, handing her friend a steaming cup of coffee. They were sitting round Gemma's one Saturday afternoon. Lovely Jon had gone off for a long cycle ride, which to be honest, was probably for the best. Since he'd come back from work on the day of the interview and Becky had screamed out her public humiliation to him, they had barely spoken. Each was now waiting for the other to make the next move; to decide whether they would give the relationship another go, or settle for becoming another one-in-three statistic and call it a day. Right now, Becky couldn't have said what she wanted the outcome to be.

Sam had gone to a mate's, and Ava and Rosie had carefully carried Ella through into the lounge where they were planning to give her 'a makeover'. Becky dreaded to think what her youngest daughter would end up looking like.

'So, what's going on with you?' It had been a while since they had last caught up, and Becky was keen to distract herself from her marital woes by finding out whether there had been any progress when it came to Gemma's love life. 'How's the Tinder traffic? Any closer to breaking your sex drought yet?'

'No! And ssshhh! Whatever you do, don't let Ava hear you. She's obsessed with sex at the moment. I thought by being open and upfront with my kids I'd have demystified it, but if anything it's the reverse. She had me panicked when she was asking me about fisting the other night; turns out she'd just got confused and thought to make a baby you had to shove your hand up the end of the man's penis in order to get the sperm out. Which, to be honest, I would rather have relished doing with my ex.'

'But you've met up with some more guys? Right? Right?' Becky looked appalled as Gemma shook her head. 'Oh come *on*! We've only got until July to get you hooked up with someone. This is Project Gemma-and-Becky at stake here! Shall I just cut to the chase and buy you a male prostitute? Would that be an easier way of getting it all over and done with?'

'Absolutely not! I just can't face another date like the one I had with Andy. That poor man. Put off from dating for ever, all because I can't hold my drink.' They both sat in silence for a moment, drinking their coffee and thinking of unfortunate, vomit-covered Andy. 'And anyway. Based on what I've seen so far, I'm just not sure that there are any decent guys out there. They've all been swept up by the likes of you.'

Becky decided now wasn't the time to enlighten Gemma on the state of her marriage. She didn't want to encourage her to give up on the dating game by giving her the proof she needed that it was all ultimately pointless anyway.

'Oh come on. Of course there are some decent guys. Just look at that lovely Mr Jones.' Becky had meant it as a passing comment, but to her surprise Gemma blushed red from her head to her toes. '*Woahhhhhhhhh*. Did I miss something, there? Are you and the delectable Tom actually fuck-buddies?'

Gemma blushed even redder, if such a thing were possible, though her face stayed perfectly composed. 'Of course we're not. Don't be ridiculous. I hardly know him. We just had one meal together.'

'YOU HAD A MEAL TOGETHER?' Becky's screech was so loud that the girls came running in from the other room to find out what was going on. Both Ava and Rosie were now sporting moustaches which, if Gemma was not mistaken, had been drawn on using permanent marker. Excellent. She couldn't wait to explain that one to the school.

'Sssssshhhhhh. It's all right girls, you can go back and play. Try not to permanently deface each other, yeah? Anyway. Yes, we did go out for a meal. After Parents' Evening. I was running late and Mr Cook was locking up the school, so

I suggested to him that we go and get something to eat. I thought I'd mentioned it to you.'

'You absolutely did *not* mention it to me, you dark horse! And then what happened? Did you end up shagging furiously in an alley somewhere? You did! I knew it!'

'We did not have sex in an alleyway.' Becky's jaw dropped, so Gemma quickly added, 'Or anywhere! We had something to eat and a few drinks and then he walked me home because Mr Cook had locked my car into the school playground, the bastard.'

'HE WALKED YOU HOME?' Becky shot up from the table, nearly taking the coffee cups with her. 'Oh my goodness. You're practically engaged. And then you got to the front door and he gave you a big huge enormous snog, right?'

Gemma threw a cushion at her. 'You are incorrigible. No, we did not snog, you horrible woman. We were just two friends, having a meal together. Not even friends, really. Acquaintances. We hardly know each other.'

Becky was not to be stopped. 'But you want to get to know each other, clearly, based on the colour of your face when I mentioned his name. Oh, this is marvellous! So much better than Tinder! We could have you married off within the year!'

Gemma was smiling but firm. 'It's not going to happen. Really, it isn't. Yes, all right. We did have a really nice time. He's great company, and he's a really good listener. I can't remember the last time I spent any time with a guy who was actually interested in what I had to say and how I was feeling. But it's not meant to be. He's Ava's teacher, for goodness' sake. The last thing he's going to want is to be dating the mum of one of the kids in his class. And it wouldn't be fair on Ava, either. So you can forget your spurious theories, and Project Gemma-and-Becky. With everything going on at work and at home, I just haven't got the time for a relationship right at the moment. Being single suits me just fine, thanks very much.'

Decisively, Gemma picked up the coffee cups and went to rinse them in the sink. In doing so, she missed the expression on Becky's face. Becky was in no way deterred by what Gemma had just said. Becky was plotting very hard indeed.

A week or so later, Becky dropped in casually one evening. Gemma was sitting at the table with Ava, whose dinner had long since gone stone cold, attempting to persuade her daughter to even vaguely consider eating just one bite of the pasta, meatballs and green beans she had lovingly cooked for her. Ava was stony-faced, and she was staring her mother down aggressively. 'You are trying to poison me, and I will not eat it,' she told Gemma decisively. It looked like they were going to be in for a long night.

'Mmmmm. Meatballs. Yummy!' tried Becky as she slid into the seat next to her. Ava slid her plate across to her. 'You can eat it. I wouldn't, though. Mum's cooking will probably kill you.' There was a glowing Trip Advisor review and a half for you.

'So . . . I was wondering.' Becky looked over at Ava, who was staring furiously at her green beans. 'Have you had any more luck on the . . . D-A-T-E front recently?'

'D-A-T-E spells date!' remarked Ava. 'A date is when you let other people see your front bottom. I am not going to have a date, ever. I do not want other people looking at my front bottom.'

'Ava, pipe down about your front bottom and eat your dinner,' said Gemma. 'No, I haven't. I told you: I just haven't got time at the moment. Plus I'm still scarred from the Andy experience.'

'Okay ... so, what I was wondering was, would you do me a favour?' Becky leant over towards Gemma. 'I've got this mate, who's really struggling at the moment. He's just moved down here and doesn't know anyone. He's desperate to meet people, to find friends as much as anything. I think you two would really get on well. What do you reckon? Would you meet him for a drink?'

Gemma sighed. Becky was unstoppable. Once she had an idea in her mind it was almost impossible to get her to let go of it. A bit like Ava, who was still staring furiously at her beans, not having taken a single mouthful.

She didn't have the energy to argue. 'Go on then. Just a drink, mind. I'm working every night after the kids go to bed at the moment; I've not got the time to be out all evening. And no telling my parents I'm meeting a guy. I'm going to need them to babysit, and if they think I'm going out on a date, they'll have the wedding venue booked by the time I get home.'

Excellent. Part A of her plan in place, Becky moved seamlessly to line up Part B.

One week later, and Gemma was heading off to meet this mate of Becky's. Simon, apparently. Learning from bitter experience, she'd touched not a drop of alcohol and had promised her parents she wouldn't be out late when they'd arrived to babysit. Her mum told her not to be silly, she should go out and enjoy herself. 'We're absolutely fine here, darling. Stay out all night, if you like.'

'Yeah, stay out all night and have SEX,' added Ava, as usual belting out what should really have been an inner monologue at a volume that could probably be heard on the other side of town.

'There will be no sex,' hissed Gemma as she ushered her daughter inside. 'No sex of any kind.'

'No,' she could hear Ava telling Sam as she left the house. 'No one will want to have sex with Mum any more, because her tummy is like a big wobbly jelly and it swings around like a bouncy castle when she walks.'

Really, she should have got Ava to write her Tinder profile for her.

Becky had been somewhat cagey about precisely where Gemma was heading off for her mystery date. 'Just jump in a taxi and get them to take you to that address. Simon should meet you there. Have fun!'

How dull and lacking in excitement her life had been before Becky had burst into it, Gemma mused in the back of the taxi. She couldn't decide whether that was a good thing or not.

Before she knew it, the taxi was pulling up. 'There you go love. That'll be ten pounds fifty please.'

Gemma looked around. There weren't any bars that she could see in the nearby vicinity. 'Are you sure you've got the right place?'

'It's the old station, yes? There you go, just over here.' The taxi driver pointed to a large stone building. It didn't exactly show many signs of life, but she would go over and take a look.

Enjoying the evening rays of sun on her face, which suggested that, at long last, summer might actually be on its way, she crossed the road and walked over to the building her driver had shown her. Sure enough, the sign on the door confirmed it to be the Old Station. There was no sign of Simon. Pushing gently on the double door, she made her way inside.

A chirpy-looking girl wearing a black T-shirt jumped up from behind a desk. 'Are you Gemma?'

'Um . . . yes.'

'Perfect. Your friend Becky told me to expect you. Do you want to come this way?'

Gemma wasn't sure whether she did or not, but the girl seemed insistent, so she followed her out of the reception area and into a darkened corridor. God, what was this place? Had Becky brought her to some kind of brothel? Nothing would have surprised her, if she was honest.

'Right then.' The girl pushed open a heavy door set to one side of the corridor and gave Gemma a gentle push inside. 'Your playing partner's already in there. Good luck! Your time starts . . . NOW!' The door slammed behind her, and Gemma was alone in the dark, wondering what the fuck was going on, and vowing to kill Becky the moment she got her hands on her.

Slowly, her eyes adjusted to the dark, and she could see a tall figure walk towards her from the other side of the room. She would have screamed, had the girl from reception not given her the heads up to expect someone else to be in there already.

'Simon?' she asked, at exactly the same moment as a voice, which seemed strangely familiar to her, said, 'Becky?'

She blinked, and as she did so, recognised exactly who it was that the voice belonged to.

'Tom!' she exclaimed, as he recognised her too, and raised his eyebrows in surprise. 'Oh my god, I can't believe Becky. That girl has got a lot to answer for!'

'So you didn't know I was going to be here?' He was dressed in navy jeans with a simple white T-shirt, and looked so utterly beautiful that for a moment Gemma felt her breath catch in her throat. She reminded herself that this was just Mr Jones, her daughter's teacher, whom for some reason Becky had thought it would be a good idea to get her to spend the evening with.

'Becky told me I was meeting an old friend of hers called Simon who'd just moved to the area and was looking to make friends. What about you?'

He smiled and ran a hand through his hair. 'She came to see me about the concerns she has about Rosie and persuaded me to come and meet her off site to talk them through. Instead of which I find she's lured me here to see you.'

Her heart sank. 'I'm sorry. I'll go and find that girl from reception and tell her we're going to go, and then you can go and get on with your evening. I don't want to ruin it.'

He paused, looking into her eyes with an intensity that left her reeling. 'There is absolutely no danger of that. I promise you.'

To hide her embarrassment at the moment that had just passed between them, Gemma went over to the door, intending to open it. To her surprise, she found it was locked. Startled, she turned back to Tom.

'I can't get out. They've locked us in. What *is* this place, anyway?'

Smiling, he passed her the leaflet he'd just discovered on the table near to them. Quickly skimming down it, she soon discovered why she wasn't able to get out.

'Welcome to the Old Station Escape Room! You have one hour to free yourselves, and your one hour starts . . . now!'

After a seriously shaky start, Gemma honestly couldn't remember when she'd more enjoyed an evening out. Becky, with her wily ways, had booked the two of them into an escape room for an evening. Typical Becky: she was going to take no chances on them having a swift drink and then going their separate ways. No, her approach was to arrange for them to be locked into a room together, where their escape depended on them working together to solve a series of logic puzzles.

Gemma had to hand it to her. It was a pretty impressive strategy.

She'd done an escape room before, not so long ago, just after Natalie had joined the business and Leroy had decided they needed to have some kind of team-bonding experience. Dave had suggested an escape room, on the grounds that it was cheap, as opposed to a weekend on the Orient Express which had been Leroy's original suggestion.

She wasn't entirely sure how bonding it had been as an experience, but it had certainly enabled them to find out a lot about each other. Dave, such a whizz with spreadsheets, had demonstrated an impressive lack of common sense when it came to working through the series of logical puzzles they were faced with. Natalie, on the other hand, the newest member of the team, was absolutely fucking terrifying, yelling at them all to focus their minds and just bloody concentrate, that she had never lost an escape room yet, and she didn't intend on starting now.

Leroy, never the best under intense pressure, had reacted in typical Leroy style, throwing himself dramatically onto the ground and lying face down on the floor, screaming hysterically at Natalie to shut up and stop abusing them, that this was supposed to be fun. And Gemma, hating every last one of them, had systematically worked her way through the puzzles and somehow got them out of there just before Natalie and Leroy had come to physical blows.

Tom was looking at her. 'Have you done one of these before? I've always wanted to have a go at one, but I've never actually found the time.'

She smiled. 'I have, but please god, let's not make this experience anything like that one was. Come on. Let's go and get started.'

Even if they hadn't had a load of puzzles to distract them, the time inside the escape room absolutely flew by. Gemma couldn't remember the last time she'd felt so relaxed with another person. As they turned their attention to the solution that would gain them access to the next stage of the room, they chatted about everything from who they thought would win the World Cup that summer – thanks to Ava, Gemma was now something of an expert when it came to both home and international football – to whether Tom had managed to stay out of Vivienne's clutches recently.

'She keeps on suggesting that I should take her up on her offer to spend Saturday evenings round at hers tutoring Satin. I'm running out of ways to say "no" politely. And who's got time for dating, anyway? Not me. I can't believe before I went into teaching I thought teachers got all that lovely time off. I sometimes struggle to fit in enough time to sleep in between all the lesson planning we end up having to do.'

'I know what you mean,' said Gemma. 'I've never, ever thought of my job as stressful, yet I'm finding myself for the first time in my life lying awake at night thinking about it. That can't be a good thing, surely?'

'It really isn't. You need to be careful.' Her face fell, thinking of Sam and Ava. As though he'd read her mind, he continued. 'Not because of your kids – I've seen them, they're absolutely fine – but because of you. Once you've crossed that line, it's very, very hard to get back.' Tom's face had lost its trademark cheer; he looked suddenly grim. 'Take it from someone who knows. Nothing's worth that amount of stress. It really isn't.' He looked away from her, his expression impenetrable.

Curiosity made her brave; she was reminded once again how little she really knew about this man. 'Did something happen? In your last job, I mean? You worked in the City, right? That's got to be stressful. Is that why you left, to move into teaching?'

Seeing her staring intently at him, he wondered how much to tell her, whether he could trust her. Tom had a hard time trusting people these days. Gemma meant well, he was sure of it. But this wasn't something he'd spoken to anyone about, ever. He was afraid that once he took the lid off it he'd never be able to go back.

Inhaling deeply, he turned to face her. 'You're right. Something did happen. And it's something I've never really talked to anyone about before. It's—'

Before he could say anything, the moment was gone as the

196

main door flew open and the space they were in was flooded with light. 'That's it! Time's up, and I'm afraid you failed to beat the Escape Room! Never mind, eh?' It was the chirpy-looking girl, still as chirpy as she'd been an hour earlier. 'We'll get a photo for the website, if that's okay. Pop your arm around her, and . . . say cheese!' They both grimaced uncomfortably as she snapped them with her mobile phone, and then told them that they were free to go, that everything had been paid for in advance by Becky. Ah yes. Becky. Gemma had an awful lot to say to Becky when she next saw her.

She was about to say her goodbyes to Tom and head for home, but he surprised her by suggesting they went for a drink. One drink turned into two, turned into three hours, and before they knew it the bar staff were calling last orders and turfing them out.

'Right then. Time to head off, I guess. I'll be round Becky's early tomorrow morning to give her what for, after the set up she's got us into tonight.' Gemma was smiling: she'd had an absolute ball.

'Yeah, make sure you give her hell. What an utterly terrible evening.' He winked at her. 'You're not far from me, are you? Want to share a taxi?'

Effortlessly, he hailed a taxi. Climbing into the back seat, they sped off home, saying very little on the journey. Having talked non-stop since they'd arrived at the escape room, they were both happy now to fall into a companionable, slightly tipsy silence.

The taxi pulled up outside Gemma's and she climbed out. Tom was just behind her, paying the taxi driver. 'I'll walk home from here. It's such a lovely evening.' The taxi sped off.

It was much later than she'd anticipated being back, but the lights were still on inside. There was also a note Sellotaped to her front door, written in red crayon by someone who was almost certainly Ava: 'DON'T DO ANY SLOPPY KISSING.'

'What's that?' To her horror, she realised Tom had followed her up the path and was standing just behind her. Before he could see Ava's commentary, she had grabbed the piece of paper and crumpled it up into her pocket.

'Oh … nothing. Just some junk mail.'

'Right then.' They both stood awkwardly for a moment, while she simultaneously desperately wished he would leave, for fear that either her mum or Ava would come out and start interrogating him, and dreaded the moment he went.

He broke the silence, looking at his watch. 'Shit, I didn't realise it was so late. I am so sorry, but I really do need to get back. I've got a full set of unintelligible Year 2 English books to mark tomorrow. The topic is My Family. I dread to think what the kids will have come up with.'

'You and me both,' agreed Gemma, imagining that she'd probably never be able to look him in the face again based on whatever Ava had decided to write. 'Thank you for a lovely evening.'

'You are more than welcome. And the same to you. Truly, I can't remember when I last enjoyed an evening more.'

'So …'

'So …'

They were standing just inches away from each other, his silhouette outlined under the golden glow of the street light. The air hung between them, taut with possibility.

And then he leant over, and their lips met, and he was kissing her, and it was quite possibly the best fucking kiss she had ever had in her entire life.

He smiled. 'I'd better go. Let's do this again some time. Soon.'

She managed to stop herself from leaping in the air, clicking her heels, and shouting 'YAHOO!' as he rounded the corner, but only just.

Fourteen

Still floating on air, Gemma fumbled for her keys, but before she could get them into the lock, the door burst open and Ava shot out, incoherent with hysterical excitement.

'Ava! What are you still doing up! It's *hours* past your bedtime.' Honestly, what were her parents like? Now she'd have a horrendously overtired seven-year-old to deal with all day tomorrow. Just how she'd hoped she'd be spending her Sunday.

Her daughter was screeching something which likely only bats could hear, such was the histrionically high level of her pitch. Kneeling down, Gemma caught her and stopped her still, her arms around her waist. 'Sweetheart, what are you talking about? I can't understand you.' In the background, she caught sight of the worried faces of her mum and dad who had congregated in the hallway. 'Is everything okay? Where's Sam?'

Ava was vibrating from top to bottom with excitement, desperate to break the news to her mum. 'Sam's fine! He's in the kitchen … WITH DADDY! DADDY'S HERE! HE'S COME BACK!'

Oh, no.

No, no, no, no, no.

Ava wasn't wrong, though. Walking into the house as though in a trance, Gemma put down her bag, just in time for Sam to rush out of the kitchen and accost her, showing more emotion than he had done in approximately the last three years of his life. 'Mum! You're back! Dad's here! Isn't it brilliant?'

That was one way of describing it, thought Gemma dryly. She exchanged glances with her parents, who gave a kind of half shrug in a 'What could we do?' manner, and watched as her ex, Nick the Dick, last seen running out of the front door into a waiting taxi – 'Don't want to miss my flight, babes, laterz!' – walked out of her kitchen, and back into her life.

Getting the children to bed took hours. It was well past their usual bedtime, and they had been hyped into a frenzy by the unexpected arrival of the father they hadn't seen for two years. Persuading them to go to bed and stay there was an almost impossible task. Having waved goodbye to her parents and promised them she'd phone them tomorrow to try and understand properly quite what the hell had happened since she'd left the house earlier that evening, Gemma eventually succeeded when Ava passed out through sheer exhaustion, and she realised Sam could be bribed with the judicious promise of a ten-pound note.

Finally, the house was silent. It was almost one in the morning. Tiptoeing downstairs, she went into the lounge, where Nick lay on the sofa, his feet up, clutching a mug of hot Ribena – a childhood habit he'd never grown out of. He had clearly made himself at home.

'Babe! Come and sit down!' He patted the sofa next to him, looking almost disappointed when she elected instead to sit in the easy chair directly opposite him. 'Isn't this brilliant! Back together again! Your mum and dad are gems, aren't they? They were delighted to see me. And the kids! They're so ... big!'

'Yes, well, children will do that, if you keep feeding them.' Gemma pulled her legs up next to her and sat back in the chair, holding a cushion protectively in front of her. Well well well. Nick the Dick, back from the dead. Over two years had passed now, and yet, looking at him, it was like no time at all had gone by. He still looked identical to the day he'd walked out of that door. Long, shaggy brown hair which, much like Sam's, was desperately in need of a cut. Wicked blue eyes, which Ava had inherited, sparkling constantly with mischief as they darted round the room, taking in everything.

'Hey, I love what you've done with this room, babe! Didn't it used to be purple?' He frowned with concentration as he looked around. The room had never been purple, but Gemma didn't say anything. She had forgotten just how irritating Nick's habit of speaking in never-ending exclamations could be. Not to mention his obsessive use of the word 'babe'. She had to write the word 'TWAT' repeatedly on the roof of her mouth with her tongue to prevent herself from articulating it out loud.

'So, Nick.' She looked over at her man-child of an ex-husband. He was wearing board shorts, flip-flops, and a T-shirt which looked like it had come out of Sam's

202

wardrobe. His long, gangly legs stretched the full length of the sofa as he sipped his Ribena and looked expectantly at her. 'Do you want to tell me what's going on?'

'I don't know what you mean, babe. Nothing's going on! I flew back into Heathrow yesterday and thought it was about time I headed over and saw you guys. It's been ... what, a year?'

'Two years,' Gemma said curtly. 'Two full years since you buggered off to go travelling with Lucy, and left me here on my own to bring up your children. Two full years without so much as a visit or an offer to pay maintenance. And now, just as I have started to get my life together, in you waltz. So forgive me, Nick, for not quite understanding what the fuck you're doing here?'

He looked wounded; like she'd walked across the room and physically punched him in the face. It was a very tempting thing to do.

'Listen, Gem. I'm sorry. I honestly am sorry. I was – well – I was a dick.' Understatement of the fucking year. 'I think it was a bit of a mid-life crisis, to be honest. I just ... I felt like you guys didn't need me any more. The kids were growing up, and I didn't have a clue how to look after them properly, and you were off smashing it at work ... and I just didn't really know what to do with myself.'

'So you got bored and flew to the other side of the world to shag your secretary. Yeah, good going Nick. That's completely what grown-ups do when they don't know what to do with themselves. For fuck's sake. Have you got any idea what you've put me – what you've put the kids – through?'

He looked contrite. 'I know. You're right. And believe it or not, I have done some growing up while I've been away.

I've been thinking a lot. About you ... about me ... about the kids. And so the reason I've come back, Gem, is to ask you ... will you give me a second chance?'

If he'd told her he was joining a monastery, she couldn't have been more surprised. Of all the reasons she thought Nick might have come back, getting back together with her was definitely not one of them. As ever, with her ex, she looked at him to try and work out what his ulterior motive might be. To her surprise, she saw nothing other than genuine contrition and even a look of ... was that, fear? Fear that she might say no? Fear that he wouldn't be given the second opportunity he so desperately wanted to be the father he had never quite managed to be, first time around?

'Fucking hell, Nick.' Gemma ran her hands through her hair, leaving it sticking up in all directions. 'Fucking hell. You can't just do this, you know? You can't just waltz in and out of my – and the children's – lives whenever you feel like it. No, you can't come back. We've got our own lives now. And you're not part of that.'

Her remark clearly hit home. 'Ouch, babe. Ouch. Look, I know I've done wrong. I know I've been a dick. But I've come back to apologise for all that. To make a new start. I'm sorry. I truly am. I was a silly little boy, and I treated you like shit. But what we had – you and I – that was something special. And I think we owe it to ourselves to try and get that back; to find the magic again.'

Finding the magic again. And what magic was that, then? Gemma's memories of her relationship with Nick were all about the latter years; the years where her husband was out all the time, clearly shagging his way around his office, while she brought up the children single handedly whilst also holding down her increasingly demanding job. Magical, it was not.

'Remember Ambleside?' He looked directly at her, his eyes pleading with her to remember.

Did she remember Ambleside? Yes, she did. A tiny town in the heart of the Lake District, nestled next to Lake Windermere. It had been the first holiday the two of them had ever taken. Madly in love, they had spent their days walking through the hills and dales of the Lakeland landscapes, stealing kisses and occasionally stealing something a bit more than just a kiss. (The expression on the face of the hill walker who had inadvertently come across them copulating al fresco next to a drystone wall when his dog had bounded up to them, hoping to join in, was unlikely to leave Gemma, ever. As was the delighted way in which Nick had gleefully proclaimed, 'He saw your pubes! He saw your pubes!' before collapsing in giggles.)

It had been utterly wonderful; even when it had rained non stop for two days and two nights, they had splashed through puddles and listened to the sound of the rain falling in the trees and sat in front of log fires drinking rough red wine from mugs and eating chips with melted cheese. It had been, it occurred to Gemma, one of the happiest weeks of her life.

Nick's eyes were bright; he could sense from her expression that he'd found a weakness. 'What we had in Ambleside, Gem – that's what I want us to get back. I love you. And I want you to be able to learn to love me again. To learn to trust me.'

'I don't know, Nick,' Gemma said carefully. 'I really don't

know. What you did to me . . . that was unforgivable. I'm not sure if I can ever get over that.'

It wasn't a flat no, and he'd latched onto that immediately. Jumping up from his prone position on the sofa, he crossed the room and knelt by her feet, taking her hands in his.

'I understand, babe. Really, I do. And I want to put that right. All I'm asking is that you give me another chance. Just one. We all make mistakes, right? And this was mine. And it was a fucking huge mistake at that. But I love you, Gem. All the time I've been away, I haven't been able to stop thinking about you and the kids. If you won't do it for me, won't you do it for them? You saw their faces; they were crazy to have me back at home. For all of us, Gem? Won't you give me a second chance?'

Shaking her head she closed her eyes; just for a moment she allowed herself to think of Tom. Her mind flashed back to the evening they'd spent together. She couldn't remember a night ever having passed so quickly; the connection between them had felt almost electric. And that kiss . . . oh god, that kiss. It seemed like a lifetime ago.

But it had been one date. Just a single evening, spent together. Their paths had barely entwined; Nick's and hers were woven together in a rich tapestry going back years and years and years. Tom would understand. He had to.

The options available to her ran through her mind. She could tell Nick where to go. Throw him out into the street, reject him in the same way that he'd once rejected her. Shout after him never to darken her doorstep again, and then see if Tom was interested in a rerun of that kiss.

Or . . . she could not. She could allow Nick to stay, give

206

their marriage another chance, let him try to be the father he wanted to be.

Because that was the crux of it, really. Wasn't it? This wasn't about her. It was about her children – about Sam and Ava. And looking at them last night, incandescent with joy at the sight of their father, Gemma realised that she didn't actually have a choice to make at all. The thought of their faces in the morning, if she'd told them that she'd sent their estranged father away again. No. She simply didn't have it in her to do that.

Opening her eyes she looked closely at Nick, trying to find a sense of the man she'd once loved. 'Fine. You can stay. For tonight, at least. Beyond that … I don't know. I need some time to think. This is a lot to take in.'

He visibly relaxed, letting out the breath that he hadn't even realised he'd been holding. 'Oh babe. You won't regret this, I promise. Thank you so much. I love you, I really do.' He leant forward to kiss her, but she turned her face and he ended up planting his wet lips onto her cheek. So much for Ava's crayoned command that there was to be 'NO SLOPPY KISSING'.

Removing her hands from his, she ran them across her face. She was exhausted. 'Cool. So, I'm off to bed. You know where everything is, yes? Or, presumably, you can work it out. I'll give you a quick tour round the house in the morning, not that much has changed. Are you okay to switch off down here before you come up?'

He walked over to the doorway where she was standing, almost drooping with tiredness. Snaking one arm around her waist, he dropped a kiss on the top of her head and whispered 'Let's go to bed, babe.'

She had rarely moved faster, putting distance between the two of them as rapidly as she was able to. 'I don't think so.' His face fell. 'Nick, I promised you you could stay – but that doesn't involve me jumping into bed with you. It's going to take me a long, long time to trust you again – if I ever can – and if you're serious about wanting to make things work, then you're going to need to give me the space to do that.'

He held his hands up. 'Babe, I totally understand. Honestly, it's fine. I can kip in the spare room. We're all good. Listen, you go and get some rest. You look exhausted. I'll finish off down here.'

Gratefully, she went upstairs, mute with tiredness and emotion. Pausing on the threshold of her bedroom, she thought better of it and went into Ava's room. Nick's acceptance of her need to take things slowly had been admirable, but she still wouldn't put it past him to decide to make a sudden nude appearance beside her bed in the middle of the night, spinning his swollen appendage like a baton twirler. No, this was definitely the safest option.

Ava barely stirred as her mum got into bed with her, attempting to move her to one side of her single bed in order for them to share. Despite only being seven, Ava's ability to take up the sleeping space usually needed by a fully grown man was legendary. Dreaming about playing attacking midfield for England, Ava kicked out in her sleep, causing Gemma to ball up in a corner of the bed about twelve inches square, desperately clinging on in order to avoid falling out altogether.

It was going to be a long night.

*

208

What felt like only seconds after she'd closed her eyes, Gemma was awoken by the sound of a frantic banging on the front door. Her mouth was dry and she suspected smelt of dead badger; the grimness of her morning breath never ceasing to appal her. Ava was still lying peacefully asleep next to her, diagonally across the bed, her relaxed composure never letting on for a moment that she'd spent most of the night kicking her mother in the vagina as she thrashed around in her sleep.

It was not solely due to her daughter's horrible sleeping habits that Gemma had had the most dreadful night's sleep. Her mind had been buzzing, full of thoughts of Nick ... and Tom. They had had such a perfect evening. She guessed it was just one of those things which was always going to be too good to last.

The banging downstairs had stopped, thank goodness. She could hear the familiar clicks of the keyboard in the room next door which told her that Sam was already on his computer. In the knowledge that her children were safe, Gemma drifted back off into a dreamless sleep.

Becky had been awake since dawn, desperate to know how the blind date had gone. She'd tried texting Gemma a couple of times but there had been no response; her phone, presumably, was turned off. That had to be a good thing, right? They were probably curled up in bed together right now, having finally admitted their lust for each other. Becky clapped her hands together with glee. Oh, how she loved it when a plan came together.

By eight a.m. her impatience finally got the better of her. Pulling on her workout gear she left the children watching some inanity involving singing vegetables on

CBeebies with Jon, and made the short walk next door to Gemma's.

Having gently knocked on the door to no avail, she increased her efforts. Surely the children must be awake by now? Eventually, through the stained glass pane, she saw a shadow moving towards her in the hallway. An adult-sized shadow. It looked too tall to be Gemma. Oh my god ... was it Tom?

The door flew open, and in the middle of the doorway stood a man she'd never seen before in her life. He was tall, and toned, and tanned, and he was wearing nothing apart from the tiniest spandex thong she'd ever seen in her life. Becky was rarely speechless, but this was one such moment. She didn't know where to look, but her eyes were inextricably drawn to the slightly pitiful-looking bulge which the spandex thong was hiding. I mean, she'd worn some fairly risqué outfits in her time, but this was something else altogether.

For his part, the man in the spandex thong was thoroughly charmed by Becky, beautiful and athletic in her running gear, with just a tantalising amount of cleavage showing above her sports bra. This was why, he reminded himself, all the money you spend on gym memberships and tanning sessions is worth it; for moments just like this one.

'Um, hi.' Becky brushed her long hair away from her eyes and put up her hand to shield them from the early morning sun. 'I'm Becky. I live next door. I was just wondering ... is Gemma in?'

'Hello, Becky,' said the hulk in the thong. 'Blimey, the neighbours have got a lot better looking since I last lived here. Would you like to come in? I can make you a coffee and we can ... get to know each other. Apologies for my lack of clothing. You just never know who's going to drop in.'

He smirked in a way that made Becky think he was all too aware that he might just as well have had his entire cock and balls hanging out, such was the lack of coverage given to them by his choice of underwear.

She was utterly confused. Where was Gemma, and where was Tom, and who the hell was this random man in a thong? Unless ... hang on a minute. Had he just said that he used to live here?

Her unspoken question was answered by Ava, who suddenly came flying into the hallway in her Barcelona football kit. 'Daddy! Daddy! Can we go to the park and play football so I can practise for when I play against Ronaldo?!'

It was two hours later, and Gemma was sitting at Becky's kitchen table with a strong cup of black coffee, Boris the fucking liability happily chewing on his dildo at her feet. She'd left the children with Nick, who'd promised to take them down to the park with a football and show them 'how we're going to smash the hell out of Brazil in the World Cup this year'.

Unusually, Jon had got up that morning and had curtly announced that he was taking Rosie and Ella off to see his parents, who lived about an hour's drive away. There was no suggestion that Becky go with them, and things between her and Jon were grim enough that she wasn't exactly rushing to spend the day in his company, which meant that the house was unusually quiet.

Gemma's eyes were ringed with black – a combination

of tiredness and being less than zealous with her make-up remover the previous night – and she stared morosely into her mug of coffee as Becky enthusiastically pressed her for details as to quite what the fuck was going on.

'So you met up with Tom? And spent the evening together? How was it? I was going to wait up for you to come back, but Ella's been teething, and I'm so exhausted that I was asleep before the end of *Britain's Got Talent*. Do you absolutely hate me for setting you both up?'

Gemma managed a weak smile. 'No. I don't hate you.' She looked up at her friend. 'It was actually a brilliant evening. We were so busy chatting that we failed miserably to crack the escape room. He's such good company. I was even getting him to open up about why he'd left the City to become a teacher.'

'And?' Becky was all ears.

'Nothing doing. At the moment he was about to tell me, the girl came in to tell us our hour was up, and then although we talked about all sorts at the pub afterwards, he never mentioned it again and there wasn't really an opportunity to bring it up.'

'So you went for drinks, and then you came home?' She looked at Gemma expectantly. 'And ... ?'

Gemma sighed. 'And ... we kissed.' Becky jumped up from the table and started doing a little victory dance. 'And, it was absolutely amazing, probably the best kiss I've ever had in my entire life.'

Becky stopped dancing and looked closely at her. 'So, you'll forgive me for stating the obvious, but aren't kisses that amazing meant to have you floating on Cloud Nine, not looking as though you've just been sentenced to watch

Fireman Sam and that obnoxious little fucker Norman Price on repeat for four hours in a row?'

'So, you've seen what's happened.' Gemma put her hands around her coffee cup and took another restorative sip. 'I get back home last night, and out of the blue, who's turned up but Nick the fucking Dick. In the time I've been out, he's infiltrated not only my house, but also the affections of my children, which makes it almost impossible to do what I should almost certainly have done and sling him out on his ear.' She sighed heavily again.

Becky was not going to have her frankly world-class matchmaking dismissed so easily. 'So? Okay, so Nick's turned up, but that doesn't change anything. He's your ex: that's the one who jilted you at a moment's notice to run off round the world with his fuck buddy. Sure, it's great that the kids will get to see him now, but that's the only change. It's full steam ahead with Project Gemma-and-Becky!'

She beamed at her friend, ready to plan her next inter-action with the divine Mr Jones, but Gemma didn't seem to share her enthusiasm. She shook her head. 'It's not that simple. He's asked me if he can stay. And I've ... I've said yes.'

'You've WHAT?' Becky's shriek was so violent that the glasses on the top shelf trembled and Boris started trying to dig himself a hole in the tiled kitchen floor. 'What do you mean, you've said yes?'

Gemma looked miserable. 'I've said yes, because what choice did I have? He's my kids' dad. It's not about what I want. It's about what they want, what they need. Come on Becky; you've got kids. You know you'd do anything for them. How could I not say yes, when I'd seen the elation on their faces when their dad had walked through the door?'

'Gemma, I know. I know you're doing all of this for the best possible reasons. But can't you see; it's not the answer. It can never be the answer. Since I've moved in here, you've never stopped telling me what an absolute fucking bastard Nick was, how him leaving was the best thing that could ever have happened to you. When I first met you your confidence was absolutely sapped. Since I've known you, since you've started dating again, I'm getting to see a whole new Gemma. One who knows she's amazing, and isn't going to settle for anything less than that. So you have to tell Nick no. Tell him you've changed your mind. Your future might be with Tom, or it might be with one of the million and one other gorgeous guys out there. But it isn't with Nick. It really isn't.'

Gemma shook her head. 'You're wrong, Becky. I'm sorry, but you're wrong. Nick made a terrible mistake. But he deserves a second chance. And I'm going to give him one.'

'But what about Tom?' Becky tried a different tack.

For a moment, Gemma's resolution wavered. 'We had an amazing night. It was an amazing kiss. But it clearly just wasn't meant to be.' She shrugged. 'So be it.'

'No!' Becky was pacing around the kitchen now, her frustration clearly visible. 'Gemma, I'm sorry – I know you probably think this is none of my business – but I cannot let you just throw this away. I get that you want to prioritise the kids' happiness. I really do. But how can they possibly be happy when their mum's dating a total arsehole?'

She had gone too far. Gemma stood up, slamming her coffee cup down on the table, spilling coffee dregs which soaked into the grain of the wood. 'That "arsehole" you're talking about there – that's my husband. My children's father. And so perhaps you'd like to think twice about your choice of words.'

Becky was unrepentant. 'He's an arsehole, Gemma. And, in your heart of hearts, I think you know that.'

Standing there in the kitchen, the two women faced each other, Becky with her hands on her hips, Gemma with her arms crossed protectively in front of her.

'I'm going to go now. I'd like you to stay away from Nick and me. Whether you like it or not, he's moved back in. Whether that means we're going to give our relationship another go, I don't know just yet. But I am damn well going to consider it. Because, if it makes my children happy –' she felt a lump in her throat catch at the thought of Ava and Sam '– it'll be worth every single moment I spend with him.'

'Oh come *on*, Gemma. How can your children possibly be happy when you're living a lie?'

Furious at Becky's audacity, Gemma walked out, slamming the door behind her.

Becky sat down at the table and put her head in her hands. Fucking hell. If she'd been looking to alienate everyone she really cared about in the world, she was certainly going the right way about it.

Fifteen

Tom sat at the tiny desk he'd set up under the window in his flat. It was a beautiful day outside; the sky was blue and the clouds moved rapidly across the sky, blown by the spring breeze. If he could make it through this pile of marking he might even manage to get outside to enjoy it.

Opening the first exercise book, and unable to stop his face from cracking into a smile as he caught sight of Simon Barnes's attempt to draw his family, resulting in a long line of what looked to be varying sizes and shapes of penis, he couldn't stop his mind from drifting back to the previous evening. Going out with Gemma had been a revelation. The instant connection they both seemed to have felt, the ease with which he had been able to open up to her, coupled with how absolutely beautiful she was, and the most amazing kiss ... he couldn't remember the last time he'd felt like this about anyone.

For almost the first time in his career, he found himself counting down the hours until Monday morning arrived and he would see her in the playground. He knew she was always rushing off to the office, but perhaps they would be able to grab a couple of minutes and he could invite her out for dinner later that week. Assuming, that was, that she felt the same way as him. God, he'd forgotten the emotional drain that was dating.

His phone lay on the desk next to him as he marked his way through Class 2A's work – failing completely to keep a straight face as Ava's essay described how 'my mum's front bottom has a beard. I hope that my front bottom never grows a beard' – and he checked it almost compulsively, hoping against hope that Gemma might send him a text or a WhatsApp. Nothing. His phone stayed resolutely silent, other than when it briefly vibrated with a text message and he almost fell backwards off his chair with excitement, only to discover that it was his local pizza place offering him their latest deal. He was depressed to see that, in the last seven days, his *only* text messages had come from his local pizza place. He really needed to reassess the state of his social life.

Contemplatively, he considered messaging her himself, even going so far as to compose several suitably casual messages on his phone, only to chicken out at the last moment. Tom had a pathological fear of rejection; sending a text message to the girl you'd been out with the previous evening, who for whatever reason had chosen not to text you herself that day, was basically asking for it.

Resolutely, he turned off his phone, finished his marking and took himself out for a long walk; his mind filled only with thoughts of Gemma.

The next morning he was up and at work even earlier than

his usual Vivienne-avoiding time. God, if she found out he'd spent Saturday evening with Gemma! He almost laughed out loud at the very thought. Gemma was going to need some kind of round-the-clock security if the two of them did decide to give a relationship a go. He stopped himself. One step at a time. He still hadn't received any confirmation from her that she actually felt the same way that he did.

Gemma's early arrival in the playground caught him by surprise. He couldn't remember a single occasion since he'd started teaching at Redcoats when she hadn't been the last to arrive, invariably sprinting across the playground with a furious Ava in tow ('Mummy, when you run like that it makes your nipples wobble and it's EMBARRASSING'). Yet now, here she was, even beating Vivienne to the classroom door.

Attempting to calm his rapidly beating heart, he leant on the door frame in a faux show of nonchalance. This was it: the moment he'd been waiting for since he'd walked away from her on Saturday night. He had better not fuck it up.

Ava ran over, her curls flying, shouting wildly in excitement. Behind her, he saw to his surprise that Gemma was accompanied by a man; a man he hadn't met before.

'Mr Jones! Mr Jones! My daddy! My daddy is here! Look!' Frantically, she jumped up and down next to him, pointing enthusiastically at the man next to Gemma. 'He's living with us now and he has got the smallest pair of pants you have ever seen! They don't even cover up his—'

'AVA.' Having caught up with her daughter, Gemma knelt down to her level, studiously avoiding eye contact with Tom. 'I don't think Mr Jones needs to know about Daddy's pants, do you?'

Ava shrugged. 'He might want to get some small pants as well. Come on Daddy, let me show you my classroom.' Grabbing the man's hand, she pulled him into the classroom, leaving Tom standing there with Gemma, thoroughly bemused.

'Um.' Gemma looked more awkward than he thought he'd ever seen her look before. 'Could we have a quick word?' She scanned the playground; Vivienne and her coven were approaching. 'Somewhere ... private?'

'Sure.' Leaving Miss Harris on duty, he ushered her around the corner of the classroom, where they could stand out of view behind the fire exit. He put his hands in his pockets and turned to face her, one eyebrow raised.

'Um. So that man there ... the one with the small pants ... that's my ex-husband. Nick. The children's father. I haven't seen him for two years, but then, when I got back to mine on Saturday night after our –' she blushed, clearly remembering the moment which had passed between them outside of her front door '– evening out, there he was. He said he'd come back to see the children, and because he wanted to give our marriage a second chance. And ... I've decided to say yes. I've decided to let him move back in.'

Tom felt his heart plummet like a stone. Surely not. After everything Gemma had told him about Nick; the way he'd undermined her, failed to support her, and totally abused the trust she'd placed in him. Surely she had more self-respect than that?

He opened his mouth to say this, but she cut him off before he could even speak. 'I know. I know exactly what you're thinking. You won't be the first to say it, either. Becky made it all too clear what she thought of my decision when I saw her yesterday. But this isn't about me. It's about my kids. When I gave birth to them, I promised them that they would always come first. They deserve the opportunity to get to live with both of their parents, if that's a possibility. And so I'm going to make sure I give them that opportunity.'

Tom shook his head. He couldn't believe she was being so blinkered. Never mind how he felt about her; even if there had been nothing at all between himself and Gemma, this Nick was clearly a complete and utter arsehole. What the hell was she doing back with him?

Disappointment and concern made him blunt. 'You're mad. You're absolutely mad. You spent all of this time telling me what a dreadful person he was, how much he ruined your life, and yet the moment he crawls back through your front door you're taking him back as if nothing has ever happened. You talk about your kids being happy, but how can they possibly grow up to respect themselves if their mum's got so little respect for herself? Come on, Gemma. You deserve better than this. You deserve to be happy. You know you do.'

She reacted as if he'd shot her. 'Oh really? And who are you to be talking about happiness? Mr Big Shot City Boy, who has probably never known a day's unhappiness in his life. You swan in here, with your privileged life, with your great job, and your good looks, and every single woman in the playground fawning over you and attempting to seduce you, with no sense of what it's like to struggle every single day to keep everything together, to keep the kids happy, to keep everything going at work and at home, to keep some vague sense of sanity. You have not a clue. Not a fucking clue.'

Tom stared at her, at her face contorted in fury. 'No,

Gemma,' he said, shortly. 'No, I think it's you that doesn't have a fucking clue. Now, if you'll excuse me. I need to get back to my class.'

Nick was waiting for her when she walked back into the playground. So was Vivienne, who stared at her suspiciously as Tom also emerged around the side of the building and walked straight into his classroom.

'All right, babe? Shall I drop you at work then?' He reached casually for her hand, and she felt that old familiarity as his fingers closed around hers. Knowing that Tom would be watching, she chose not to pull away.

Gemma visibly exhaled as she arrived at Zero and walked into the office. Sure, work might be complicated – but compared to her personal life at the moment it looked like fucking child's play.

Her feelings of relief were short-lived, however. Leroy and Dave were sitting in the glass-fronted meeting room, brows furrowed, staring at Dave's laptop screen. Leroy, clad today in a hot-pink T-shirt and lime leather trousers – Gemma had learnt over the years that the more panicked Leroy became, the more outlandish his fashion choices – looked up to see her passing and beckoned her in.

'Morning, Gem. Come and join the fun. Dave here's just taking me through our latest forecast. It's a fucking riot a minute in here, I'm telling you.'

Gemma slid into the chair next to him and looked at the forecast. You didn't need to be a finance specialist to know that things didn't look good.

She pointed at the line showing cash. 'Is that ... ?'

'Yep.' The finance director ran his fingers across where

his hair would have been, had he had any. 'We heard this morning that Vanity aren't going to pay. I think the technical term is that we're basically fucked.'

'Oh Leroy.' Her boss had his head in his hands and looked like he might cry. 'Is there nothing we can do? What about all of those ideas for expansion and diversification that you told me about?'

He shrugged. 'Fucking pointless, aren't they? You can't expand or diversify without investment, and there's absolutely nobody out there wanting to invest into a fashion software business run by a dickhead who wears green trousers.' He looked up at Gemma and Dave. 'Let's face it, guys. Dave's right. We're basically fucked.'

Back in the classroom, Tom was having an equally shitty day. He'd had to remove Noah Hardcastle from assembly after he'd elected to announce to the entire hall that 'my willy is going massive, and I can't get it to go down', and Mrs Goldman had looked as though she would quite like to drop kick both Tom and Noah out through one of the hall windows. Then, when he'd got back to the classroom, Ava had threatened to bite off Satin's little finger on the grounds that 'she keeps touching my air, and I don't want her to'. There were some days when he was truly glad that he had never had an opportunity to have children.

He looked over at Rosie. Unlike the rest of his class, Rosie could consistently be relied upon to work hard and not cause problems. Unfortunately, this was because she had become so introverted and so separated from the rest of the class that she barely spoke a word other than when he directly asked her a question.

At break time, he was surprised to see Ava not rushing out into the playground to play football with the group of boys that she usually hung around with, but waiting to talk to him.

'Everything okay, Ava?'

She considered his question for a moment. 'No, I don't think it is. Can I tell you something, Mr Jones?'

He crouched down on the floor so as to be at the same height as her. One rarely lauded benefit of KS1 teaching was just how hard it worked your thigh muscles; he'd barely had to touch the Stairmaster in the gym since he'd started working here.

'Of course you can. What's up?'

Ava stared at him intently with her brilliant blue eyes. 'I saw Satin being mean today. She was being mean to Rosie. She went over to her, after we came back from assembly, and you were trying to sort Noah's willy out.' Tom physically recoiled; there was a rumour he was going to need to address before Ava repeated that back to everyone she met. 'And she said something to her. I don't know what she said, because she said it really quietly, but Rosie didn't say anything, and after Satin went away she was smiling in a really nasty way but Rosie looked really sad and I thought she might cry. Like I did when Sam once ate all the chocolates out of my advent calendar and pretended Father Christmas did it.'

A light bulb went off in Tom's head. Now he came to think about it, he'd seen Satin and Rosie together on quite a few occasions. Rosie had never seemed to have any particular friends, but Satin was often over talking to her, and Ava was right, Rosie had never appeared to seem especially happy. What was Vivienne's daughter saying?

He looked at Ava. 'Thank you very much for telling me, Ava. It must have been tough to speak up –' goodness, he knew about that all right '– but you've done absolutely the right thing.'

'Of course I have.' Ava was entirely dismissive of his claim that speaking up was tough; she couldn't have looked less concerned about the fact that she'd been the one to break ranks and speak with him. Not for the first time, he wished that he had just a tenth of her self-confidence and devil-may-care attitude. 'Our school values tell us that we should always be kind, and I didn't think Satin looked like she was being very kind, so that's why I told you. Will you give me ten house points now?'

Tom smiled at her shameless request. 'Maybe not quite ten house points, but I agree, you've been a huge help. I wonder ... would you be able to help me a bit more?'

Ava looked at him suspiciously. 'And then will I get ten house points?'

'If we get to the bottom of this mystery, almost certainly. I need to find out what's making Rosie so sad. Do you think you could help me?'

Ava thought about it for a moment. 'Okay. I bet it's Satin, though.'

Tom didn't say anything, but he had a sneaking suspicion that Ava might just be right.

Over the next few weeks, Tom observed Ava going out of her way to get close to Rosie in an effort to find out what – or who – was making her so unhappy. When the boys she usually hung out with clamoured for her to come and play football with them, Ava silenced them with one wave of her hand. 'No. I can't play football today. I'm doing something for Mr Jones.' Uncomplaining, the boys went off to set up their pitch without their star striker.

At first, Ava had no more success than anyone else in finding out what was upsetting Rosie. While Rosie liked Ava, and was used to her from the many times they'd hung out at either one of their houses, it didn't mean she was prepared to open up about what was going on. She was no match for the sheer willpower of Ava, though. Ava wasn't used to taking no for an answer, and gradually she whittled away at Rosie's insistence that there was nothing wrong.

'But you're sad,' persisted Ava. 'So there must be something wrong.'

'I told you, I'm okay,' replied Rosie.

'No, you're not. That's like when my mum says that she's okay when she puts us to bed, but later I sneak down the stairs and I see her crying on the sofa and doing really bad singing like a cat being strangled while she listens to sad songs. She pretends she's okay, but she isn't really. And you're doing the same.'

Rosie was affronted. 'I don't sound like a cat being strangled when I sing.'

'Yes, but you know what I mean. You have to go and talk to Mr Jones.'

'But he's a teacher.'

'Of course he's a teacher. That's why you need to talk to him, because he will sort everything out.'

'Really?' Rosie looked up, her eyes bright for the first time in what felt like for ever.

'Definitely.'

'Will you come with me?'

Ava shrugged, secretly delighted that she would get to be in the thick of the action. "Course.'

Tom could barely believe his eyes when, that lunchtime, Rosie, accompanied by Ava, walked towards him where he was on playground duty.

'Mr Jones, Rosie wants to talk to you. Can we go into the classroom?' Ava was walking on air; her ten house points were practically in the bag.

Quickly finding cover for the playground, Tom walked into the classroom, both girls following in his wake. He sat down on the carpeted area, encouraging them to do the same.

'So then. Rosie. What's going on?' He spoke softly, determined to encourage the little girl to speak up.

Rosie looked uneasily at Ava, who nodded encouragingly. 'Don't forget, once you've told Mr Jones you'll be able to come and play football with me and the boys. I think you'll probably be really good in midfield.'

'It's Satin,' whispered Rosie. 'She's not being very nice to me.'

Tom exhaled. So Ava had been right. What the hell had Satin been up to then?

'What sort of things has she been saying?' He was willing to put money on Satin threatening to leave Rosie out, not invite her to her party – the usual kind of seven-year-old unkindness.

Rosie looked at Ava again, who reached into her pocket and took out one of her favourite Match Attax cards, featuring a hologrammed Eden Hazard. She gave it to Rosie who stroked it reverentially. 'That's my absolute best card, but you can have it to keep for *ever*, because that's the sort of kind thing you do when you're friends with someone.'

Eden Hazard gave Rosie the confidence she needed to speak up. 'She's been saying mean things to me. She's been telling me ... that I look funny. Because of the colour of my skin and the fact that my granny and granddad come from the Philippines. She keeps telling everyone in the class to stay away from me and not sit next to me, or she's going to get them. And I don't want people to get got.'

Rosie looked sadly down at Eden Hazard, and Ava gave her arm an encouraging squeeze. Tom, meanwhile, sat there with his mouth open. He was appalled. Funnily enough, racism had been the one thing he'd never expected to encounter at school, particularly in a primary school of Redcoats' standing. It had been rife in the City – he shuddered just thinking about it – but he'd actually found children to be far more receptive than adults to embracing each other's differences. It horrified him to think that all this time, Satin had been running an undercover campaign directly designed to exclude Rosie from her new class-mates – purely because of the colour of her skin.

Composing himself, he spoke gently to Rosie. 'Rosie, that's terrible. That's an awful, awful thing to do to some-one, and I am so, so proud that you felt able to come and talk to me about it. I'm going to speak to Satin, and I'm going to make sure that no one ever speaks to you again like she's spoken to you.'

'She says my face looks funny,' said Rosie quietly, still looking down at Eden Hazard.

'But that's nonsense, isn't it!' said Tom encouragingly. 'Your face doesn't look funny at all. I mean, you don't look at my face and think that I look funny, do you, just because I've got different colour skin to you?'

The girls thought about that for a moment. 'Sometimes your face does look a bit funny,' said Rosie. 'Especially when you are telling us off and it goes all crumply and weird.'

Okay, so that hadn't gone quite as he'd planned. It had broken the tension though, as Ava and Rosie were now laughing their heads off, presumably at the thought of his funny-looking face.

'But I think it's good that we're all different,' said Ava, pausing in her mirth. 'It would be boring if we were all the same. It's like Daddy wears tiny little pants, and Mummy wears big huge pants to hold up her wobbly tummy and her big bottom. Being different is fun.'

'It certainly is that,' agreed Tom, firmly refusing to allow his mind to drift onto thoughts of Gemma's bottom. 'So, Rosie, I'm going to speak to Satin. And Ava, can I ask you to keep on being Rosie's special friend at school and making sure she's not being left out?'

Ava nodded. 'Of course I will. Come on Rosie, let's go and play football. I'll teach you to do a rainbow flick.' Laughing, the two girls ran out of the classroom, only pausing for Ava to shout, 'And don't forget my ten house points, Mr Jones.'

Finally. He'd got to the bottom of what was bothering Rosie. Now all he needed to do was work out how to resolve it.

Sixteen

In the end, he'd elected to speak to Vivienne first. Part of him had wanted to jump straight on the phone to Becky to let her know that he'd finally worked out what was so upsetting her daughter, but he'd decided against it, until he'd actually sorted out a resolution. Which would involve speaking to Vivienne. Something he was looking forward to about as much as root canal surgery.

He'd broached it with Vivienne that he would need to speak with her, urgently, when she'd come to collect Satin from school that day. Immediately, she was all ears. 'But of course,' she'd purred. 'Just let me drop Satin back home with the nanny. I'll slip into something more comfortable, and then I'll be back.' She'd made it sound like a threat.

Quaking in his size-twelve loafers, Tom whiled away the time before Vivienne returned by attempting to get the interactive whiteboard to work. It had been playing up recently, frequently switching itself on and off, and once, to his utter mortification, breaking into a medley of Tom

Jones hits. His class had been delighted yet nonplussed, not being familiar with the classics from the elderly Welsh crooner; Miss Harris, on the other hand, had been beside herself and had actually had to go out into the corridor for a moment to compose herself.

Just as he thought he'd detected the source of the problem, there was a tap on the classroom door and in walked Vivienne. Tom had to bite his bottom lip to prevent himself from laughing out loud. Good grief, what *did* she think she looked like? She was wearing a dress which his rather conservative mother would likely have described as a top; it covered her pelvic region more by accident than design. Paired with fishnet tights and a pair of Perspex heels which Tom thought he'd last seen on Katie Price, the overall effect was one of a hooker – and not the ones in Ava's wardrobe – whose best days were behind her.

'Mrs Avery. Come in, please.' Tom sat down behind his desk and gestured for her to take a seat opposite him.

She waggled her finger at him, fluttering her eyelashes seductively as she did so. 'Now I've told you before, you naughty boy, it's Vivienne. There's absolutely no need to stand on ceremony.'

God, she was an awful woman. The thought of Satin's sustained campaign against Rosie gave him an energy and confidence that he'd never usually felt in her presence, and he bluntly explained to her that this was a formal meeting about an extremely serious matter which had occurred at school. Briefly, he outlined Rosie's claims.

Vivienne denied them, as of course he had known she would. 'I think you must be mistaken, Mr Jones. That can't be Satin. Satin would never do something like that.'

Tom was unmoving. 'I'm afraid she has. It's testimony which is backed up not only by Rosie's statement, but also by the claims of a number of other children in the class.' Once Ava had led the way, he had been both appalled and encouraged by the number of others who had also felt able to mention to him that they had seen Satin deliberately trying to exclude Rosie – the only child in the class who didn't come from a strictly white British heritage. Tom suspected that there was a good chance Satin felt threatened by Rosie's stunning good looks and outstanding academic abilities, and had therefore attempted to make the transition into her new school as difficult as possible for her. Thank goodness for Ava, who had spotted what he had so miserably failed to see.

In the weight of such damning evidence against her daughter, Vivienne attempted to make light of the situation. 'You know what children are like, Mr Jones. I'm sure she was just having a laugh.'

Tom's face told her exactly what he thought of this statement. 'I'm afraid there is absolutely nothing to laugh about, Mrs Avery. We take racism extremely seriously in this school, and I will be referring the matter to Mrs Goldman. She will be in touch with you in due course. I must make you aware that the possible sanctions for Satin may be anything up to expulsion. Redcoats will not tolerate any kind of discriminatory behaviour, and to see such a sustained campaign against one individual, at such a young age ... I can only say that this is a matter of grave concern. I will now pass it to the head for her to make the ultimate decision on how it is addressed.'

His mention of possible expulsion appeared to have got

through to Vivienne where everything else had failed. She covered her glossy pink lips with her hand, horrified at the thought of what her daughter's behaviour could mean. For the first time, her face was that of a parent who finally, perhaps, was starting to realise that she had certain responsibilities in life when it came to her children's upbringing; responsibilities which she was maybe not quite fulfilling.

'Thank you, Mr Jones,' said Vivienne, in a voice lacking her usual brash confidence. 'I will see myself out.'

Tom exhaled with relief as the classroom door closed behind her. Now for Mrs Goldman. Fuck, he had probably completely circumnavigated some essential school process by speaking with Vivienne directly without first informing the head. Already in her bad books, this could be curtains for him.

To his surprise, he found Mrs Goldman in a conciliatory mood. Privately, she had felt slightly guilty about her reaction to the disastrous school trip, and had been secretly looking for an opportunity to make it up to Mr Jones, who was fast turning out to be one of the best teachers she'd ever had. The skills he'd learnt working in the City enabled him to communicate effectively with children, parents and teachers alike; he could easily be a candidate for deputy head in a couple of years' time.

Having listened carefully to everything he had to say, she congratulated him on the way he had handled the matter and assured him she would be making an appointment to speak with Vivienne the very next day. 'It has occurred to me that we may have let that woman have rather too much rope in this school,' Mrs Goldman mused. 'Sometimes I think she walks around the place like she bloody owns it.

And what *does* she look like in those clothes she wears? Does she think she's walking into a nightclub every morning rather than the school playground?'

Tom smiled. Mrs Goldman was not the sort of person he imagined would even know nightclubs existed, let alone be aware of the kind of thing one wore to them. Just went to show that you should never judge a book by its cover.

'I'll be getting on home then, if that's okay?' It was getting late and he still had the latest fractions homework to mark for his class, which was bound to send him over the edge into slamming his head gently into the wall as he explained to Simon Barnes once again why one half plus one half did not equal forty-seven.

'Of course it is. And Tom ... well done. You're a credit to this school.' Smiling, Mrs Goldman held the door open for him as he left her office.

He allowed himself a brief moment to glow in her admiration before ... was that his imagination, or did she *wink* at him?

Oh fucking hell, it was never-ending.

The next morning, Becky was surprised and concerned to be told by Miss Harris, looking more like she'd picked the wrong vocation than ever, that Mr Jones needed to see her. For the first time, Becky thought Rosie had seemed brighter when she'd come home from school yesterday; she was full of tales of the brilliant game of football she'd played at lunchtime with Ava and the boys. Had she imagined it?

She hadn't. Taking her into the hall, which was empty, Tom explained to her what had happened. Becky was silent throughout; he had no inkling of what she was thinking.

When he finished speaking, he was surprised to see tears in her eyes.

'Hey, it's nothing for you to be upset about. You haven't done anything wrong.'

Becky shook her head. 'How do you know that? My daughter was being bullied at school – for an entire term and a half – and I couldn't see it. And being excluded because of the way she looks? It wouldn't have even occurred to me that that was a possibility. I suppose – when you're so comfortable in your own skin, and have always encouraged your kids to be the same ... I had just never thought that how Rosie looks could be a problem for her.'

'And it won't be,' Tom reassured her. 'Your daughter is beautiful. Unfortunately, she happens to be in a class with a child who has a difficult lesson to learn about friendship and differences. The good news is that we've worked out what's been going on; Mrs Goldman is going to speak with both Satin and Vivienne; and it sounds like we're going to be getting a new midfielder for the England ladies' team.'

Becky smiled; Rosie hadn't stopped going on about football when she'd got home last night. It was clear to them both that Ava's friendship was going to be very, very good for her.

'Speaking of Ava,' Tom continued casually, 'how's Gemma?'

Becky shrugged. 'Not a clue. I haven't spoken to her for weeks, since the Morning After The Night Before, when I knocked on the door to see if you two were having wild passionate sex and instead got accosted by a man in a thong and then she turned up at mine to say that it was Nick the Dick and she was planning to live happily ever after with

234

him, so I told her she was a fucking idiot and she stormed out and told me to leave her alone.'

Tom sighed. He'd been hoping that his pep talk to Gemma would have somehow got through, but it seemed Becky had been just as spectacularly unsuccessful as he had when it came to making her see sense.

'I don't know what to do, to be honest,' continued Becky. She looked him square in the face. 'She's my friend. She's the only real friend I've made since I've moved down here. And when you count the fact that I'm not really speaking to my husband on the grounds that he's a complete and utter cockwomble – don't ask, it's a long story – it's all a bit shit, really.' She sighed. 'Doesn't seem like there's much chance of Project Gemma-and-Becky succeeding now.'

'Project Gemma-and-Becky?'

'Oh, the night I first met Gemma – the evening we got introduced to you as the new Year 2 teacher – we went out to a bar and got drunk and we thought up Project Gemma-and-Becky. The deal was that she'd help me with my job search – which is going so badly, it's laughable – and that I'd get her a shag by the time she turned forty. Well, her birthday's in July, and the current status is that we're not speaking and she's shacked up with that absolute bloody twat, who I can't bear to think of her having sex with, so it seems like any which way, we lose.'

Tom sighed. It didn't seem like anyone was doing very much winning right at that point in time.

If she was honest, Gemma felt the same. Sat on the toilet one morning, attempting to have a wee in peace and listening to the chaos unfolding around her, she wondered why she had ever entertained the concept of letting Nick back into her life. Oh, he meant well. He genuinely did. The trouble was, his emotional age was stuck firmly at twelve, meaning that, far from having an extra adult to share the load with, it was more like she'd brought a third child into the mix.

From outside the toilet door – from which, regrettably, she'd had to remove the lock after the memorable evening when Ava had locked herself in there, completely lost her shit and the fire brigade had had to be called – the sounds of warfare emerged.

'MUM.' Ava burst in through the door; personal space was in short supply in this household. Frankly, Gemma was so used to carrying out once-private tasks with an audience, that she'd once contemplated selling tickets the next time she changed a tampon.

'Ava, could you maybe at least think about knocking before you barge in? I was trying to have a wee.'

Ava cared not one jot for her mother's desire for privacy whilst she carried out her basic bodily functions. 'Sam is *annoying* me.'

'And why is Sam annoying you?'

'Because he keeps looking at me.'

'And? He's allowed to look at you. It's a free country.'

'No he's not. It is my face, and he is NOT to look at it.' She looked furious.

'Okay ... so, I'm just finishing up in here, so could you possibly ask your dad to deal with Sam looking at your face instead?'

Her daughter shook her head. 'No. He's not as scary as you are.'

Marvellous. Terrifying: totally the parenting vibe she was going for.

The door swung open again; this time it was Sam. He saw Ava already there and looked mutinous.

'Mum, Ava's being unreasonable. She keeps telling me that I can't look at her face. I can look at her face if I want to. They're my eyes.'

'Yes, and it's *my* face, and I am telling you that you CANNOT LOOK AT IT.' Ava made a noise which sounded suspiciously like a growl.

Gemma put her head in her hands. 'All I want – *all* I want – is just five minutes' peace while I have a wee. Is that honestly too much to ask?'

Both of her children looked at her in surprise. 'Um, yes,' they said in perfect unison. As it was the only thing they'd agreed on all morning Gemma wasn't going to bother arguing with them.

Before she knew it the door swung open again. This time it was Nick, who raised his eyes in surprise as he saw the three of them crowded into the tiny bathroom, Gemma still sitting with her knickers round her ankles. 'There you all are. I wondered where you were. Wondered what I was missing.'

'What you are missing,' said Gemma, through gritted teeth, 'is the two minutes I was hoping to call my own to urinate in peace. Now, is there any chance you could possibly take responsibility for your two children just long enough to allow me to wipe, flush and wash my hands?'

He looked surprised. 'Of course, babe, no drama. Come on, kids, Mum wants to be left in peace while she has her wee.' He said it in a tone that suggested her expectations were set far too high; which, to be fair, they probably were.

At last. Peace, perfect peace. Gemma relaxed her pelvic floor, finished weeing and looked around for the toilet roll. Naturally, there was none, because the very concept that you could finish one toilet roll and replace it with another, as opposed to leaving the empty roll for the next person to find, was frankly preposterous.

Nick was never going to be capable of operating in a proper partnership, she realised, as she looked for a new toilet roll in the cupboard under the sink and sighed in frustration as she wiped stale piss from the lino round the bottom of the toilet bowl, before ... God, was it up the walls as well? She'd overheard Nick telling Sam about the time he'd won a competition at school to see who could pee up the wall the highest. This, clearly, had been Sam's practice attempt.

The wee on the wall couldn't have made things any clearer for her: this wasn't working. Much as she hated to admit it, both Becky's and Tom's words had been ringing in her ears over the last few weeks, as Nick had asked her repeatedly if she was ready to give their relationship another go and she had told him to back off. Slowly, she was starting to realise that, actually, maybe she did have a right to be happy. And that it was a state she was unlikely to be able to reach with Nick *in situ*.

Of course, this meant she was going to have to pick her moment to break this to him and thereby ruin the lives of both her ex-husband and her children. Sighing heavily, Gemma washed urine off her hands and wondered quite how she'd managed to get herself into such a mess.

The only saving grace was that things at Zero were so horrendous, they were distracting her completely from the dramas she had going on at home. Having finally found some toilet paper and packed Nick and the kids off to school (he was in theory only meant to drop them off, but she often wondered whether he'd benefit from joining Ava's class while he learnt how to operate like a normal functioning human being), she'd arrived at the office to discover that Leroy had called an Extraordinary Board Meeting. Half suspecting that he'd only done it because he liked the name, she arrived to find a room of sombre-looking faces.

'Hey, Gem.' Clad today in an all-in-one playsuit which was bright blue and peppered with crudely drawn images of pink and white seashells, Leroy didn't need to open his mouth for Gemma to know that today was not going to be a good day. He couldn't even crack a smile as Dave bustled around them, handing out packs of paper. Leroy dropped his on the desk in front of him and looked despondent.

'Right then,' said Dave, seeing that Leroy was in no fit state to take charge. 'Shall I—'

'Oh, what's the bloody point?' said Leroy, raising his hands in the air. 'We can sit and go through these sodding spreadsheets until the cows come home, for all the good it will do us. Gemma, Natalie – we're fucked. I have tried everything I can – truly, I have – but we're at the end of the line. We're out of cash and the future isn't fucking bright, it's fucking grey and miserable. I'm so sorry. I'm the worst fucking boss in the world.'

'Now now,' said Dave consolingly. 'It's not quite so bad as all that. There is some hope. But it's going to require drastic action. Basically, if we want to ensure the future of the business, we are going to have to slash headcount.'

Dave made a dramatic and somewhat unnecessary slashing motion through the air, Mask of Zorro style. He was thriving on this, Gemma thought; he looked more animated than she'd ever seen him.

'Okay, so what does that mean?' Natalie, ever pragmatic, was up and drawing on the whiteboard. 'We've got – what – ninety, one hundred staff? What are we talking? 10 per cent cuts? 20 per cent?'

Leroy looked ashen. 'It means ... that we will be working with an HR consultancy to put all employees into a formal consultation period based on the fact that their jobs are at risk. It means that I can't guarantee a job for anyone, any more.'

Her mouth dry, Gemma asked the question that she didn't want to know the answer to. 'Even us?'

Leroy couldn't meet her eyes. 'Even us.'

Seventeen

Driving home that evening, her car stereo for once silent and not belting out power ballads, Gemma felt empty inside. So this was it. Her time at Zero – the only job she'd ever known – was about to end. Things were moving so quickly, too. Dave, experiencing a new lease of life in his self-appointed role as the Grim Reaper, had already appointed an HR consultancy firm, who had come in to meet with himself and Gemma that very afternoon. The consultants they'd met with had been both kind and reassuring, but there was no escaping the fact that this was absolutely bloody awful. And she hadn't even got to the point of having to break it to her staff yet. Oh god, Siobhan. How the hell was she going to tell Siobhan that, after all these years of working together, the answer to her daily question of 'Am I sacked?' was actually going to be 'Yes.'

She desperately wished there was someone she could talk it all through with. Her parents were amazing, but they were worriers by nature, and she just couldn't bear the thought of months of anxious looks as she went through consultation. No, she'd tell them when there was something concrete to say, not before. There was Nick, of course, who was still intent on his efforts to woo her back, none of which were working. If anything, they'd only served to remind her of all the reasons why they had broken up in the first place. To be honest, for all the help he'd be, she might as well talk to the kids instead.

The person she really wanted to talk to, she realised, was Becky. Becky always had a brilliant knack of simultaneously making her feel like everything would be okay and at the same time coming up with a load of – often, admittedly, insane – ideas as to how she could get herself out of the situation. If only she could go round to Becky's with a bottle of wine and sit with her on the sofa while Boris chewed his dildo and they put the world to rights.

But she couldn't. Becky had made her feelings about her and Nick clear, and so that was that. Gemma was still appalled that the friend she'd only known for a matter of months thought she knew enough about Nick to flat out declare he wasn't the right man for Gemma.

I mean, he categorically wasn't, but that was for her to say, not for Becky.

Becky was at home, attempting to deal with the disastrous aftermath of Boris getting hold of one of Ella's dirty nappies. She'd been under the mistaken impression that she'd developed some kind of resistance to dealing with bodily fluids and was now able to clear up pretty much anything without her gag reflex kicking in. This particular incident was proof of just how wrong she was. Boris, the absolute fucking liability, was licking his lips like he'd just been treated to the seventeen-course tasting menu at The Fat Duck, as opposed to hoovering up a bag full of shit. God, animals and children were foul.

She'd texted Jon on her way home from the school, telling him briefly of her meeting with Tom and how it looked like they'd got to the bottom of Rosie's unhappiness at last. To her surprise, Jon had replied within seconds, telling her that was great news and that he would be home by seven so they could sit down together and talk it through properly. Obviously, she'd believe it when it actually happened, but it was a nice thought.

As she scooped up shit, her spirits were at least slightly lifted by the fact she'd finally found a journalist who was interested in the treatment she'd received at her very first interview at the solicitors. Sure, it was the local *Gazette*, as opposed to the *Guardian* or *The Times*, but beggars couldn't be choosers, and the lady she'd spoken to had promised she would run a well-researched piece which talked about the difficulties of mothers with children getting back into the workplace, as opposed to a *Daily Fail* classic 'sad face' number.

Unfortunately, that was where her good news had stopped. Despite her best efforts – and Becky was nothing if not persistent – the few job interviews she had managed to secure had dwindled into nothing, and her rejection rate thus far was a staggering 100 per cent. To her shame, she'd even attempted going along to the last couple minus her wedding ring, in the hope that the panel would think she was some kind of free and easy single girl without any of those blasted family responsibilities which might prevent her from working around the clock for them. But nothing doing. The doors to gainful employment remained firmly closed.

With the kitchen bleached to within an inch of its life, Becky went to check on the girls. They were both in the living room, totally absorbed in a recorded episode of *Match of the Day*. Ava's influence had spread far and wide, and Becky could not be more grateful for the role she had played in ensuring she had her happy little girl back again.

It was just a shame Ava couldn't perform the same trick on her own mum.

Making the most of the fact that no one was screaming or threatening to kill anyone else, she legged it upstairs for a scalding hot shower, to destroy any last traces of shit which might be remaining in her hair or under her finger-nails. Honestly, never mind being in the trenches – half the time parenting was like spending your life in the middle of a farmyard.

To her surprise, she heard the front door slam. Galloping down the stairs in a towel to ensure Rosie hadn't followed through on one of her frequent promises to leave home 'because you and Dad are so *embarrassing*', she found Jon.

'Hi!' He was clutching an enormous bouquet of red roses, which he held out to her. 'Um ... these are for you.'

'Why? What have you done?' He looked at her askance. 'I mean ... thank you.' Top on her list of resolutions for next year was going to be practising more social niceties, instead of displaying her internal monologue all over her face. Becky wasn't so much an occasional sufferer of Resting Bitch Face as the pioneer of it.

Grabbing her towel to prevent it from falling to the ground – though she knew Jon would appreciate the view, she wasn't sure she was ready to resume marital relations – she reached over and took the proffered flowers. 'They're lovely. Thank you.'

'And ... ta-da!' From behind his back he revealed a bottle of Veuve Clicquot, already chilled. 'Thought we could sit down and drink this together.'

Now she was really suspicious. Something was definitely up. Although he probably hadn't lost his job, if he was still buying Veuve.

Her heart sank. Since the Night of the Fire Brigade, she'd never completely plucked up the courage to ask him where he'd been, when he was supposed to be meeting the mysteriously absent Mr Matthews. It had crossed her mind, multiple times, that he could have been with someone else. Another woman. She wouldn't entirely blame him, given the depths their relationship had sunk to since they'd moved in here.

'Where are the girls? Watching TV?' She nodded. 'Right, you go and finish your shower, then sit down and relax. I'm going to put them to bed, and then you and me, we're going to spend the evening together.'

Ah yes. Jon's idea that they would have a romantic evening together. She'd experienced her husband's idea of a romantic evening together before. It consisted of him, her ... and his work iPhone, which he grabbed every time it bleeped with an incoming email, tapped at it frantically, staring at the screen, and occasionally looked up from his obsessive emailing to promise her that he would 'just be five minutes'. Which inevitably turned out to be five hours, during which time she'd drunk his share of the wine, lost her shit with him and gone to bed.

He saw what she was thinking, and shook his head. 'Nope, this time it really is going to be just you and me. In fact ... here.' He extracted the loathed object from his suit pocket and passed it to her. 'Go and put it somewhere out of sight for the evening. Tonight really is all about me and you.'

She remained cynical, but by the time he'd crashed his way around upstairs with the girls (with a delighted Boris in tow), managed to get them showered, teeth brushed, and into bed, and had even prevented Rosie from playing five hundred rounds of the game she'd learnt from Ava – 'I Can't Go To Sleep Because ...' – with the promise she'd get to stay up late at the weekend if she just stayed in her own bed that night, Becky had allowed it to cross her mind that maybe, this time, he actually meant it.

'So.' He sat opposite her at the other end of the sofa, the champagne fizzing in two flutes on the coffee table next to them.

'So.'

'We need to talk.'

'We do.' She paused and took a deep breath. 'Jon ... I need to know something. Have you been seeing someone else?'

He looked appalled. 'My god, no. What in the world has made you think that?' He took her hands in his and she didn't pull away. 'Becky, I love you.'

Briefly, she explained. Janet had promised he'd be home, his dinner with Mr Matthews had been cancelled; and yet he wasn't home, he was out until the wee small hours and returned smelling of drink and cigarettes. What was she supposed to think in those circumstances?

'God.' He ran his hand across his forehead. 'I'd had no idea you'd spent all this time worrying about that. Why didn't you say anything?'

'Given I don't think we've said anything beyond barked instructions regarding the girls for the last few weeks, it would have been a bit difficult.'

He had the good grace to blush. 'Yeah, that's a fair point. But honestly, sweetheart, you don't ever, ever need to worry about anything like that. You're my girl, and there's no way I'd ever do anything like that. Even if you *do* attempt to burn the house down in my absence.'

She managed a weak smile. 'So Mr Matthews?'

'He did cancel, Janet was absolutely right. But then he called my mobile to tell me his flight had been delayed, and he was going to be in town after all, and could I still squeeze him in. Given he's probably brought me about half of all of my commission for this year, it was a tough one to say no to. And I had no idea you were planning anything.'

'You wouldn't. Janet promised me she wouldn't tell a soul.'

It felt like a weight had been lifted from her; she hadn't realised how long she'd been carrying around her concerns. So, her husband wasn't having an affair. However, they still had some significant work to do on the state of their marriage.

As though he'd read her mind, he continued, 'It's been a pretty rubbish few weeks, hasn't it? And I know I'm mostly to blame for how things have been. If I hadn't dumped you in the shit with that interview, we'd probably still have been talking, right?'

She shrugged. 'I'm sure I had a part to play too ... no, actually, on second thoughts, you were a bit of an arse.' They laughed in unison; it struck her it was the first time she'd heard her husband laugh in weeks and weeks. 'It's been both of us. We've been too stubborn to make it up; too stubborn to admit that either of us was wrong.'

'So how is the job hunting going? Have you had any joy?'

She sighed and pulled her legs up under her. 'Not a fucking bit. Rejected, every single time. Reckon I could add "100 per cent rejection rate" to my CV? It seems wanting to work part time around the needs of your children makes you pretty much unemployable.'

'But your experience before you had kids—'

She cut him off. 'Counts for nothing, it seems. It's fine. I'll just spend the next eighteen years of my life cleaning bodily fluids off soft furnishings instead of in an interesting job that actually stimulates me. I mean, who wants to do something that provides actual job satisfaction and gives you a sense of self-worth? Not me, that's for sure!'

She attempted a laugh. It came out as a half-sob; he could see tears sparkling in her eyes as she picked up her champagne flute and drank deeply.

'Listen, Becks. I'm not having an affair, but I have got something that I need to tell you.'

'Oh god.' Her face fell. 'You *are* sacked.' She went to pour the champagne back into the bottle. 'Reckon we can return this?'

'I'm not bloody sacked! Though it speaks volumes for your belief in my employability that that's always the first conclusion you jump to!' He winked at her.

'So ... you're having a sex change. Or you want us to

think about having a threesome. Or you've noticed just how hairy my toes really are and have decided that you don't want to be married to a half woman, half ape. Come on, which is it?' She stared him straight in the eyes, daring him to laugh at her.

'Oh Becky. Becky, Becky, Becky.' He took her hands, pulling her towards him. 'No, I don't want a threesome; no, I'm not having a sex change; and no, I definitely am not put off by your hirsute toes. I love you, troll feet and all.'

'Tell anyone else about my troll feet and I'll kill you. So what is it? Tell me.'

He took a deep breath. 'What I've realised is that right now, I'm really not being a very good husband.' She went to interrupt him and he stopped her. 'No, hear me out. Some of the things you've said hit home, because you weren't wrong. I have prioritised what I've wanted over what you've needed, and marriage shouldn't be like that. It's meant to be a partnership, and we need to get back to ours being a proper partnership.'

She tried to speak again but he was having none of it. 'Seriously, hear me out. I've been thinking a lot over the past few weeks, and what I want, more than anything, is to make you happy. I thought – mistakenly – that me taking on the burden of being the sole breadwinner would allow you to do all of the things that you wanted to do, but that's not the case. And so –' he took a deep breath '– I've made a decision. I've spoken to my boss today, and it's all agreed in principle ... if, that is, you decide that it's what you want to do. I've agreed that I'm going to drop down to working a three-day week. That will mean that I can spend the remaining two days at home, taking full responsibility for the girls. Hopefully, that will give you more options when it comes to finding a job that you really want to do. Or, if you decide that you actually don't want to work, you could have those two days as days for you. What do you think?'

She was silent for a moment, clutching her champagne flute tightly. 'Can we afford it?'

He smiled. 'As you know, we're pretty fortunate in that respect. To be honest, it will probably only have minimal impact on my commission, and with the backdated pay increase they've promised to give me off the back of that tender I turned around the other month, I think we'll be more than fine, even if you decide you don't want to work.'

'Oh I do. I absolutely do. I mean, there's the minor fact of being able to persuade any employer out there that I actually have skills worth having, but that little tiny issue aside, I so do.' Already, her face was cracking into an enormous smile at the thought of being able to get a break from the daily routine. God, she might even be able to have a wee *all by herself* once in a while. 'But are you sure? Are you really, truly sure? Isn't this going to set your career back?'

He shook his head. 'I honestly don't think so. And even if it did ... Someone's got to start to lead the way, haven't they? If I prove that part-time, flexible working can work for everyone, not just mums with children, then maybe we'll get more men in our office doing the same, which will make it more acceptable for everyone to be doing it. I've been genuinely shocked by what you've experienced when you've gone out to look for work. We have to change that. And I want to be part of driving that change.'

In the whole of their relationship, Becky thought she had never loved Jon more than at that moment.

Such a momentous announcement called for a celebration. It came in the form of wild and insatiable sex on the kitchen floor, which even Boris the fucking liability bounding into the midst of couldn't stop from being absolutely bloody mind-blowing and reminding them both of every single reason why they'd married each other.

Eighteen

Gemma was absolutely dreading Sports Day, on a number of different levels. Sitting in a field watching her children ineptly attempt to take on their classmates in a number of different sporting activities was not exactly high on her list of great ways to spend a day's annual leave. However, she had always promised her children that, while she probably wouldn't make it to the class assemblies, or the phonics training mornings, or the recorder concerts (thank fuck), she would guarantee to be there for Sports Day.

Sam and Ava differed in their approaches to Sports Day; both had the potential to be incredibly embarrassing in their own special ways. Sam had inherited his mother's athletic ability; that is to say, he had absolutely none. From his very first Sports Day, back in Year R, when he'd ended up tripping over in the three-legged race and being dragged along the field by the ankle by his brick shithouse of a partner, Sam had made it very clear that he was unlikely to be representing the family in the Olympics any time soon. He was consistently the only person on the field on Sports Day who seemed to be enjoying himself even less than Gemma.

And then there was Ava, who, frankly, was a law unto herself as to what she was going to do next. Ava was uber-competitive but, despite her skills on a football pitch, was completely lacking in grace or sense of direction. This had led to a few memorable moments, like the year she'd headed completely the wrong way round the track and ended up trampling the toddlers as they waited for the toddler race. Ava was oblivious to the wailing destruction she'd left behind her as she sprinted the wrong way across the finish line and celebrated her victory by running around the track with her school shirt pulled over her head, much to Mrs Goldman's horror.

They nearly hadn't made it out of the house at all that morning, thanks to Sam coming into Gemma's bedroom to announce that he could not go to school, 'because Ava is wearing my pants'.

'Why is she wearing your pants?'

'I don't know. She's Ava.'

'Well, get them off her then.'

'I can't. She growled at me.'

'Sam, you have about twenty pairs of pants. Could you possibly, just for today, consider wearing one of the other nineteen pairs?'

'I can't find them.'

Gemma had sighed heavily. 'Then I don't really know what to suggest.'

Defiantly, Sam had crossed his arms. 'Fine. I'll wear some of your pants.'

Yet another of those parenting scenarios they had never covered in NCT classes.

Thoughts of what carnage Ava might cause that year, and the knowledge that this was one of her so-called days of 'holiday' – oh, how she laughed, in a hollow and slightly hysterical manner – were not the only reasons Gemma was dreading Sports Day. She was almost guaranteed to run into Becky who, since the morning of Nick the Dick and the Spandex Thong, she had been completely blanking. This hadn't been easy, what with them living next door to each other, but she had successfully managed to stoically ignore her neighbour, even hiding behind the wheelie bin one morning until she could be absolutely certain that Becky had left on the school run.

By contrast, Becky saw Sports Day as a serious opportunity to get everything sorted out. Gemma was, frankly, being ridiculous. Nick was … well, a dick – and Gemma and Tom were clearly meant for each other. She was going to get them together, if it was the last thing she did.

Somewhat against her better judgement, but working on the basis that there was safety in numbers, Gemma persuaded Nick to accompany her to the school. Thus far, despite her cajoling, he'd failed entirely to obtain any kind of gainful employment – 'I'm on it babe, don't nag me' – and so was more than happy to do so. This was primarily on the grounds that he remembered the generally strict school having an unusually liberal policy when it came to providing a Sports Day bar, which had served Pimm's and bottled beer from the incredibly civilised time of nine a.m.

Gemma was about to disappoint him. "'Fraid not. Not

this year,' she said, as he looked around thirstily for the jugs of Pimm's.

'What? But that was the only reason I agreed to come. I mean –' taking in Gemma's blistering look '– wasn't that one of the biggest fundraisers for the school all year?'

'It was,' Gemma agreed grimly. She would miss the bar too; it had made Sports Day vaguely bearable. 'Unfortunately, though, Leticia Swift's mother enjoyed the bar rather too much last year. Ended up having actual sex in the middle of the long jump with her latest squeeze. Tried to persuade the school it would save them having to teach sex education. Don't ask me how I know this stuff. I wanted to bleach my brain when I found out. Becky, on the other hand, thought it was hilarious.'

'How is Becky, anyway?' asked Nick curiously. He had hoped to get to spend rather more time with the stunning woman he'd met on the doorstep the morning after he'd moved back in, and had been incredibly disappointed that not only did it not seem to be an option, but Gemma wouldn't even allow her over the threshold, for reasons she refused to share.

Gemma shrugged. 'Don't know, don't care. Come on.' She put her arm through his companionably and dragged him over to the lines of tiny chairs, where they would be destined to spend all day sitting with their knees somewhere up round their ears. 'If we get a spot in the front row we'll be in pole position to watch Ava take out this year's quota of toddlers.'

Becky watched Gemma and Nick carefully from her vantage point over by the Year 2 classroom. She'd been waiting to catch Tom and persuade him to act as her co-conspirator.

In the event, he took very little persuading, agreeing entirely that the whole thing had become ridiculous, and that this was the perfect way to resolve things.

And maybe, if he was really lucky, even get him one step closer to another evening out with Gemma.

The races dragged on. Sam sloped his way through his, feet dragging miserably, arms raised towards his parents as if to say, 'Honestly, what do you expect me to do?' Ava came running over excitedly to tell them that 'Sam has got a new school record, it is the slowest that anyone has *ever* run fifty metres! Even that boy in Year R who was sick halfway through the race last year, he still got to the finish line quicker than Sam did!'

'I feel strangely proud,' said Gemma. 'I don't come from a great line of sporting achievers; now my son has a school record in the fifty metres. We'll just maybe not mention it was for the slowest time ever.'

Ava ran her races with panache, trampling – sometimes literally – her classmates on the way to the finish line, and then celebrating in typical Ava style.

'Oh my god, she's twerking,' said Gemma, head in hands, as Nick laughed his head off and Mrs Goldman looked appalled. 'Marvellous. Just the reputation I was hoping this family would be cultivating. Come on Ava, why don't you just cut to the chase and streak round the field?'

'I wouldn't encourage her,' said Nick nervously, who was secretly mildly terrified of his batshit crazy daughter.

Ava's twerking marked the end of the class races. At the start line, a crowd of harassed-looking parents were attempting to corral a group of unruly under-fours in preparation for the toddlers' race. To Gemma's relief, her daughter was several metres away from them, still revelling in her latest victory.

'So what happens now?' asked Nick, as the last wailing toddler crossed the line, covered in grass and snot.

He was answered by Mrs Goldman, who took hold of the tannoy system and announced, 'And now, ladies and gentlemen, boys and girls, it is time for the Redcoats Sports Day Mummies' and Daddies' races!'

'Oh fucking hell,' groaned Gemma. 'I'd forgotten about this. Don't you remember, that first year Sam was here and you got overly competitive in the dads' race and broke that poor man's collarbone?'

Nick wasn't the only one to get overly competitive in such circumstances. All around them, parents had risen from their uncomfortable vantage points on the tiny chairs and were limbering up in such a manner that suggested they'd been training for this for years. In fact – was it Gemma's imagination? – had Vivienne and her coven brought a coach with them?

'They do three-legged races these days. I think they thought it might be a safer option than the obstacle course.' Gemma elected not to remind Nick that the obstacle course had been immediately cancelled after the year he'd lunged over the gym bench for the line and had broken Toby Abbott's poor dad's collarbone in the process.

'Brilliant!' Nick was standing up. 'You and me then?'

'Absolutely not. Fortunately, it's strictly single-sex races only. You can go and find some other poor sucker to be your partner.'

Nick didn't need to be asked twice, galloping off into the distance to persuade some unsuspecting father to accompany him to the finish line. She didn't miss the way his tongue nearly fell out of his mouth as he passed Vivienne, who today was clad in scarlet Lycra hot pants and a neon yellow bralet top, looking more like she was on her way to film a workout video than she was to be a casual spectator at her children's Sports Day.

Relaxing now that Nick had left her, Gemma slumped back into her tiny chair, wishing that she'd actually followed through with the hip flask she'd threatened to bring with her. To her surprise, her attention was caught by her name being shouted at high volume from across the track.

'GEMMA-GEMMA-GEMMA!' chanted Year 2, led by a delighted Ava. Nonplussed, Gemma looked around, only to discover a defiant-looking Becky walking towards her.

'Right then. You and me. Mums' race. Are you in, or are you in?'

Gemma pursed her lips and shook her head decisively. Oh no. Becky wasn't going to use the cover of Sports Day to attempt to wheedle her way back into her good books.

From across the track, the chant changed. 'ROSIE AND AVA'S MUMMIES, GO GO GO! ROSIE AND AVA'S MUMMIES, GO GO GO!' Suspiciously, Gemma cast a sideways glance at Tom, whom she'd thus far managed to ignore entirely. His face was inscrutable.

'Come on, Gem. We can't let the girls down. Just look at them.' She gestured at Ava and Rosie, who were holding hands in the front row and yelling their little heads off. 'Let's go and run the race together. For the kids.'

Gemma couldn't decide who she hated most right at that moment in time – Becky, for putting her in an impossible position in front of the entire school; Tom, for very clearly being in on the whole thing; Vivienne, for being the competitive twat who had suggested the school needed to have parents' races in the first place; or Nick, simply for the fact he was an utter dick. But what choice did she have? Ava was clearly never going to forgive her if she didn't get herself roped to Becky in time to make the start of the race.

'Fine.' She spoke quietly, avoiding eye contact. 'I'll run the race with you, because I don't want to let our daughters down. But it doesn't change anything.'

The start line was a throng of mums and dads twelve deep. Not for the first time, Gemma cursed the fact she'd chosen to send her children to such a high-performing school; it made the vast majority of the parents ridiculously competitive.

Somehow, Becky wangled them a place in the front row. There were four sets of mums running in the race, which would take them once round the field – themselves, four other mums whom Gemma knew only by sight, and Vivienne, with her partner Kristin, one of her inner circle.

The two other pairs were laughing as they reached down to tie their ankles together and put their arms around each other, but Vivienne and Kristin were stony faced and incredibly focused as they took up their starting position, all the time listening to advice from their coach – Gemma hadn't imagined it; Vivienne had actually brought one – on the sideline.

'Where does Vivienne think she is? Crystal fucking Palace?' muttered Becky as she ensured the knot between them was tight and slipped her arm around Gemma's waist, pulling them together. Reluctantly, Gemma placed her opposite arm round Becky's shoulders. At least this way she didn't actually have to look at her.

Mrs Goldman was getting ready to fire the starting pistol – actually an old water gun, which Mr Cook the caretaker stood behind and shouted 'BANG' at the appropriate moment – but Becky was still talking as they set off. Vivienne and Kristin streaked ahead of them in a manner so synchronised it suggested they'd probably been training for this moment since this time last year.

'Gem, honestly, this is ridiculous.'

'You're right, it fucking is.' Gemma was already breathing heavily; she kept meaning to find some time to fit in exercise around her busy schedule, but given that would probably have meant working out in the time she had allocated for sleeping or taking a shit, it had somewhat gone by the wayside. 'I can't believe you're making me do this.'

'Not the race. Although you're right, that is also fucking ridiculous – Vivienne will actually be lapping us in a moment – but it was the only way I could get you to talk to me. I miss you, Gem. I really really miss you. There's so much that I keep wanting to talk to you about, but I can't, because every time you see me you go and crouch down behind your wheelie bins until I go away, like some actual lunatic. Listen, I'm sorry if you don't agree with what I said about Nick. I'm not sorry about saying it though, because truly, Gemma . . . you deserve so much more than him. I'm sure he's got his strengths, but being a doting husband is not one of them. Look at him, perving at Vivienne's arse.'

She wasn't wrong. Nick was practically drooling as Vivienne and Kristin sprinted past and Vivienne's breasts threatened to break free from their Lycra casing.

'All I'm trying to tell you,' continued Becky, 'is that you're amazing. And you deserve someone amazing. Maybe that's Tom, and maybe that's Andy – actually, it's probably not Andy, given he's probably now voluntarily placed himself in solitary confinement to avoid ever having another experience like the one he had with you – or maybe it's some disgustingly good-looking man that you haven't even met yet. Whoever it is, you'll be able to tell they're the right one for you because they make you happy. Happy in a way that I don't believe Nick has ever made you. Not really.'

Gemma would have sighed, had she had the breath left in her body to do so. Her heart was going like the clappers as they rounded the second corner of the field. Becky had surprised her by really going for it, and she was having to focus all of her energies into simply staying upright and keeping pace with her. Falling on her face in front of the assembled parents, children and teaching staff would probably mean she'd have to consider leaving the country, such would be her total and abject humiliation.

To her surprise, Vivienne and Kristin appeared to have passed the finish line, but were still running in perfect unison around the field. 'Please tell me this isn't a multi-lap race,' gasped Gemma. 'I bloody well hope they've got a defibrillator waiting on the finish line.'

'Come on,' encouraged Becky. 'We can do this! And, when we do, I've got premixed gin and tonics in our picnic for us to toast our clear victory over the rest of the field.'

Wearily, they stumbled on, but to their horror, Vivienne and Kristin were gaining on them. 'Fucking marvellous. Not only are we going to be last, we're going to be lapped . . . in a race which was only ever one lap in the first place! Come on, let's move out of their way.'

Quite what happened next, no one was entirely

sure. With Becky pulling, and Gemma stumbling, they attempted to move towards the inside of the track in order to allow Vivienne and Kristin to pass. A personal best clearly in sight, though, Vivienne and Kristin were unwilling to relinquish the inside lane. Consequently, the next thing Gemma knew was she was face down in the mud, her ankle still attached to Becky's. From somewhere above her head she could hear screeching.

'YOU! I might have guessed that it would be the two of you. Always causing problems, always ruining things for everyone else. And now ... look at the state of me!'

Vivienne had a point, Gemma thought as she raised her head. She did look something of a state, clutching her left ankle, streaks of grass and mud down her face, and half of one nipple exposed after her sports bra had given up the fight entirely.

Like a pig snuffling out truffles, Nick had shot into sight at the first sighting of areola, and was already offering his assistance to the injured Vivienne. Cutting the rope that still bound her to Kristin with his penknife, he picked her up in his arms, and was audibly heard to mutter to her that he knew a great way of distracting her from her pain.

Becky and Gemma, caked in mud, looked at each other. For a moment, neither spoke.

And then they laughed as though they would never stop, great, belly-aching laughs, until tears ran down their cheeks and Ava announced to her entire class that this was more embarrassing than Sam wearing a pair of his mum's pants to school, and Sam looked like he wanted the ground to open up underneath him.

*

'I've got something to confess to you,' Gemma announced as they sat later that afternoon in the sun drinking their cans of gin and tonic, watching Ava terrorise the Year 6 boys into giving her their football and immediately smashing it past them into the goal. 'Nick and I never actually got back together. I agreed to allow him to move back in so that he could see the kids, but we're not back in a relationship. Not for want of trying on his part, mind.'

A vision snapped into her mind of the moment Nick had materialised in her bedroom doorway one morning last weekend, a tiny towel draped suggestively around his hips while he gyrated to his own karaoke version of 'Sex Bomb'. 'Come on, babe. What do you say? You ... me ... humpy humpy?' She had thrown a pillow at him and told him to go and take a cold shower. As his departing back left the room her mind had drifted inexorably to Tom. Nick's choice of soundtrack had been somewhat unfortunate in that respect.

Becky's eyes were wide. 'So you ... Nick ...?' She made the universally recognised 'shagging' sign with her index finger and her left fist, leaving Gemma screwing up her face in disgust.

'Absolutely not. And stop that: knowing my luck Sam will see you and start imitating that gesture in the classroom. Mrs Willoughby still isn't over the interrogation he gave her on orgies.'

'But I thought ...'

'I know. You thought, and Tom thought, and it seems quite a lot of other people thought.' She gave a wry smile. 'And I suppose I can kind of understand why. There was even a part of me that wanted to give it a go. To be a perfect

263

family again. Only trouble was, I worked out that we could never actually be a perfect family.'

Becky was watching her intently. 'And so?'

'So,' considered Gemma, 'I'm probably going to go home and tell him that it's time for him to move out.'

'And the kids?'

'They'll be fine. Turns out, their happiness is very much linked to mine. Or so a very wise person once told me.' She winked at Becky and they clinked their cans together.

'To happiness.'

'To happiness.'

In the end, emboldened by her midday gin and tonic, Gemma decided not even to wait until she got home to tell Nick it was game over for the two of them. As the teachers took their classes back indoors at the end of the day to change from their PE kits back into their school uniforms – a process which you would have to pay Gemma three times her annual salary to oversee, based on Ava's gleeful report of the time 'Simon's pants once went onto Noah's head, and they had *poo* on them' – she went over to retrieve her ex from the inner circle of Vivienne and her coven. Sprawling on deckchairs, their lean tanned limbs on full display, they looked up at Gemma in disdain as she wandered over. For once, she couldn't have cared less.

Grumbling, Nick relinquished his plastic champagne flute of Prosecco and followed in her wake, dragging his feet behind him like a truculent teenager, but not before kissing each member of the coven multiple times on each cheek and promising he'd see them 'soon. *Very* soon'. If any of them had a spare room, Gemma suspected they might be seeing him even sooner than they thought.

'What did you have to do that for? Kids aren't ready yet, are they?'

She shook her head. 'No, but there's something I need to talk to you about.'

His face lit up. 'Babe! You and me! Are you saying we're back on?'

If she'd hoped he was going to make the process less painful for her by second-guessing what she was about to say, she was clearly kidding herself. Taking a deep breath, she went for the jugular.

'No, Nick. We're not back on. In fact … I'm going to ask you to leave.' She held up a hand. 'I know, I know. You wanted to make this work. And I was prepared to give you a chance. But it's just not working. We're not a partnership; we can never be a partnership. You're just too—'

'Adorable? Good looking? Blatantly the man of your dreams?' Ever the optimist, Nick still had a half smile on his face. 'Come on, babe, you know it'll be worth it! I'll change! Promise!'

She shook her head sadly. 'No. You won't. You're you, and you don't need me – or anyone else – trying to change that. Besides, I'm sure somewhere out there there's a woman who's waited all her life for a man who is going to piss up the walls of the downstairs loo.'

He looked immediately guilty. 'That was Sam.'

'And who gave him the idea?'

'Um.' He looked sheepish. 'That might have been me.'

'Nick, I genuinely believe that you mean well. You can be a bit of a dick – no, you can – but underneath it all,

265

you're a good person. But you and me, we're never going to work. So let's cut our losses, shall we? You can still see the kids – we'll work all that out. Let's walk away while I can still look at you without wanting to punch you in the face. And before I need to get specialist damp coursing laid in the downstairs loo.'

Silent for a moment, her ex-husband looked down at the ground. She couldn't tell what he was thinking as he shuffled his flip-flopped foot against the grass, back and forth, back and forth.

'So.' He lifted his head, his trademark grin back on his face. 'Does that mean you're okay if I go back over and rejoin those lovely ladies over there?'

For a moment, she contemplated hitting him, before realising, with blissful relief, that not only was what Nick did not her problem any more, but that she genuinely didn't care what he did either. She clapped her hand to her forehead and laughed out loud. 'Be my guest. Just maybe pop your chastity belt on first.'

Nineteen

Tom found it hard to believe that more than six months had passed since he'd joined Redcoats. It was the last day of term, and Miss Harris was helping him take down the wall displays while their class ran around in the playground like they were on crack. He'd been amused to see Ava walk over to Satin, who had become quite isolated since Tom and Ava had unmasked her behaviour towards Rosie, and tell her, 'You can come and play with us, but only if you're going to be sensible and not be an idiot.' Satin hadn't quite conceded to give up all idiotic behaviour altogether, but was now standing on the sidelines of the makeshift football pitch Ava, Rosie and their gang had put together, and even looked like she might be thinking about smiling. Once again, he had to hand it to Ava. That kid was going to go far.

Miss Harris sighed as she pulled some cardboard monstrosity that the class had created down from the wall. It was meant to be a castle but, thanks to their choice of brown papier mâché as a building material, it looked more like an enormous lump of shit. Later on, Tom would pull names out of a hat to ascertain which lucky family got to take it home with them. He was already intending on rigging it to ensure that Vivienne was the lucky recipient; nothing said sweet, sweet revenge like a giant lump of excrement that your small child insisted you display in pride of place within your interior-designed home.

'You sound like you're as ready for the summer holidays as I am,' said Tom. The amount of work he still had to do over the summer to get ready for his new class was horrible, but he planned to ignore it all for at least a week while he lay face down on his living room floor with a continuous supply of intravenous alcohol being pumped into him.

'Well.' Miss Harris looked suddenly coy. 'There's something I need to tell you. I've decided ... that actually, teaching isn't for me.'

Tom's face fell. Miss Harris – Anna – had been a huge source of support to him over the year, and he had hoped he might be working with her again during the next academic year.

'Blimey. That's a massive decision. What do you think you're going to do instead?'

She smiled. 'You'll probably think I'm mad, but I've been accepted to be a trainee prison warden. I figure a load of violent criminals can't be any worse than trying to get thirty six- and seven-year-olds changed after PE.'

She had a point. Wishing her all the luck in the world, Tom finished helping her remove the giant lump of poo from the wall and rang the bell to call his class inside. Just two more hours to go.

*

They were the two longest hours he could ever remember experiencing. The children were tired, emotional and over-excited at the thought of the long break approaching. If he was honest, he felt the same way. Eventually, Miss Harris – god, he would miss her – captured all of their attention by sitting down and reading a chapter of *The Witches* to them. I mean, none of them would go to sleep with the light off until they were at least eighteen as a result, but it was worth it for the half hour's peace it brought him to sort through their reports and count down the minutes until his charges were off his hands.

As he listened to Miss Harris's impressively convincing Grand High Witch voice, his mind drifted, as it did so often these days, back to Gemma. He'd hoped Sports Day would provide him with an opportunity to break down the wall which seemed to have formed between them, but to his dismay she'd turned up with that useless bloody ex of hers in tow, wearing trousers so tight Tom reckoned he could draw the outline of his cock and balls from memory. His retinas scarred, he'd turned away, only to miss the moment when Gemma and Becky had finally rekindled their friend-ship after he'd got his class piling on the pressure with their self-composed chant across the track.

By the time Gemma and Becky were sitting on the grass with their G&Ts, he was embroiled in an intensive discus-sion with a little boy called Harvey about all of the reasons why no, Mr Andrews (Year 6 teacher) didn't look like a penis, and even if he did, that wasn't a very nice thing to say about someone, and if you are going to call someone a penis, you probably shouldn't shout the word 'PENIS' quite so loudly … and before he knew it, Gemma had left and the moment had gone.

The one cloud hanging over the prospect of the break ahead was the fact that there was a strong likelihood he wouldn't see Gemma at all until September. Their paths had never inadvertently crossed outside of school, and short of him going and lurking outside her house – which probably wasn't ideal, 'stalker qualities' not usually being one of the traits one looked for in a prospective life partner – he was at a loss as to how he might find the opportunity to speak to her.

The playground outside was filling up with parents, though there was no sign of Gemma's distinctive curls through the crowd. Miss Harris had finished reading, leaving the class with a delicious cliffhanger to start their holidays, and the classroom descended once again into noisy chaos as children collected their book bags and PE bags and lined up by the door, ready to leave.

He handed each child an envelope containing their school report and ushered them out of the door. Vivienne, of course, was at the front of the queue, practically snatching the envelope from Satin's hand and tearing it open to see whether her daughter's brilliance had been recognised by him.

She was going to be very disappointed.

On the plus side, Vivienne's attempts to seduce him had reduced considerably, he suspected in no small part as a result of Nick the Dick's clear interest in her nipple region at Sports Day. Vivienne loved to be admired, and loved even more getting one over on one of her sworn enemies. Ava's unmasking of Satin had sent Gemma right to the top of Vivienne's hit list; attempting to sleep with her ex-husband would be the perfect way to exact her revenge.

Becky poked her head round the classroom door as the last few stragglers were filing out, Ella waving delightedly at him from her pushchair. 'Hiya. Bet you're ready for a stiff drink. Has Gemma turned up yet?'

He gestured to Ava, who was standing, alone and somewhat forlorn in the middle of the classroom. 'Nope. Reckon she's remembered there's no after-school club today?'

'Knowing Gemma, almost certainly not.' Becky looked over at the little girl. 'Ava, do you and Sam want to come home with me? I could burn some fish fingers for you to have for tea and then you could play football with Boris in the back garden.'

Ava was out of the door before she'd even finished speaking, gripping Rosie's hand and leaping in the air with delight. 'YEEEESSSSSSSSSSSSSSSSSSSS. Come on Rosie. You can play mid, and I'll be up front, and we can make Sam go in goal so we can kick the ball at his face and see if he cries.'

Texting Gemma to let her know she'd collected the kids, Becky left. Tom was about to close the classroom door when, to his horror, he saw Vivienne advancing towards him like an angry rhinoceros. School report had gone down well then, clearly.

Miss Harris had already left to go and get ready for her leaving drinks, and the classroom was empty as he bolted back inside. Shit, where could he hide? There was absolutely no way he was going to spend the first two hours of his summer break defending the – perfectly reasonable – statements he'd written about Satin to her mother, who clearly thought that anything less than 'Satin is the greatest student I have ever taught in my career' was entirely unacceptable.

271

Vivienne was approaching fast; he could hear the click of her heels on the tarmac. There was nothing else for it. Opening the arts and craft cupboard, Tom hurled a load of tissue paper out of the way and crammed himself into it, shutting the door behind him.

From outside the cupboard he could hear Vivienne's strident tones. 'Mr Jones. Mr Jones! Where are you? I request you come and speak with me *immediately*. You have clearly issued Satin with a report card meant for another student. The SATS scores you have given her show that she is working at the expected level. Satin is *not* working at the expected level! She exceeds expectations in every single area! I don't know where you are, but I really must insist that you come here and speak with me.'

She had to be fucking joking. Trying not to make any sudden movements that would give away his position, Tom buried his face in a pile of sugar paper, waiting for her to get bored and go and harass the head instead. Mrs Goldman was paid about four times his salary; she could have the pleasure of being the recipient of Vivienne's diatribe.

At last, Vivienne did indeed get bored. He could hear the sound of her heels clacking off down the corridor, and thought in grim satisfaction of the experience Mrs Goldman was going to have when she found her. That would teach his boss to wink at him suggestively.

The classroom quiet, Tom leaned against the cupboard door to free himself. To his horror, it stuck fast. The latch on the door had been problematic for some time, and great care had to be taken to lift it in precisely the right way to be able to gain access. Now, with him stuck inside, the latch had fallen back down into place and he had no way of getting back out. He made repeated and increasingly desperate efforts in the cramped space to dislodge it with his shoulder, to no avail. The door remained firmly shut.

It was fine, he told himself. Someone was bound to be along to rescue him soon. Or would they? It was the last day of term. The playground was empty. Soon the remaining teachers would be leaving for their holidays and Mr Cook would be locking up the building. Unless he came and checked in here first, Tom could be in a pretty desperate situation.

Panic rose in his throat and he banged frantically on the door. He would even accept a two-hour interrogation by Vivienne if she just got him out of this bloody cupboard first.

Silence. He was all on his own, with no possible way out.

Gemma had had an utterly torrid day. It had been the day she'd been dreading since she'd first realised they were out of options at Zero; the day she'd had to tell Siobhan that, for the first time since they'd been working together, the answer to her hourly enquiry of 'Am I sacked yet?' was, in all probability, about to be 'Yes.'

In some ways, it had been easier than she'd imagined, mainly because Siobhan's natural inclination was to assume the worst. She'd been on at Gemma for weeks, knowing that something was up and driving herself insane panicking over what it could be. Still hoping against hope that a last-minute solution would be found that would save Zero, Gemma had remained tight-lipped. As Siobhan had proved herself to be absolutely trustworthy over the years they'd worked together, Gemma typically told her pretty much everything. Consequently, Siobhan had correctly interpreted that there could be only one thing that her boss could be keeping from her.

With consultation for all employees starting on Monday, Gemma knew she was out of time. Having put off the evil moment for as long as she possibly could, when she turned to Siobhan and asked her if she could have a word, her assistant's face told her everything she needed to know.

They left the office and took the five-minute walk down the road to the Royal Oak, their favoured local haunt which did amazing morning lattes and bacon sarnies. Gemma wondered if she could persuade Bill, the manager, to sneak a couple of shots of brandy into Siobhan's latte. She had a feeling she might need it.

'Come on then,' said Siobhan, once they were seated at a little table by the window. 'Hit me with it.' Her nails were chewed down to the quick, Gemma saw, and she was systematically shredding her bacon roll into tiny pieces. If you looked up the dictionary definition of 'stressed', Gemma was fairly certain you'd find an image of Siobhan and her shredded bacon sandwich.

'There's no easy way to say this,' Gemma said, taking a deep breath, 'so I'm just going to go right out there and say it. It'll be just like ripping a plaster off. Except hopefully not the plaster I ripped off Ava's knee the other day, when I ripped off a load of skin with it and blood went absolutely everywhere and she started trying to grab my phone off me and screaming that she was going to phone Childline.'

Siobhan sat there opposite her, staring down at her shredded bacon roll. 'You can say it. I'm sacked, aren't I?'

For a moment there was silence, other than Bill stacking glasses into the glass washer behind the bar. Gemma found she couldn't speak; it turned out, she didn't have to. As Siobhan looked up, startled by the lack of immediate rebuttal to her question, she met Gemma's eyes, and knew everything she needed to know.

They both burst into tears.

'Now then,' said Bill, bustling over to them. 'Come on, we can't have you two crying in the window; you'll put all the punters off. What is it? – lovers' tiff? Here you go. I've brought you some tissues –' he plonked a large, industrial-sized toilet roll in the middle of the table '– and some of my homemade flapjack. On the house. Just mind you take your dentures out before you eat it; you could build roads with this stuff, you could.'

Both women gratefully took a piece of tissue from the enormous roll and dried their eyes as Bill placed a tub full of flapjack between them. 'You get your choppers around that. There'll be no more crying; you'll not be able to when you've got a lump of flapjack gluing your teeth together.' Satisfied he'd dealt with the immediate crisis, he shuffled back off to his glass washer.

Gemma took a deep breath, wiping mascara from her cheeks. 'I'm so sorry. That was horribly unprofessional of me. I just . . . well, actually having to tell people. Tell you, in particular. It's just . . . it's fucking awful isn't it?' A wave of emotion overwhelmed her, and another mascara landslide threatened her clear-up job.

Siobhan sniffed noisily. 'It's fine. I mean, obviously it isn't fine, it's about as far from fine as it can be. Oh god, this is karma, isn't it? I've ended up getting us all sacked because

I've been asking about it for so long. God, why am I always such a fucking dick?'

Reassuring her that this definitely had nothing to do with karma, that it was simply to do with the finances of the business, Gemma talked her through the facts as she knew them. Zero was running out of money. If the company was going to survive, drastic changes would need to be made. Starting from Monday, every single person in the organisation would be placed in a consultation period, while it was determined who would survive the cull and who would be asked to leave.

'So what does that mean for me? For us? Will we still have jobs?' Siobhan clung onto the one crumb of comfort she'd been able to take from Gemma's words. She knew how much Leroy valued Gemma – and by association, herself. Surely this meant they had a chance.

It was a question Gemma had been asking herself for weeks on end, ever since she'd first become aware that this was the likely outcome; it was a question she still didn't have an answer to. 'I don't know, Siobhan. I just don't know.'

Bill's flapjack had been left, uneaten, as the two women picked up their bags and left, thanking him as they did so. He shrugged, unperturbed. He'd have no shortage of willing customers to try that out on later. Maxine Sanderson, for one. Bloody woman would never stop talking; well, let her try with a mouthful of that, Bill thought in satisfaction to himself.

The rest of the day had passed in virtual silence. It was most unlike Zero, where Gemma had often wondered if she'd need to go out and purchase Tena Lady as a result of the fits of giggles she would find herself in with her colleagues. Siobhan had said to Gemma on the walk back that she understood, that she didn't blame Gemma in any way, but Gemma wasn't sure she believed her.

Now, Gemma looked across at Siobhan, still at her desk and typing furiously.

'You should get off home. What are you doing, anyway?'

Siobhan shrugged, still typing. 'Trying to see if I can get some more business in. If we got enough business, maybe we wouldn't all have to get sacked.'

Gemma forced a smile. 'Even if we do have to make changes, you won't be getting sacked. You'll – we'll – be made redundant. Nobody's going to lose their job because they've done something wrong.'

Siobhan paused in her typing for the first time, and turned to face Gemma. 'It doesn't matter though, does it? We might as well just call a spade a spade. We're none of us going to have jobs, and so the end result will be exactly the same.' She looked away and returned to her typing.

There wasn't a lot Gemma could say in response to that. She trotted out a few platitudes, but her heart wasn't in them, and she knew Siobhan could read her like a book. Cutting her losses, Gemma packed up and headed out to the car park. Next week was D-Day, the point of no return. God, there really were times when she absolutely hated being a grown-up.

Arriving at the school, she realised to her horror that most of the building was locked up. Shit, it wasn't early finish day was it? Yes. Yes, it was. Of course. Her hand to her mouth, Gemma realised she'd completely forgotten that it was the last day of term, when the after-school club didn't run. Nick – who was currently sleeping on the sofa at a mate's – wasn't due to have them until the weekend, and her parents were away in Tenerife. It was usually her mum who reminded her the children would be breaking up early, and did Gemma want her to collect them for her.

Oh crap. Fumbling in her handbag for her mobile phone, Gemma found a series of unread WhatsApps. Scrolling through them, she saw that they were from Becky, her very own guardian angel who had stepped in and prevented the children from feeling like they had been entirely abandoned. From the selection of photos she had sent through, they were clearly having the time of their lives, as was Boris, who in the last photo was somehow wearing Ava's Barcelona shirt as she sat astride him feeding him her discarded cremated fish fingers. Oh, and Ava had announced that her mum was having another baby, which was why her tummy had gotten so big, and did Gemma have anything she wanted to tell her.

Her mind filled with thoughts of what she would be saying to Ava when she got home. Her heartbeat subsiding a little, Gemma walked towards reception. Ava would almost certainly have forgotten the carrier bag full of family photographs which she'd brought in to accompany her My Family project. She'd been promising Gemma faithfully every single day for the past week that she would bring them home; needless to say, they were pretty much guaranteed to still be hanging on her peg.

Mr Cook was hoovering the reception carpet when she arrived and looked at her suspiciously. Only her persuasive arguments that she just needed to grab a carrier bag, that she wasn't going to be more than five minutes and that she was wearing white-soled trainers which wouldn't mark the parquet flooring in the school hall that he'd just spent over an hour polishing convinced him to let her in.

Tracing her way through the school to the Year 2 classroom, right at the back of the building, she could hear raised voices coming from Mrs Goldman's office. It sounded like Vivienne, and from the tone of her voice, she clearly wasn't happy. She hurried her pace and walked past.

The classroom was empty and, as she'd suspected, Ava's carrier bag was hanging on her peg. Classic Ava. Carefully unhooking it, she was about to leave the room, when she heard a thudding noise, followed by the sound of a voice. A male voice. It was hard to make out, but . . . was that 'Help!' it was shouting?

Her heart pounding in her chest, Gemma followed the source of the sound. It led her to the large cupboard in the corner of the room, which she had a feeling was used to store art materials. 'Hello?' she tried. 'Is anyone there?'

In response, there was more frantic hammering and a muffled cry of: 'Oh thank god. Let me out, please!' Quickly, Gemma unlatched the cupboard door, and then watched in utter disbelief as the door opened and Tom slid out.

'Oh my god, am I relieved to see you. Thank you so, so much. I thought I was going to be stuck in there all summer – the most embarrassing death of all time. Honestly, you are an absolute legend. I could kiss you.' He stopped abruptly, appalled by the inappropriateness of what he'd just said.

Gemma too was startled out of speech, her close proximity to the man she'd been thinking about – not to mention having slightly debauched fantasies about – for what felt like weeks making her completely tongue-tied. Awkwardly, she stood there as Tom brushed pieces of tissue paper from his shirtsleeves and ran his hands through his hair.

'So ... um. Why don't you have a seat?' Desperate to cover up the awkwardness of the fact that he'd basically just told the woman he wanted to kiss most in the world that he wanted to kiss her, Tom proffered Gemma a chair. A tiny chair, obviously. Obediently, she sat. He pulled up a similarly tiny chair next to her and slumped over on the table in relief.

'I honestly thought that was it for me. I know that sounds ridiculous, but I just couldn't work out how I was going to get out. Looks like my guardian angel turned up just in time.' He smiled at her and she blushed furiously, her traitorous body deciding to betray her feelings by plastering them all over her face. Marvellous. So much for playing it cool.

Tom looked around the room, as though expecting to see someone else there. 'Where's your husband? Ex-husband, I mean. Or ex-ex-husband. Nick. Is he not with you?'

Briefly, Gemma filled him in, the initial suspicion on his face fading rapidly to relief as she explained that they had never been back together, that she had simply allowed him to move in to see whether he was capable of being a responsible father to the children again. The answer, clearly, had been no.

'And Sam and Ava?'

'Fine. They've been absolutely fine.' They really had, much to Gemma's surprise.

Sam had told her it was okay, because he and Nick would be able to chat over Skype while they played no doubt horrendously inappropriate computer games together, and

Ava had nodded her head when Gemma had told her that Daddy would be moving back out again. 'It's because he kept weeing on the floor next to the toilet, isn't it? I told him to sit down and have a wee, so it wouldn't go everywhere, but he just wouldn't listen.' Ava looked wistful. 'I wish *I* had a willy to wee out of onto the floor.'

Yes, bar Ava's frustration that she still wasn't able to wee standing up, there had been remarkably little fallout from Nick moving out. And with things between herself and Becky patched up, not to mention Lovely Jon and Becky being as loved up as they'd ever been – Gemma had found herself babysitting not once, not twice, but three times in the last week for Rosie and Ella for an hour so that Becky and Jon could shag like newlyweds – it seemed like everything had all ended up happily ever after.

I mean, there was the minor detail that, as of Monday, she was highly likely to find out that she no longer had a job and was going to be joining Becky in queuing up at the Job Centre, but who needed gainful employment anyway? Secretly, Gemma was absolutely terrified. She could cope with fucking up her marriage and being destined for a life of singledom, but the thought of losing her home and not being able to afford to feed and clothe her children was more difficult to bear.

Tom was watching her carefully. 'So, you and Nick ...'

'Over.' She was categorical. 'One hundred per cent, over. To be honest, I'm just not really sure that relationships are my thing.'

Tom looked as though he was going to say something, but thought better of it. 'But that's good, right? That Nick's left. I mean, if you weren't happy together ...'

'No, you're right. It is good. It's just ... well.' Tentatively, she explained to him the situation at Zero, going into more and more detail as she realised he was genuinely interested and not simply listening to be polite.

'And so you see, come Monday, there's a strong chance I'm not going to have a job any more. To be honest, I'm absolutely terrified. Working at Zero is all I've ever known. The thought of having to go out there and start from scratch, find a new job which pays enough to cover the mortgage and bills *and* allows me to work around the children ... you've seen how much luck Becky's had. It's the fucking holy grail. I might as well put the house on the market now and tell my parents I'm moving back in with them. And then maybe get a T-shirt printed which says I HAVE FAILED AT LIFE, because, let's face it, with a divorce and a redundancy behind me, that will basically be the truth.'

'Oh come on, now. You've met your children, yes? No one who's managed to produce two kids as bright and switched on as your two can ever truly claim to be failing at life. Even if Ava does still slightly terrify me.'

Gemma smiled. 'You won't be alone in that, that's for sure. Did she tell you about our trip to the dentist the other day?' Tom shook his head. 'We went for a check-up, and she was terribly quiet throughout the time we were there, which is always a worry – as was the dentist, for that matter: he seemed weirdly distracted – and then we got into the car to drive home, and she suddenly piped up from the back seat, "Mummy? You know that dentist? When his hand was in my mouth, I was licking his glove", and Sam went so hysterical with laughter that I had to pull over so he could pee at the side of the road. That poor dentist, getting licked by Ava.'

'Oh my god. That poor dentist indeed. That's Ava, right there. Why go and behave like a normal person at the dentist's when you can lick them instead?' Tom wiped tears of mirth from his eyes. 'Brilliant. But tell me more about Zero. This Leroy guy sounds fascinating.'

The sun streamed through the windows as Gemma told him the full story of Zero. How she had joined when none of them was sure it was even going to get off the ground; and how now it had a multi-million-pound turnover and was set to embark on its next stage of growth. 'The problem is cash. We need to diversify, but we're not able to follow up on any of Leroy's amazing ideas if we can't get the upfront money to invest in them. We've exhausted every possible avenue. Much as I hate to say it, I think it's time to admit defeat.'

'But there must be a suitable investor out there. I mean, how much are you talking?'

Gemma told him.

'That's small change to most of the investment houses out there.'

'That's the problem. The large companies don't want to invest in us; we're not worth their time and effort. And the solo investors get nervous; they view Leroy as a loose cannon and they don't want to put all their eggs in one basket. Truly, we've tried everything. Believe me, if I thought there was another option out there, I'd be looking at it. The thought of having to leave Zero breaks my heart.'

Tom was looking at her curiously. 'You really love it, don't you?'

She smiled. 'Like I can't even describe. It's not just a job ... it's my life. I wake up every day, and I'm excited to get up and go and start the day at work. You only have to scroll down social media to see how unusual that is. Leroy's created somewhere incredible to work. He actually wants his employees to be happy. And we are. We really are.'

For a moment, Tom closed his eyes, finding himself swept back to a world that he no longer wanted to be a part of. Angrily, he shook his head, dismissing the memories, and turned back to Gemma.

'Gemma, you can't give that up in a hurry. You mustn't. Believe me, what you've got at Zero is something special. You don't know how many people would give anything to be able to work in that kind of environment; how many people's lives are destroyed because they're not able to work somewhere where people want them to be happy ...' Trailing off, he looked down at his hands.

'Tom, what happened? With your old job, I mean. When we were in the escape room together, you were going to tell me, but that woman opened the door and you never got to finish whatever you were going to say. You left a prestigious job in the City to come and work in a school, but you've never explained why. It doesn't make sense. What happened to you?'

Tom fought the tide of anxiety rising inside him. His palms were sweating and a chill ran down his spine. What happened to him ... well. That wasn't something he'd ever spoken to anyone about, not since that final day, when he'd walked out of his old life and never looked back.

But maybe it was time he did.

Twenty

Gemma was watching him intently, her curls pouring out of the band she'd attempted to secure them in and forming spiralling tendrils around her face. Her face was flushed from the warmth of the classroom, and her mascara had smudged down below one eye so that she looked rather as though she'd come off worst in a fight. To Tom, she was absolutely beautiful.

He took a deep breath. 'What I'm going to tell you, I've never told anyone. Ever. So you're going to need to bear with me, because this probably isn't going to be easy for me.

'When I graduated from university, I got taken straight onto a graduate scheme with one of the major banks. I was so proud of myself. It was one of the best graduate programmes in the country, and they'd picked me. I knew I'd have a career there for life.

'I worked hard and quickly got promoted – a bit like you did. As I worked my way up the ranks, my salary and my bonus increased exponentially. Trouble was, so did the hours that I was working and the amount of stress. The culture at the bank was one of blame and of pointing fingers. Everyone was terrified of ending up in the firing line and so we were all desperately trying to always cover our own backs. You couldn't trust anyone. I actually made some quite good friends there, but it was a dog-eat-dog world. When I reached management level, I had to sack the guy I'd graduated from university with; we'd been working together ever since. He was in tears, telling me that I was ruining his life, that he'd have to sell his house because he wouldn't be able to afford the mortgage repayments. His wife was pregnant and his parents were elderly and frail, but it didn't even register with me emotionally.

'The trouble is, working somewhere like that – your emotions start to get dulled. You stop caring. You stop caring, because the prospect of doing so, and of getting hurt as a result, is too terrible to contemplate. And so you build up these protective walls around you, to allow you to survive – and to thrive – in such an environment. I became hardened to it. Brutality became normality.'

He took a deep breath, steeling himself to go on. Gemma was listening intently, her elbows resting on her faded jeans.

'My job didn't give me a huge amount of time for a social life. I'd had a few casual relationships, but nothing serious. That all changed about four years ago, when I met Jo.

'I'd been aware of Jo for a while – she was one of the few female graduates who had stayed the course and shot up the ranks. She'd actually been promoted ahead of me, and ended up becoming my line manager. We spent a lot of time together. I admired her self-confidence, her intelligence … oh, and the fact that she was fucking gorgeous didn't hurt either.' He smiled, wryly. 'At the Christmas party we both got wankered on disgustingly expensive champagne, and we ended up sleeping together.

'I'd assumed it would just be a one-night thing, but Jo surprised me. She was keen to settle down; she wanted a serious relationship. I was totally in lust and completely starstruck by the fact that the rising star of the business wanted me, thought I was worthy of her time and affections. We moved in together within a month.

'Then something happened. At work. I became aware that there was some insider dealing going on within the bank. I'd always suspected that this kind of thing went on, but this was the first time that I had real, hard evidence. At first, I wasn't sure what to do. I decided to tell Jo.

'For a short time, our relationship had been amazing, but the cracks soon started to show. I had been doing well at the bank, and was bringing in a lot of new clients. Jo didn't like that; her sales were down, and she felt that I was only doing it to show her up.

'When we got home that evening I told her what I'd discovered. She was silent while I told her. At first, she tried to dismiss me, told me that I was talking nonsense. When she realised I was serious, and that I wasn't going to let it go, she told me that I had to forget all about it. That this kind of thing probably went on all the time, and that I should just put my head back into the sand and get on with my job.

'I thought about what she'd said, and for a few weeks I didn't say anything, but it kept eating away at me. It was wrong. I knew it was wrong, and I'd always promised myself that I would speak up if I ever saw anything like that. I told Jo that I was going to formally report it under the company whistleblowing policy.

'She went berserk. She stood in the kitchen screaming at me. I told her that this was my decision and mine alone, that she didn't need to get involved, that it had nothing to do with her. She screamed that of course it had something to do with her, that her card would be marked by association. That she had worked her arse off to get to where she'd reached in her career, and that she wasn't going to risk throwing all of that away just because some "stupid prick" – her words, not mine – couldn't sit down and shut up and stop trying to play the hero.

'I thought she'd come round, that she'd see that it was the right thing to do, but when I woke up the next morning, all of her personal belongings were gone. When I arrived at work she completely blanked me; it was like I was invisible.

'As I'd said I would, I reported what I'd found out through the official channels. I was promised that it would be investigated and that it wouldn't count against me. Turns out, that wasn't quite the truth.'

The room was silent. Gemma could see dust motes floating through the rays of sun which shone through the windows. Tom looked down, avoiding eye contact. His hands were clenched into fists.

'From that day onwards, my job became pretty much untenable. Jo was hugely influential at the bank. It didn't take long for the word to get out that I'd spoken up about some alleged insider dealing. Jo made it clear to everyone in our department – and half the rest of the business – that

I'd been spreading spurious rumours which had no grounding in fact.

'I don't know if you've ever been bullied?' Gemma shook her head. 'I had, as a kid – but this was on another scale altogether. No one would speak to me – Jo had turned them all against me. I'd go into a room and everyone would stop speaking. I thought about reporting it to HR, but what would have been the point? You're unlikely to win when half the business are determined to ensure that you lose.

'I've always been comfortable in my own skin, but such a sustained campaign against me changed the person I was. I stopped speaking to people – I mean, there wasn't a huge amount of point trying, was there, given that most of them behaved as though I didn't exist.' He attempted a laugh; it didn't quite come off. 'Instead of living it up out on the town every weekend, I just started staying in my flat, lying on the sofa, staring at the ceiling. It felt like every single part of me had been squeezed dry; all that was left was a shell.

'One Monday morning I woke up. I say I woke up – I don't remember ever having been to sleep. I lay in my bed, and I looked out of the window, and it was a beautiful sunny day, the sky was blue ... and I just thought, what is the point? What is the point of any of this? For the first time in my life, I didn't think I could go on.

'Thank goodness for my parents. When I'd failed to turn up for work, and HR had been unable to contact me – I'd seen my phone ringing, but never answered it – they'd followed the process to contact my next of kin. Also unable to reach me on the phone, my mum and dad drove to get me. They took me home to theirs.

'I spent the entire summer in my childhood bedroom in some kind of daze. I struggled to get myself out of bed every morning; I loathed myself. I was a failure – a useless, worthless failure. Jo and most of the people we worked with had been telling me so for weeks, and now I finally realised that they were speaking the truth. I didn't think I could ever be happy again.

'This went on for weeks, and then one day, my sister came to visit. She brought my nephew Isaac with her; he was four at the time. Isaac had been told to leave me in peace, but he broke ranks and came and found me in my bedroom, lying on my bed, staring at the ceiling. He asked me why I didn't come out, and I told him that I didn't think I could. He told me that I was being stupid. He was right.

'Isaac and I spent the rest of the day together, and gradually I started to feel some sense of the old me flooding back. Isaac didn't care about what had happened to me. All he cared about was whether I would play football with him, and if I knew what would happen if the sun exploded, and if I could tell him who would win out of a Tyrannosaurus Rex and a great white shark in a fight.

'And what I slowly realised was that this kind of human interaction . . . this was what I'd been missing. The bank did everything they possibly could to dehumanise you completely. I should have cut and run the moment I had to sack Jack, my mate from uni – he didn't deserve that; there's no way that decision was fair. But I'd stopped being able to see clearly. I'd lost that human side of myself.

'My time with Isaac was the start of me getting better. He was the start of me learning that actually, I still had a lot to offer the world. And that not everyone out there thought I was a useless, miserable failure. Isaac and I hung out a lot over the summer, and it was that time with him – watching his wide-eyed curiosity at the world, his endless fascinated questions – that made me decide that I wanted to give teaching a go. I wanted to change lives instead of destroying them. I handed in my notice – the bank couldn't accept it fast enough – and registered for a teacher-training course. It was the first positive thing I'd done since leaving the City, and I loved it from the very first day. Gradually, I got better. Gradually, I found me again.'

Gemma was motionless. A solitary tear snaked down one cheek, but she made no attempt to brush it away. 'Oh my god. I had no idea.'

He laughed. 'I wouldn't expect you to have done. And it's fine; really, it is. It's taken a lot of therapy – and a healthy dose of antidepressants – but I honestly am back at my best. Everything happens for a reason, right? Although I still think that I could have learnt that particular lesson in a slightly less traumatic way! But, honestly, it's made me give grateful thanks for every single day. Even the ones where I end up getting locked in the arts and crafts cupboard.'

Sitting facing her, he leant forward and brushed the tear from her cheek. Her skin tingled at his touch. 'But that's what I'm trying to say. That time I worked at the bank ... I was more miserable and alone than I think I've ever been in my life. By contrast, you're working in a job that you love surrounded by great people who really care about you. You've got to do everything you possibly can to hang onto that. You deserve to be happy, Gemma. We all do.'

She hardly dared to breathe as he moved closer to her, filling the empty space, until their faces were almost touching. Softly, looking into her eyes, he whispered: 'And being with you, that's what makes me happiest of all. What do you reckon? Fancy giving it a go?'

She responded by kissing him so fiercely and with such passion that the tiny chairs gave up the fight entirely and tipped them onto the floor, where they tumbled, still kissing, as though their lives depended on it. Laughing through their kisses, Gemma pulled him close to her, revelling in the soft touch of his lips and the caresses of his fingertips as they ran down her spine.

So engrossed were they in each other, that neither of them heard the approaching footsteps. The first they knew was when, to their collective horror, they heard the distinctive tones of Mrs Goldman saying: 'So, Mr Cook, what do you reckon? Shall we hose them down, or shall I throw the interactive whiteboard at them?' Appalled, they both sprang to their feet, frantically brushing down their clothing as though nothing had happened.

Mr Cook was brandishing a mop in their general direction, and appeared to be so furious that he was struggling to get his words out. 'Adults ... *teachers* ... in the Year 2 classroom ... having INTERCOURSE.' It was too much for him; he looked as though he was going to burst into tears.

Mrs Goldman looked Tom straight in the eye. He wondered for a moment whether she was about to march him out and tell him that he could consider himself sacked with immediate effect.

Instead, with a glint in her eye, she turned to Mr Cook and said: 'Oh, piffle. Intercourse, indeed. If you think that sort of pathetic fumble counts as intercourse, then all I can say is how desperately sorry I am for your poor wife.' Then she turned on her heel and marched out of the room, with Mr Cook frantically jogging along in her wake, and Tom and Gemma laughed so much they thought they might never stop.

Twenty-One

It was early evening on 31 July and Gemma looked at herself in the full-length mirror. All things considered, she hadn't scrubbed up too badly at all. Admittedly, it had taken Becky a good couple of hours, and every single item of cosmetics from her box of tricks, but now she was primped and preened to within an inch of her life, and actually, she thought she was looking pretty good for someone who was newly forty. Slipping her feet into another pair of Jimmy Choos which Becky had generously lent her for the night and which perfectly complemented her cream and crimson dress, she could almost feel beautiful for a moment.

'Urgghhh, why are you pulling that stupid face? You look like a fish.' Ava, of course, bounding into Gemma's bedroom dressed in her Chelsea kit. 'Are you wearing that perfume which smells like the stuff we kill nits with?'

'No I am not! And what perfume is that? I don't have perfume that smells like the stuff we kill nits with.' Gemma sniffed herself cautiously. Did she?

'Of course you do. SAM!' Ava bellowed her brother's name at approximately the volume she'd need to use if he was standing down the other end of the street. 'Doesn't Mum's perfume smell like the stuff we kill nits with?'

'What?' Sam materialised from the gloom of his bedroom, clad only in his blue towelling dressing gown, which seemed to have become something of a second skin for him and had to be prised off him at intervals in order to be boil washed. 'Mum, my balls are getting properly hairy now.'

'Good. Marvellous. I'm so proud. No, Ava, get off him ...' Ava had rushed over to attempt to stare at her brother's balls, and Sam pulled his dressing gown protectively around him and told his sister to get her own balls and to stop looking at his.

'To be fair to Ava, it's quite hard not to stare at your balls if you will insist on walking around the house with them hanging out.' Gemma woke up every single day hoping that Sam might have developed some sense of modesty; at the moment, it seemed she'd be a long time waiting. 'I sometimes think I should be setting another place at the dining room table for your balls, so prevalent are they in our family life. Anyway. Do you suppose, what with today being my birthday, that either of you might consider wearing something smarter than a smelly old dressing gown or a football kit when we go out for dinner?'

'My dressing gown isn't smelly! How dare you!' retorted Sam, as Ava explained to her mother that it was critical that she wore her Chelsea kit, 'because what if the Chelsea scouts are at the restaurant, and they see me, and then they want me to show them my skills, so that they can give me a job playing for Chelsea and I can earn millions and millions of pounds and buy a massive mansion and we can all live in it, apart from you, Sam, because you are a smelly boy and I do not like smelly boys.'

Gemma sent the children in opposite directions before they could come to actual physical blows over the imaginary mansion that Ava didn't actually have. 'Thirty minutes until it's time to go. Fine, Ava, wear your Chelsea kit, but no, you can't wear your studs in the restaurant. Sam, if you really want to wear your dressing gown out then go for it. Obviously, there's always a chance that one of your mates might see you.' That did the trick. Muttering about how of course he wasn't *actually* going to wear his dressing gown to the restaurant, Sam disappeared back into his bedroom, presumably to extract some item of clothing covered in dubious-looking stains from the pile of crumpled shirts and trousers which had a permanent home on the floor next to his bed.

Descending the stairs, Gemma poured herself a glass of champagne from the bottle she and Becky had opened earlier as they got ready. Sipping from it deeply, she thought about how much her life had changed in just a few short weeks. She had a surprisingly good feeling about her forties.

The doorbell rang and Ava charged down the stairs. 'I'll get it! I'll get it!' Panting, she fumbled with the lock before pulling the door open wide. 'Mr Jones! Shall we do some quick penalties before tea?'

Gemma would have been deeply nervous about introducing any new man into her children's lives, but her concerns had ramped off the scale when she considered the fact that this particular new man was a teacher at their school. Her heart in her mouth, she had introduced the topic to them after her third date with Tom in as many days, one that had finished with him pulling her close to him and her almost physically panting with desire. God, she wanted to shag him, but on the grounds that not only was she probably a bit too old and sensible to have sex standing up in an alleyway somewhere, knowing her luck, she'd almost certainly get caught on CCTV and have her naked arse plastered all over the internet, she was going to need to get the children comfortable with him coming into their home first in order to be able to secret him up the stairs and into her bed.

As was so often the case with her children, they had taken her by surprise. Ava had been completely uninterested ('Yes, I know, you want to do lots of sloppy kissing with Mr Jones. Can he come in the back garden and play football with me first?'), and while Sam had been initially appalled – 'Oh my god, Muuuuuuuum, that is *disgusting*' – he'd been swift to see the potential benefits of this new relationship. In the two weeks that Tom had been coming over to theirs, Sam had alternated between dragging him upstairs so he could watch him play new Minecraft 'mods', and desperately trying to persuade him that the perfect way of ingratiating himself with his new girlfriend's son would be to give him all the answers to his holiday homework.

As a result, Tom had become a firm fixture in their household after an incredibly short period of time. Gemma had wondered if it was too much, too soon, but she was so utterly besotted, she was struggling to keep her hands off him. The sex, when the children had finally gone to sleep and they'd been able to barricade themselves into Gemma's bedroom, had been *in-fucking-credible*. Gemma had forgotten what it felt like to have anything more than an inanimate bit of plastic giving you pleasure, let alone having someone giving you pleasure who actually cared about you having a good time. Tom's gentle, caressing approach was in stark contrast to Nick, who had once memorably brought himself to climax by slapping her on the arse as she sat miserably astride him, yelling 'Who's a lucky girl?! You are! You are! YOU ARE!'

God, she'd had a lucky escape.

Tom barely had time to drop a kiss on her lips before he was dragged through the back door by Ava. 'I'm going to bury you, Mr Jones!' were the last words Gemma heard Ava shriek before the door slammed behind them. Poor Tom. She hoped he was prepared for what he was getting into.

By the time they finally dragged Ava off the football pitch and walked the short journey down the road to the restaurant – a local French bistro which was always packed tight with clientele enjoying the excellent food and even more excellent wines – they were running late. Tom held the door open as the kids ran in, Ava shrieking with excitement as she spotted Rosie sitting at the large table at the back of the room, and running over to her.

'Oh my god, Gemma, you look amazing!' Becky clapped her hands in delight as she stood up from the table and embraced her friend.

'Of course I do, you lunatic. It was you who spent hours getting me into this kind of shape. Poor Tom: he's going to wake up next to me tomorrow and feel like the prince who kissed the princess and found she turned into a frog.'

'Please.' It was Tom, his arm round her waist. He kissed her gently on the top of her head. 'You look beautiful every single day to me.'

'Oh god, I think I'm going to vom.' Becky mimed sticking two fingers down her throat and turned to Jon, who was patiently entertaining Ella in her high chair. 'Come on, gorgeous husband of mine. Let's stop these two having actual sex on the table and get the drinks in.'

It was a glorious meal. The wine flowed as course after course of delicious-looking dishes was placed on the table in front of them. Ella slept in Jon's arms and Rosie and Ava sat together down one end of the table, in fits of hysterics at something none of the adults had a clue about. Sam had done his best to look interested and engaged for his mum's special birthday meal, but the smile had soon slipped and he'd ended up slumped over on his elbows, looking as though he'd rather be anywhere else. Until, that is, Becky slipped him her iPhone and provided him with access to the internet, 'So long as you keep it out of sight of your mum.'

Becky filled them in on the latest rumour circulating around the school mums, fuelled no doubt by Vivienne's coven. 'Turns out, the word on the street is that your ex-husband is doing the down and dirty with the Grand High Witch herself.'

Goodness. For a moment, Gemma wasn't quite sure how she felt about that. Vivienne and Nick? Really? Was this the moment that she was meant to collapse in floods of tears and realise how much she loved him?

The sensation she was actually feeling, she realised, was one of abject relief. The others round the table were looking at her, curious to see how she was going to react. 'I think,' she concluded, 'that it probably couldn't happen to a more screwed-up couple.' And they all laughed until their stomachs hurt.

It occurred to her, Gemma realised, that it was a very very long time since she'd felt this comfortable on one of her birthdays. She'd either been dealing with Nick's neurotic and egotistical behaviour, or she'd been sat by herself with a bottle of wine, promising herself that next year it would be different. This year, for the first time, she felt like she belonged.

'So, I've got some news,' announced Becky, swaying slightly as she sat back down after a trip to the loo. 'You will remember, Gemma, that a little over six months ago we both signed up to Project Gemma-and-Becky. Our shared objective was that by the time you turned forty, you would have got a shag –' Jon hushed her, but the children appeared to be oblivious '– and I would have got a job.

'Well, from the look on your face and the amount of time Tom here has been spending round your house recently, I'd say that number one of those was in the bag.' At this point Gemma covered her face with her hands and Tom laughed his head off. 'But part two of Project Gemma-and-Becky has remained somewhat elusive.

'Or has it? Because ... breaking news ... as of yesterday, yours truly is gainfully employed! Yes! It's true! I'm going back to work!'

'Oh my god, Becky, that's incredible news!' Gemma got up to hug her friend. 'I can't believe you didn't mention it earlier!'

'I wanted to save it until we were all together. I can't entirely believe it myself, to be honest.'

'So tell me! What's the job?'

'It's a funny thing.' Becky took another sip of her wine and stroked the sleeping Ella on the head. 'Do you remember that horrific interview I had with those two absolute perverts, all those months ago?'

Gemma grimaced. 'Like I could forget. Please don't tell me you're going to go back and work for them.'

'As if. Over my dead body. No, but I did eventually manage to get the story in the local paper. I couldn't imagine it was going to go anywhere, what with that particular newspaper having a circulation of about three people – all of whom work for it – so you can imagine my surprise when I got a phone call from the journalist who'd written my story the other week. She'd been contacted by a woman who'd read it, and who wanted to talk to me about a potential job.

'So I phone her back, and it turns out to be the HR manager I met when I took this one here along to interview.' She gestured at Ella, who babbled incomprehensibly in her sleep and snuggled further into Jon. 'She was appalled I'd been treated like that, and asked me to meet with her. Turns out she'd moved job, to a charity who are working with organisations to bring flexible working opportunities to everyone. From my remarks in the paper, she knew it was something I was passionate about. My shitty LinkedIn profile also came in useful at last, because she'd looked me up and had seen I had a background in marketing.

'Long story short, I'm going to be their marketing and social media manager! I start next week, two days a week plus flexibility to work from home, which couldn't work out better with Jon's new working hours. It is an actual fucking dream! Oh – and that solicitor firm is now being formally investigated by the SRA for malpractice.'

'Oh Becky, that's absolutely fantastic! I am made up for you. So we did it! We made it!'

'Yes, but what about you?' Becky's face was suddenly serious. 'What about your job? You haven't said anything, and I haven't wanted to ask. Does this mean . . .'

Gemma and Tom exchanged glances. 'So, actually . . .' began Tom, at the same time that Ava shrieked, 'LEROY!' and shot across the restaurant.

Ava and Leroy had always had an affinity. From the moment they'd first set eyes on each other, when Gemma had brought a tiny Ava into the office when she was just weeks old, she'd made a grab for Leroy's fluorescent tie with bright purple squid painted all over it, and Leroy had immediately announced that they'd found a synergy. He didn't profess to understand Ava's obsession with football, and she was frequently scathing about the colour he'd dyed his hair or the way he wore his jeans, but something in their mad little minds had clicked, and they'd been soulmates ever since.

'Goodness, speak of the devil,' said Tom, getting up to shake Leroy's hand as Ava clung to his (turquoise, spangled) trousers, before also greeting his partner Jeremy, who was just as charming as Leroy, if somewhat less outlandishly dressed. 'We were just talking about you.'

'What?' Becky was shaking her head at Tom as Leroy and Jeremy joined the gathering. 'How do you and Leroy know each other?'

'We don't,' said Leroy. 'Or rather, we didn't. Happy birthday, darling.' He handed Gemma a bottle of champagne and kissed her flamboyantly on both cheeks. 'I hope you don't mind me popping in. I just thought it might be appropriate to raise a glass in celebration . . . a double celebration.'

'WILL SOMEONE TELL ME WHAT IS GOING

ON?' shrieked Becky, so loudly that she woke Ella, who gave her mother a totally disdainful look before immediately falling back to sleep.

'I might just have a little bit of news too,' confessed Tom, making space for Leroy and Jeremy to pull up chairs around the table before popping the cork on the champagne. 'Because, in the last couple of weeks, I've gone into business.'

'Oh my god,' wailed Becky. 'You're going to leave the school and we'll end up with some teacher who smells of wee and cabbage and hates children, aren't you?'

'Categorically not,' confirmed Tom. 'I have no intention of going anywhere ... assuming, that is, Mrs Goldman can wipe from her memory the last day of term and never mention it to me again.' Gemma sniggered. 'But I have made a decision to invest in a business. A local business ... a business I believe is going to go on to do some really rather incredible things.'

Even with Tom, Jeremy, Leroy and Gemma all grinning like Cheshire cats, it took a moment for the penny to drop with Becky.

'Oh my god, you haven't, have you? You've saved Zero? But how? I thought they needed millions of pounds?'

'What do you take me for, young lady?' asked Leroy in mock affront. 'Just how much of a big spender do you think I really am? I don't need *millions*. Just, maybe ... one or two millions.'

'But ... you're a teacher.' Becky was looking at Tom now. 'You haven't got one or two millions.'

'Not any more I haven't,' Tom joked. 'Leroy's had those off of me. Yes, you're right, I am a teacher, and no, teaching

303

jobs don't tend to come with utterly obscene bonuses attached to them. But my old job did. And I was very good at it. I've been lucky enough to squirrel away quite a bit of money over the years, and even luckier to have invested it wisely. It's been sitting there, and to be honest, I've always wanted to find a business to invest in. To have found a business which I think has potential, which actually gives a shit about the people it employs – oh, and which happens to employ my most favourite person ever – frankly, it seemed like something of a no brainer. I met Leroy, I had a chat, and the long and the short of it is that I'm going to be his new – silent, I hasten to add: my skills when it comes to clothing sizing are probably not likely to be in demand – business partner.'

'Oh Tom,' said Becky. 'I honestly do think you might be the most perfect man in all the world.' Lovely Jon coughed loudly next to her. 'Oh, obviously apart from you, darling, that goes without saying.' She kissed him passionately, until it was Gemma's turn to cough loudly.

'And that's not all. Tom investing means we can finally diversify out into some of the other incredible ideas Leroy has come up with. The next big thing is going to be bras. Imagine – being able to order a bra online which you knew would fit, wouldn't leave you with double breasts or with permanent scarring due to bastard fucking underwires breaking free and stabbing you repeatedly in the side of your tit.' The women sighed in recognition. 'The ultimate dream.'

'Only problem was,' said Leroy, winking, 'I needed someone absolutely fucking awesome to run it, who was brilliant at managing people, brilliant at getting shit done,

and brilliant at putting up with me. Oh, and who understood bras, because, frankly, they scare the shit out of me.
There could only possibly be one person for the job.'

'And ... your new MD will be working just four days
in the office, the remaining day at home, to make sure
she's both there for her children and leading the way
when it comes to senior positions being worked flexibly.
So Sam – I've kept my promise to you. I'll be home much
more frequently so there won't be a hope in hell of you
"forgetting" to do any of your homework from now on!'
Sam groaned and buried his head in his hands. He knew
he should have been careful what he wished for.

'THIS IS THE BEST NIGHT EVER!' shrieked Becky,
high on life and champagne. 'So now I've got a job, and
you've got a job – a new and fucking *amazing* job, you
corporate high flier, you – and you've finally broken your
fifty-year sex drought, or whatever it was, and forty is to be
honest the new twenty, I mean, apart from the fact we've
both now got tits that hang down to our knees without
some serious scaffolding – thank heavens for your new bra
business, frankly – and so Gemma, I say, here's to you.
Here's to me. Here's to us!'

'Here's to us.' And, raising their glasses, they toasted
each other, surrounded by their friends and family. Even
Ava crawling out from under the table to belt out, 'MUM,
WHAT'S A SHAG AND CAN I HAVE ONE FOR
CHRISTMAS?' while Sam threatened to leave the country
on the grounds that his sister was so abjectly mortifying –
and the other diners in the restaurant killed themselves
laughing – couldn't diminish Gemma's perfect bubble of
happiness right then.

Despite her best efforts over the last few years, she'd worked out that it simply wasn't possible to have it all, and anyone who told you otherwise was kidding you. Yes, she had an amazing new job, two gorgeous children, and – eek! – what appeared to be a brand new and seriously hot boyfriend. But she also had a house that looked like a shit-tip, an out-of-control arse, and a pelvic floor which was waving the white flag of surrender. She was unlikely to ever be able to get Sam and Ava to school on time, and would be destined to spend her morning routine screaming 'TEETH! HAIR! SHOES!' until they left home. Oh, and of course nothing screamed Sex Goddess like nipples which hung down to your knees.

So she didn't have it all, far from it. But she had enough – oh, she had more than enough. And right there and then, with everyone she loved around her, and Ava sitting under the table delightedly teaching her self-composed 'Labia! Labia! Labia!' song to Rosie, she felt like the luckiest woman in the world.

Acknowledgements

There are so many people without whom this book would never have been written, and top of that list is my real life Fairy Godmother. Maddie West turned my life upside down in the best possible way when she got in touch with me out of the blue on a grey spring day when I'd spent the best part of a week clearing up vomit (a family dose of norovirus) and the most exciting thing to happen to me prior to her email was keeping down a dry piece of toast. Maddie, you have allowed me to fulfil the dream I have had since I was five years old, and I will never be able to properly thank you for that.

Thank you so much to everyone at Sphere/Little Brown who has worked so hard to bring my book to life – each and every one of you have been absolutely incredible.

My amazing blog readers! To every single one of you – from the Original 108, to those who have joined more recently . . . thank you so much for being a part of the madness. If it wasn't for all of you, this genuinely would never have happened.

Alice, thank you so much for not only reading a very early draft and providing some first class feedback ('I didn't hate it' – best review ever!) but for also being the person who first inspired me to start blogging. Basically, this is all your fault. Love you, dude.

Helen, thanks also for your brilliant early feedback ... and for always being just suitably scathing enough – in the way that only siblings can – about the blog to keep my feet well and truly on the ground. Love you.

Ian and Eileen, and Harry and Grace – my amazing in-laws and step-kids – you put up with me regularly turning up at yours and then ignoring you completely while I sat glued to my laptop and frantically typed up the first draft. Your support is so appreciated ... and the mint tea was amazing, Ian!

JAAAAAAMS! I mean, let's be honest – you had fuck all to do with this book coming together, but when it comes to hysterical gin-fuelled celebrations about the fact I have written An Actual Book, I could ask for no better BFF in the world. You can guarantee that Gemma and Becky had at least one drunken night where they walked in their dressing-gowns to get more wine from the Co-op. LOVE YOU.

I couldn't possibly parent without my village, and central to that village is the amazing Vee – my Proper Grown Up! (She'd deny it vehemently!) Vee, I can't describe how grateful I am for your unquestionable willingness to step in and pick up multiple parenting duties while I fucked around writing a book. Absolute legend.

Teachers everywhere, I have so much admiration for the job that you do and the way that you change lives, every single day. I was lucky enough to have a number of wonderful teachers over the years, but head and shoulders above the rest was my Prep V teacher, Mrs Stone. Mrs Stone: you taught me to tell a story, taught me the power of 'funny', made me believe in my writing and convinced me I could one day write a book. Thank you so much.

Mummy, the hours you spent teaching a precocious two year old to read and write weren't wasted! (I'm really really sorry for all the swears!) You have always made me believe that I could do anything I put my mind to, and I'm sure I wouldn't have achieved half of what I have in life without you instilling that in me. I love you.

Yo Pop! Thanks for always being so incredibly proud of everything I do ... whether that's writing a book ... or having 30 million people read about my #celebrityflaps ('I have no idea what a celebrity flap is, but I am always proud of you.' Brilliant) ... or that time on the packed number 82 bus when I phoned you after my first ever smear test to tell you that the nurse had told me that I had a really accessible cervix. #lifegoals. I love you.

In hindsight, Wrenfoe, our marriage vows should probably have read 'I promise to love you ... in sickness and in health ... and in that fucking mental year when you decide it will be a good idea to juggle a full-time job with parenting two children, writing a book, updating a daily blog – oh, and occasionally remembering you're married to me'. You have been an unwavering supporter of my writing and my work and I couldn't have done any of this without you. I love you so much. I'm Spartacus!

And, last but so definitely not least ... Jamie and Beth, you two have changed my life in every single way, and oh, so much for the better. (Other than the sleep deprivation, which was truly shit.) I can't imagine either of you ever being particularly inclined to read this book, what with it failing to feature either Tom Gates or Harry Potter, but I want you both to know that none of my dreams would ever have happened without you. It doesn't matter how many words I write, I will never ever have the right ones to explain to you both just how much I love you. Love you for ever. Mum xxxxxxx

PS Now could you PLEASE tidy your rooms.

Now read on for more adventures with Gemma and co in

Winning at Life

'MUM! Ava keeps showing me her vagina.' For approx-imately the three thousandth time that long, hot day, it appeared World War Three was threatening to break out.

Wearily, Gemma left the dinner she was preparing and headed up the stairs. 'What's going on, guys? I told you, you need to get your stuff ready.'

'And I'm trying to get my stuff ready, but Ava keeps coming into my bedroom with her vagina hanging out, and I don't want her to,' Sam retorted grumpily.

'Ava.' There was no response. 'Can you come here, please. Sam, I'm sure she's not really—'

'It's not a vagina, Sam. Vaginas don't hang out. It's my VULVA,' Ava announced loudly. Not for the first time, Gemma really really wished her seven-year-old daughter came with an inbuilt volume control.

To be fair to Sam, he wasn't entirely wrong, Gemma decided as Ava appeared with rather too much on display beneath the summer dress she had attempted to squeeze herself into.

Gemma ran her hands across her face. 'Ava, what are you doing? Go and find some proper school uniform that fits. And where are your pants?'

'This is my proper school uniform.' Ava looked appraisingly at herself in the hall mirror. 'I think it might be a bit short.'

'A BIT? Ava, you told me last week that you definitely had all your uniform ready for going back to school. So what's happened?'

Ava stared back at her mum mutinously. 'Nothing's happened. I have got all my uniform, and here it is. And I am not wearing any pants, because the only pants left are the ones that Granny bought me, and they're PINK.' She looked appalled at the very concept of pink pants.

Gemma buried her head in her hands and let out a groan. It didn't matter how hard she tried, it seemed she was destined to spend the last day of the holidays trapped in her own personal *Groundhog Day*, as she once again proved herself to be miserably lacking in the key parenting skills of basic preparation and organisation.

She turned her attention to the problem at hand. 'Okay. Ava, you cannot have actually grown that much over the last six weeks. Let's go and have a look in your wardrobe. And Sam: congratulations, now that you're about to start Year 6, it's officially your responsibility to go through the festering hideousness that is the interior of your book bag. Personally, I suggest you tip the whole lot out and put it straight into the bin. Maybe even burn it. Just check there's nothing important you need for tomorrow, yes?'

Taking her daughter by the hand, Gemma walked across the landing and attempted to open her bedroom door.

'Ava, what's the matter with your door? Why isn't it opening?'

'Um.' Ava looked vague. 'Maybe because there is something in the way of it.'

I ABSOLUTELY MUST
WIN THIS FANTASTIC
PARENTING PAMPER PACK

We're offering one lucky reader the chance to win a parenting pamper pack containing everything you need to survive and thrive as a parent! Each pack contains the essentials:

A bottle of Gin

A bottle of Cava

 Copious amounts of chocolate

Bubble bath

Scented candles

Parenting reward stickers

TO ENTER SIMPLY VISIT
HTTPS://PAGES.LITTLEBROWN.CO.UK/PAMPER

Terms and conditions available online.